Praise for Jezzy Wolfe

"Jezzy Wolfe covers a lot of weird territory in this book, from the lighthearted and satirical to the odd and disturbing. And it's all great stuff! Treat your brain to *Strange Doses*—it'll thank you!"

– Jeff Strand, author of *Freaky Briefs.*

"*Strange DOSES* delivers a rich and unforgettable world of stories and poems with deliciously twisted tales that keep strange secrets and reveal hellishly cruel surprises. Weaving science with supernatural and otherworldly possibilities, Wolfe introduces worlds where everyday problems blur into stinging, surreal situations. Throughout the collection Wolfe dares to explore the dangerous spaces where risk intersects with punishment and reward, and the results are full of magic, love, and fury."

– E.F. Schraeder, author of
The Price Of A Small Hot Fire

"Jezzy Wolfe presents you with stories that you think you know. She lets you walk into them all comfortable and cocky. Then she smacks you upside the head with a depth of emotion and empathy that makes those stories something wholly other and much more scarring."

– Anton Cancre, author of *This Story Doesn't End the Way We Want All The Time*

"I'm envious of those taking their first trip with Jezzy Wolfe's fiction and poetry. The seventeen tales and six poems show a fondness for the unusual and macabre, but often with tongue in cheek, and always with a love of language. You'll find here work that will elevate your blood pressure due to fear or spice or humor, and sometimes all three, and before it drops to normal you're crawling back for more. Take a hit. Scream like a queen. Giggle like a loon. And be prepared for Jezzy Wolfe to be your new addiction."

– Derek A. Johnson, author of *The Faith*

"I don't think I've ever used the phrase "uproariously funny" before, but it is the first that comes to mind after reading Jezzy Wolfe's collection of fanciful what-the-fuck in *Strange Doses*. This collection is exactly what I crave: weird, hilarious, the right amount of twisted, and clever as all get out."

– Bridget D. Brave, weirdo and author of
A Piasa for Christmas

"You do not have to read far into Strange Doses before you realize you've found something different, something special. Jezzy Wolfe is a master storyteller who quite literally deserves a genre unto herself."

– Stony Graves, author of
At the End Of All Things

"An odd collection, both eclectic and electric, Strange Doses boasts a wide array of prose and poetry reflected perfectly by the gorgeous patchwork cover. These tales come from a place both alien and very much human, pressing horror through insecurities and captivating depravity as something beautiful through its raw poetic nature. Jezzy spins a web of unpredictable storytelling that shifts moods on a dime."

– Robert Royal Poff, author of
Sleeping Among Wolves

"Jezzy's poetry is divine, and her stories are like the lost episodes of Twilight Zone that never aired because they were too scary."

– Sarah Hans, author of *Entomophobia* and *Asylum*

"It's not an easy thing to balance wit, dark humor, and originality, but Jezzy Wolfe accomplishes just this. From haunting poetry to stories that speak volumes between the lines, Wolfe wastes not a word to deliver bizarre circumstances that will thrill and entertain as well as haunt. A keen eye for the human condition, Wolfe shares a peek at our flawed existence. Unnerving, it's hard not to see a glimpse of self staring back from her work. These are indeed *Strange Doses*, but Wolfe sweetens the bitter truth with black humor creating a collection of prose and poetry that will remain on the palate long after the last page has been devoured."

- Angela Yuriko Smith, two-time Bram Stoker Awards® winner,
and author of *Bitter Suites*, and *Inujini*.

Strange Doses

a collection of weird by

Jezzy Wolfe

Strange Doses

a collection by Jezzy Wolfe

The content of this collection was published by various publishers from 2009 to 2023.

ISBN: 979-8-218-37696-3

Cover art by Don Noble
Edited and formatted by Kody Boye Publishing Services

Dedication

My deepest appreciation goes to the friends who have helped me along the way, by being my eyes and, often, voice of reason. Skip Novak, Derek Austin Johnson, Jim Kelley, Will Prescott, and Anton Cancre – *thank you* for your time, advice, suggestions, guidance, pats on the head, and sometimes, much needed shots of liquor. Without you, these stories would never have seen the light of day. Look at you, making that much of a difference to some weirdo like me! But you did, and you do, and there are no words that express this better than "ARGWARGARBLE."

Many thanks to Kody Boye for your fantastic editing and formatting, and to Don Noble for the stunning cover art. You both made this collection look SO much better. Professional, even! Also, a big thank you to Angela Yuriko Smith. Your encouragement and advice helped more than you know, and I'm so grateful to know you. And my eternal gratitude to Cindy O'Quinn for the wonderful introduction. I am incredibly honored by your kind words.

Much love goes to my hubs and kids for putting up with me all these years, even when I talked your ears off about plot holes and typos and weird YouTube channels. Thank you for your patience, and for being equally as goofy as me. I am grateful for our many hours of laughter and Tik Tok video swaps. Did you see that last one I sent? The one with the cat?! You *have* to watch it!

And, as always, thank you Mom. I hope wherever you are that I still make you proud. I would not be who I am if it weren't for you. I love you, and I miss you deeply…

Wait for me by the tree.

Table of Contents

Introduction

Welcome to the wonderful world of weird horror, as only Jezzy Wolfe can create. Her collection of short stories and poetry, *Strange Doses,* is the perfect example of Wolfe's unique way of putting the "weird" into horror.

I first read her brilliant style of writing, in *Monstrum Poetica,* a collection of poetry, and was completely blown away. If you have not read it yet, I highly recommend you do so.

With Wolfe's new collection of both stories and poetry, she takes somewhat ordinary things in life and twists them until they reach the epitome of Weird Horror. The first story, "Locks of Loathe," shows exactly what I am talking about. Alopecia is something many can relate to, but what extreme measures is one willing to go through to have a thick head of hair again? Wolfe takes us there and then some. All the stories will touch in one creepy way or another.

The poetry exemplifies Wolfe's gift of imagery through her words, and the way she slices her way into your mind. Ready or not. Two of my favorites are Unfortunate Victim, and Those Of Us Who Eat Brambles. Words from the latter, "Daggers in our throats savoring Songs from lacerations", quite the image left for one to ponder a while.

Thank you, Jezzy Wolfe, for the invitation to write this introduction. It truly is an honor to read your work before it is released into the wild. You have taken me on a rollercoaster of weird delight. And to all who read *Strange Doses,* enjoy the ride.

Cindy O'Quinn, Author
Four-time Bram Stoker Award® nominee
Elgin, Rhysling, and Dwarf Star nominated poet

Locks of Loathe

Alesha Aldopita's head resembled a butchered Barbie doll. Scant threads of dull brown gossamer barely covered her pasty scalp. Growing up, she envied men with comb-overs. Her peers in eighth grade nicknamed her 'Alesha Alopecia,' and it followed her through high school. The more her beautiful but vicious classmates ridiculed her, the more she grew angry and resentful. She'd missed out on sleepovers with the girls at school, staying up past midnight putting crooked braids in each other's hair. Prom was out of the question, along with every other dance and party the typical teenager begged to attend.

After graduation she moved across the country to attend college and never left her dorm room without a hat or scarf covering her cranium. Needless to say, she stayed as lonely as she was bald. A lifetime of poorly disguising her condition had passed, and she was tired of hiding.

Hell yeah, she was bitter.

"Have you considered wearing a wig?" This was her first

therapy session with Dr. Wiston, a woman possessing more hair than the entire high school varsity cheerleading squad combined.

Alesha glared, regretting her choice of doctor. Taking advice from her would be the equivalent of a morbidly obese person taking nutritional suggestions from an anorexic.

“Hair salons donate hair to an organization that makes wigs for cancer patients and people with other illnesses,” the doctor continued. “That would be an easy solution if you’re so insecure about your appearance. Would you like me to give you their number?

Alesha knew about them as well, but wigs were uncomfortable. They made her scalp itchy and sweaty, and she feared they would fly off her head at the worst possible moments.

“Wigs give me rashes. Isn’t it bad enough that I have to wear sunscreen under my scarves? I’m tired of living like a freak!”

Dr. Wiston squirmed in her seat as she scrutinized Alesha’s chrome dome.

Great. She’s captivated by the drops of sweat covering it. They’re probably reflecting tiny rainbows all over the room. I’m a human disco ball, whee!

“At the risk of sounding simple, many women flaunt a shaved head. Perhaps, rather than cursing your condition, you can turn it into an asset?”

Alesha practically hissed. "Absolutely not!"

"Okay," Dr. Wiston said calmly, "there are many advancements in hair replacement now. While the majority of patients looking for hair replacement are men, it is certainly not limited to them."

"If you are talking about Rogaine, it didn't help."

"There's also Propecia, Dithro-Scalp, cortisone injections, and hormonal modulators."

"You don't think I would've tried them already? I've seen at least four different specialists, and it's cost me more than a few years' salary. The only progress I've seen is the ability to have lots of sex now without getting pregnant, thanks to the contraceptives they told me would spur more hair growth." Alesha struggled to keep her voice steady. "But hey, the pill works. Since it didn't make my hair grow, no man will touch me with a ten-foot penis."

"You're an attractive woman, Alesha."

"Right."

"Have you looked into hair plugs?"

"Have you looked *at* hair plugs? Don't I look weird enough?"

Alesha regretted her misdirected hostility, but she felt powerless to control the emotions dominating her reactions. She couldn't stop staring at Dr. Wiston's thick mane of spun gold. *She can't take me seriously because she doesn't understand how I feel.*

"How are your finances now?"

She didn't even listen to what I just said! "Uh, few years' salary, remember? I'm broke."

Dr. Wiston studied her again, eyes squinted and brow creased as she tapped her pen against her lower lip.

"I am not supposed to do this; it is a violation of policy. But if you promise to keep this disclosure completely confidential, I might be able to help you."

Alesha smirked. "How will you do that? Hair extensions and super glue?"

Dr. Wiston went over to her desk and opened a drawer, pulling a flat black box from under a stack of papers and laying it on her desk blotter. Resettling in a chair by the desk, Alesha watched as the therapist slowly lifted the lid of the box.

In the box rested only one simple business card.

Dr. Wiston started to hand her the card, but pulled back when Alesha reached for it. "Dr. Pift was disbarred six years ago, but he still practices from a private location. Some believe his methods were unethical and grossly negligent, and had his license removed." She glared a warning at Alesha. "If I give you his number, you cannot tell anyone that you're seeing him. Should complications arise from whatever procedure you agree to, you will not be able to seek medical help from a hospital or outside doctor."

Alesha's heart pounded erratically and sweat rivulets raced down her temples.

"Because he has a humanitarian streak, his fees are reasonable. He continues his work because he believes in helping people like you... those who have tried every avenue they could afford without success."

Still not convinced, Alesha shrugged. "That's great, but is he any good?"

Dr. Wiston rounded the desk and squatted in front of her, eyes glittering above her twisted smile. She shook her head and a bounty of golden silk tumbled over her shoulders.

"You tell me. What do you think?"

Dr. Pift waited quietly behind an oversized steel desk as Alesha studied the sheet he handed her. It read like a menu, but rather than food, a list of surgical procedures and brief descriptions were laid out next to dollar amounts.

Her stomach dropped. *I can't even afford an appetizer...*

"I appreciate you stopping in to see me. Dr. Wiston is a long-time friend. How is she looking these days?"

"Perfect," Alesha mumbled.

"Indeed. You know, there was a time her head was as bald as yours." He paused as Alesha's jaw dropped. "Unusually bad reaction to the chemo, I'm afraid. For many, the hair will return, but in her case..."

"How did you fix her?" Alesha ran a hand across her scalp. When she looked at her palm, she saw four strands of baby fine hair caught on her fingers.

"I'm sure you've heard of hair plugs." As disappointment registered on her face, he chuckled. "I'm not suggesting a traditional process of hair plugs, of course. You have no hair to re-harvest. But after experimenting with a combination of techniques, I've discovered that healthy hair can be achieved on even the most barren head. What I'm suggesting for you is a full thickness skin graft. We replace your scalp with the scalp of a healthy head and their hair becomes yours."

A vision of Frankenstein fluttered through Alesha's mind, complete with oversized metal sutures and neck bolts. "I... I don't know, Dr. Pift. That sounds outrageous."

"Why? Successful skin grafts are performed all the time on burn victims. Hair plugs themselves are just smaller patches of transplanted skin."

"Yeah, but isn't the skin their own?"

"Most of the time, yes. But skin is an organ, Miss Aldopita. And organ transplants are hugely successful with the medications now available. Skin can be transplanted from a donor and treated just as if the recipient received a kidney or a liver. Once the body has successfully merged the new scalp into your system, the healthy follicles will continue to regenerate new hair."

"It sounds pretty fantastic, but I'm not sure I can afford this," Alesha said, dollar signs swimming in her vision.

Dr. Pift watched as tears welled in Alesha's eyes. Pity—or something close to it—poorly disguised his smile as he leaned across the desk and offered her a tissue.

"Usually when a patient comes to see me, they've already exhausted their resources to find a cure. I never refuse to treat a patient based on their inability to pay." His smile warmed. "I came from a very poor background myself, but now I live a comfortable life. I'm not greedy."

He stood, and he looked like a giant as he came around the desk and offered his hand to her. "Let me help you, Miss Aldopita. I promise, soon your bald past will be nothing more than a faint memory."

She was caught off guard when he explained the procedure in detail, but really, what did she expect? After all, you can't order scalps from a catalog, and how many women were willing to donate their entire head of hair to a stranger? They had to scalp someone. There'd be hell to pay if anyone found out what they were about to do. The agreement they made was unconventional, immoral... criminal. But Alesha would sell her soul to the devil and tell him to keep the change, just to wake to the possible experience of bad hair days.

He warned her of all the usual risks—potential scarring, serious infections, and the possibility of tissue rejection if her medications weren't monitored carefully. But after twenty-three years of humiliation and insecurity, those risks were insignificant. Alesha's only real concern remained in finding the one head of hair that would be the envy of everybody she'd meet.

She found the hair sooner than she'd anticipated.

The sun bathed the sidewalks in an intense heat that bounced around the moving crowds in waves. Alesha stopped outside a tinted coffee shop window, debating on the purchase of a frozen beverage as she studied the street at her back in the murky reflection. The glazing transformed the passing people into indistinct shadows that floated by. A sudden shock of glowing copper invaded the chiaroscuro—a manifestation of gilded snakes that slithered across the glass and disappeared into the door frame. Frappuccino forgotten, Alesha trailed the hallucination to an office building a couple of streets over.

Perched on a bench outside the building, she searched the throng of executives and secretaries that flooded the sidewalk that evening. In a sea of carbon copy grey suits and skirts, the lush sheen of long henna curls caught her eye. They bounced in the early evening breeze, beckoning her closer. Alesha hid in the crowd, following just near enough to keep her sights locked on the shimmering strands that fluttered like a flag at dusk.

When the young woman entered an apartment building less than a mile from Alesha's walk-up, she waited a beat and entered the lobby, just in time to see a door on the second-floor landing slam closed. *This is it. She's practically in my own back yard!*

The initials on the mailbox read 'A. A.' It was the only sign she needed.

Hiding under a stairwell, Alesha clenched and unclenched her fists to stop their shaking, fighting against a myriad of 'what ifs.' For instance, what if the woman fought back? What if the chloroform didn't work? What if her boyfriend happened to be a police officer who randomly stopped by for an unexpected booty call and had his own set of keys and burst into the place after the woman was unconscious but before Dr. Pift arrived to collect her body?

She checked her watch. 1:30 A.M. Curls still hadn't returned home. Alesha's stomach sank as another 'what if' came to mind: what if she doesn't come home tonight?

The lobby door creaked as it swung open, and Alesha reached for the bottle in her jacket pocket. From the shadows she watched as the woman checked her mailbox, and then ascended the stairs. Alesha tiptoed to a back stairwell that she discovered earlier and climbed them two at a time, the soft soles of her sneakers muffling the sound of her steps.

Copper Curls fumbled with her keys, dropping them with a mumbled curse. Alesha prepared to sprint, cloaked in the dark doorway. *Okay, get ready now...*

As Copper Curls pushed open the apartment door, Alesha sprang from the doorway, chloroform-soaked rag in her hand. In a fluid motion that could've been rehearsed, she cupped the towel over Copper's nose and mouth before she could struggle. Alesha levied her weight against the woman and pushed them both into the apartment. Shoved towards a squat sofa, Copper went limp and sprawled like dead weight over the cushions. Alesha rushed to retrieve the keys and close the door, locking the dead bolt as she fumbled for the light switch.

The woman splayed across the couch like she'd had too much to drink. Alesha pressed two fingers to her limp wrist. Copper's pulse was a little uneven, but strong. She pulled her cell from her pocket and called Dr. Pift.

While the doctor was en-route to collect the donor, she studied the woman's cascade of curls. They appeared wet to the touch, the color gleaming, shifting between penny copper and fire-red. In direct light the effect looked holographic. She slid her fingers into the silky weight, stunned by how cool it felt as it twined around her skin. Searching for the base of Copper's skull, she lifted the heavy tresses, breath caught in her throat as her fingertips caressed her skin. No clips. No weaves. Not even discolored roots.

My hair.

Clara, Dr. Pift's assistant, helped Alesha into her surgery gown. While they retrieved the donor, Clara had been prepping the operation room for the procedure. Heart monitors, I.V.s, breathing masks for the anesthetic, several metal carts with various instruments, and needles lined both beds. The doctor wanted to begin the transplants before sunrise.

"Are you allergic to shellfish, strawberries, kiwis, bananas, or poinsettias?"

Alesha climbed onto the gurney. "No... why?"

Clara checked off boxes on a chart. "Standard questions. We need to know if you are allergic to iodine or latex."

"No allergies that I'm aware of." Alesha shrugged. After a moment, she cleared her throat and said, "You know, I probably should've asked before, but what is going to happen to the donor after the transplant?"

She focused so much on acquiring the donor that she hadn't thought about the aftermath. How would Dr. Pift keep them both out of danger once the transplant was completed?

"The doctor has a plausible explanation for her 'accident.' After the transplant he will also monitor her recovery, but you will be in different wings of the building. She will have no suspicions of foul play." Observing Alesha's apprehension, she added, "Dr. Pift has performed dozens of these transplants so far and they've been quite successful. You needn't worry. You're in the best possible hands."

Alesha nodded and tried to relax. *No backing out now.* She watched the second hand on the clock circle around as Clara started an I.V. on her arm and began adhering the electrode patches for the cardiac monitor to her chest. Once she was situated in the hospital bed, Clara placed a mask over her face and told her to count backwards from twenty.

The scream was so distant she thought she must already be

dreaming.

Daily she downed as many anti-rejection medications as she did food. Gengraf, Prednisone, Cytovene ...the names blurred together in a chemical cocktail designed to keep her body from killing the new flesh sutured above her scalp. The only medication she enjoyed was the morphine they administered in even higher doses to dull the crippling headaches. But her discomfort was outweighed by excitement.

Ten days after the transplant, Dr. Pift removed the bandages. Sitting with her back to a mirror, she kept her eyes closed tight. For the first time in her life, she would see herself with a full head of hair. Even as she faced her reflection, she didn't peek.

The copper curls were now just coarse waves, the color dull and greasy. She smiled regardless. They'd been wrapped in a turban of gauze for a week and a half, of course they were grimy. All that mattered was they were hers now. She met Dr. Pift's eyes in the mirror. He frowned.

"Is something wrong?"

He didn't answer, just circled around to inspect her scalp. His fingertip, though barely grazing the incision, felt like a razorblade slicing her open.

"Clara, take some fresh samples and send them to the lab, please."

He turned to leave as she grabbed his arm. "What's wrong?

I see it in your eyes. What's happening?"

"Most likely nothing, but I need to make sure you're not in the early stages of rejection." As the color drained from her face, he continued, "Try not to be alarmed. Almost all transplants try to reject in the beginning. I expected this would happen. We will adjust your medications and monitor you, but I'm sure you'll be fine."

She faced her reflection, this time staring closely at the incision. Practically indistinguishable from her new hairline, she almost didn't notice the slight puckering, or the yellow stain that seemed to bleed onto her forehead. Gently, she touched the ruched seam, wincing at the sharp sensation that squeezed her skull. Then she noticed the odor, a faint rotting that reminded her of two-week-old roadkill.

Deep down, she'd known the transplant was failing. The odor that grew stronger every day, the puckering that deepened around the edges of the incision... to make matters worse, some of the hair started falling out. Dr. Pift upped the dosages of steroids, readjusted the Gengraf, but still it continued. Her head was decaying.

"You're in acute transplant rejection," Dr. Pift confirmed. "The only real remedy is another transplant."

"This is my hair, Dr. Pift." Alesha panicked. "I don't want another transplant. There has to be a way to save it!"

He shook his head, his eyes answering before he said, "Not with medicine, I'm afraid."

* * *

Dr. Laurie Middleton looked nothing like the woman Alesha pictured when she made the appointment. She answered the door with a tight smile and perfectly coifed hair, dressed in a floral sweater and tweed skirt. Alesha expected tribal gowns, and perhaps a bone piercing or two.

Dr. Laurie Middleton was a shaman.

As per the agreement, she avoided hospitals and doctors, but after a few holistic attempts ended in heightening infections, she decided to look for a less conventional solution. Dr. Pift suggested she see a different sort of healer. "Sometimes, such a crisis can only be cured with faith," he said. During a brief telephone interview, Dr. Middleton agreed to meet with Alesha in her home office.

After a cool handshake, Laurie led her to the study. "Please have a seat while I ready the room for the ceremony."

Alesha watched Laurie place stone bowls filled with branches on either side of a chaise. As she lit the stems they smoldered and caught flame, swirling pungent smoke into the air. She then turned on a small stereo resting on a nearby shelf. The faint sound of drums whispered through speakers mounted in the corners of the room. Once her ministrations were complete, she settled on the chaise and smiled at Alesha, then closed her eyes. They sat in silence for several minutes.

When Alesha softly cleared her throat to speak, Dr. Middleton's eyes opened, and she smiled again. Her voice was calm, like she could drift to sleep mid-sentence. "I sense you are missing a part of yourself. Something has been lost, and until it is brought back, you cannot be whole. As a shamanic healer, I can do several things to alleviate such situations, but in your case, what would serve you best is what we call a soul retrieval."

"I don't know what that means," Alesha shrugged. "And I'm not all that religious. What am I supposed to do?"

"All I need is for you to remain quiet and open your mind. I will do the rest. This will require a spiritual journey, during which I will slip into a trance. Once I emerge, your healing will be complete. There may be instructions for your aftercare, but I will explain them to you before you leave. Do you have any questions before we begin?"

"How will I know it worked?"

"My dear, you will know without words. You will feel it–" Dr. Middleton laid a hand over her heart "–in *here*."

"But I'm not sick there..."

The doctor shot her a look that could quiet baying wolves. "When you are sick, you always need healing in your center. Now, if there are no other questions, are you ready to begin?"

"Sure, I guess," Alesha mumbled.

Laurie pulled her legs onto the chaise and reclined, her eyes closed as she hummed a tuneless melody. The humming faded into deeps breaths while the woman relaxed, her chest rising slow and even.

Alesha watched the woman sleep, her own eyes growing heavy. Between the acrid smoke and the soft deliberate rhythm of ceremonial drums, it took all her willpower not to doze off. She studied her nails, tried to read the titles of the books on the shelves, even tried to make a song from the drumbeats. But despite her most valiant efforts, sleep took over.

She hovered in a black abyss, her body numb and heavy, like an ocean buoy suspended mid-air, waiting to hit the waves below. When she opened her mouth, she couldn't speak. Couldn't scream. Couldn't even gasp. Confusion and panic gripped her, but oddly enough, she didn't feel her heart race.

An electric current ripped through her, and as it did, she was submerged into light and sound. Chills washed over her as she awakened, disoriented and overcome with vertigo. *Where am I?*

A quick glance around did nothing to ease her growing anxiety. She sat on an unfamiliar couch in a stranger's living room. *How did I get here? Shouldn't I still be at Dr. Pift's clinic?*

Then she remembered. *I'm at the shaman's house.*

But the room didn't resemble the traditional décor of Dr. Middleton's home. A widescreen television hung on a far wall, the furnishings pristine and contemporary. Various polished picture frames on the end tables held snapshots of people she'd never met. She searched the room for anything that would jog her memory, but nothing rang a bell. She ran her hand over a lush velveteen sofa cushion.

Come to think of it, she'd seen this couch before. But where?

The room was immaculate... except for the dozens of empty yogurt cups that littered the floor.

Alesha's stomach rolled. She hated yogurt. The vile sour taste, the thick creaminess... she couldn't eat as much as a spoonful without gagging. And yet here she sat, surrounded by empty containers, including an empty cup in her left hand with a spoon resting inside. It had been licked clean.

Repulsed, she threw the cup down and stood slowly, immediately noticing a pain in her joints similar to the aches she felt after rigorous exercising. Groaning, she dragged her feet through the sea of Dannons and Yoplaits, looking for her purse and her bottle of painkillers. No sign of either.

She located a telephone in the kitchen and dialed Dr. Pift's number. As she waited for an answer, she caught sight of her reflection across a polished refrigerator door panel. Her hair looked fantastic. So did her clothes.

Too bad they weren't hers.

Dr. Pift answered before she had time to end the call. "Yes?"

"Dr. Pift? It's Alesh..."

"Where the hell have you been?" He roared in her ear. "Have you broken our agreement?"

His reaction sent another chill through her. "What do you mean? I had an appointment with Dr. Middleton, remember? I think I fell asleep."

"You've been asleep for three weeks? You need to come back to the clinic so I can monitor your recovery. Being off your anti-rejection meds that long will surely create dire complications."

Alesha couldn't speak. She was numb with shock. Her voice cracked when she found it again. "I've been gone for three weeks?"

His voice was tense, like he was speaking through clenched teeth. "Miss Aldopita, get back here at once. Your very life could be in jeopardy."

She ran a finger gingerly under her hairline, waiting for the jolt of pain. Nothing. She didn't feel as much as a scar. "Of course, doctor. I'm leaving here now. I should be there shortly."

If I can figure out where 'here' is...

She explored the rest of the apartment, finding a bathroom and bedroom. No sign of any of her belongings, other than her purse, which lay on top of a tall bureau. Reaching for it, her eyes fell on a picture in a small frame nearby.

Copper Curls. Or, as the diploma framed and displayed over the bureau clearly stated, Andrea Aimes.

"Oh god, I have to get out of here!" She looked around, making sure she hadn't left any other personal belongings behind. If Copper discovered her in the apartment, wearing the stolen hair, she'd have Alesha behind bars faster than she could blink. Hopefully she was still under treatment at the clinic.

Which is where I haven't been for the past three weeks...

She checked the bathroom once more, making sure there were no traces of her visit. Then a dark puddle in the tub caught her attention. Jerking back the shower curtain, she almost screamed. The clothes she'd worn to Dr. Middleton's house were heaped in the basin. Soaked in blood.

Sinking to the floor, she cradled her head in her hands, fighting a wave of nausea.

I'm in Copper's apartment, wearing her clothes, because my clothes are ruined. Why can't I remember the past three weeks? What happened at Dr. Middleton's house?

Dr. Pift might not have answers, but certainly he knew where Copper was. That little bit of knowledge was better than nothing. She would get back and let him finish her therapy so she could begin her new life.

A mile from the apartment, with her purse and a black garbage bag full of bloodied garments clutched in her arms, it occurred to her—for all the blood on her clothes, there was no blood anywhere else in the apartment.

Dr. Pift regarded her as if she'd laid a golden egg. Once he determined that her scalp had completely healed without the aid of repression therapy, he sat at his desk, looking dumbfounded.

She would have been amused were she not scared shitless.

"Dr. Pift, is my donor still in the clinic?"

"No." He looked away, busying himself with desk papers, and said, "I didn't want to tell you, but I suppose you should know."

"Know what?"

"While you were being prepped for your surgery, there was a bit of an accident. A freakish mishap, you might say. Your donor woke unexpectedly as we were getting her ready for the procedure. A struggle ensued before we could sedate her, and she thrashed about so much, her neck snapped." Both his face and voice conveyed no emotion. "It was an unfortunate situation, and by that time you were already under sedation. Don't worry though. We incinerated her remains. Neither you nor I will be implicated if she is reported missing."

Alesha was torn between terror and relief. Her palms were clammy, trembling so badly she kept them tightly clasped on her lap.

He seemed oblivious to her panic, instead hitting the button on the intercom. "Clara, can we get some samples from Alesha? I need to readjust her immunosuppressant therapy."

Clara responded quickly, entering the office with a tray of syringes, vials, and rubber tourniquets. "Wow," she said, "you healed better than anyone I've seen so far. Now, didn't I say you were in the best hands?"

Alesha nodded, unable to speak around the lump in her throat. She waited as Clara extracted three vials of her blood and left the room. "Dr. Pift, something is not right. I don't remember leaving Dr. Middleton's house. I don't have any memory of the last three weeks. When I called you, I had just woken up. In the donor's apartment."

Dr. Pift stared, speechless.

"Plus, I seem to love yogurt now, which is weird, because the stuff usually makes me throw up. And that's not the worst of it..."

"Yes?"

"These aren't my clothes. I woke up in them. My clothes were in her tub, covered in blood."

If he was worried at all, she couldn't tell. He rubbed his chin thoughtfully before replying. "The Cytovene you're taking is known sometimes to cause changes in taste. Not unheard of. Just means we need to lower your dosage. Prednisone often comes with a host of complications, including confusion and a difficulty in your perception of what's real and imagined. I'm sure all this can be fixed with your medications. As soon as your tests come back, we'll see where your levels are and make the necessary changes." He quickly added, "I will test the blood on your clothes. We need to know if you were hemorrhaging."

"But isn't that unlikely? I don't even have a scar."

"You are a very fortunate young lady," he agreed. "I suspect you'll be on your way much faster than anticipated."

But his unflustered optimism was clouded with concern when Alesha met to discuss the results of her lab work.

"The tests results came back with unexpected information. I'm not sure what to make of it, honestly."

Alesha braced herself for the bad news. Did they find a tumor? An impending aneurysm? Was she on Death's doorstep?

"Before the surgery, your records all indicated your blood type was A negative. The samples we just tested are O positive."

"Is that possible?"

"I wouldn't think so. Coincidentally, your donor's blood was also O positive, so most likely it was an error somewhere in our paperwork."

Alesha frowned. "But my blood type has always been A negative. I used to donate..."

"That aside, everything looks good. I'm giving you scripts for the lowest possible dosages of your medications, and we can look you over in a couple of weeks to see how you're doing. Meanwhile, relax." His demeanor was brisk, his smile tight and businesslike. "You finally got your dream come true."

* * *

"I love your eyes."

Alesha didn't realize the cashier was speaking to her at first. But the clerk smiled wider as she handed back her credit card. "Thanks. That's kind of you to say."

The woman laughed. "I'm sure you get compliments like that all the time. Men can't resist pretty redheads with big green eyes."

Alesha smiled nervously and shrugged. "I guess so." She took her bag of groceries and left without mentioning that her eyes were brown. *She'd have to be colorblind not to notice that!*

She was still adjusting to the attention she received now. While she expected people would stop staring at her like she was a freak, she never thought she'd get so many compliments. Men and women both seemed fascinated with her looks. Not used to all the praise, she found herself often at a loss for words. Sure, she'd always had a pretty face, but adding a head of hair wouldn't transform her into a supermodel.

The cashier's comment really bothered her. Her eyes were so brown they were almost black. When she arrived home she headed immediately for the bathroom.

"Holy shit!"

They weren't green... they were emerald. And for some reason, rounder. Not even the most expensive contact lenses to create the shade staring back at her. Those weren't her eyes.

* * *

She woke from her nap feeling heavy headed and drained. Standing up, she stretched, rubbing her eyes. Shuffling a few steps, her toe kicked something on the floor. Opening her eyes wide, she gasped. An empty cup of blueberry yogurt rolled across a designer rug. Copper's rug.

She crossed to a desk and brought up the screensaver on a laptop computer. She hovered over the time in the bottom corner. *Four days.*

The blackouts continued, sometimes for just a day or two, sometimes for weeks. Every time she woke, she found herself in Copper's apartment, wearing her clothes, eating her yogurt. But Copper wouldn't be needing it anymore. In fact, she was contemplating moving in permanently, especially when she discovered the checkbook to Copper's fat bank account.

It didn't hurt that Alesha discovered she could sign Copper's name perfectly.

She no longer panicked when people paid her unexpected compliments. Before her last blackout, a flirtatious waiter called her 'freckle face'... she discovered afterwards that her pale cheeks had turned golden, sprinkled with sandy speckles. To her amusement—and delight—her breasts outgrew her brassieres by a whole cup size. Fortunately, Copper had extravagant taste in lingerie, and it all happened to fit Alesha perfectly. Almost everything about her changed in the months following her surgery, and for the better.

The only lingering concern was the bathtub full of bloody clothes that came with every black-out. She immediately dumped them in the garbage incinerator and would forget about them. *Out of sight...*

Life was perfect now that Alesha Alopecia was history.

Copper's apartment proved a much better fit for her new life, as long as she remembered to check the calendar. Once she forgot, and discovered later that she had blacked out when she went for a shower and stepped into a bloody tub. She only needed to make that mistake once.

She even remembered to respond when people called her Andrea.

Spring cleaning Copper's closet felt like an Easter egg hunt. Looking through boxes and drawers, she found photo albums, journals, budget planners, and keepsakes. Judging by the treasure trove of mementos, she gathered Copper accumulated a lot of frequent flyer miles.

Humming a song she didn't know, she pulled a stack of hatboxes off a shelf and placed them on the bed. Most of the boxes contained hats. But when she opened the largest one, she found a jumble of mismatched sleeves.

There were different colors, different fabrics, different sizes. The only commonality they shared was that they were all men's sleeves. Some were torn off at the shoulder seam;

others appeared to be hacked off with scissors. One by one, she laid them in a neat pile. Twenty-three in total.

Underneath the sleeves was a metal lockbox, but the hasp was unlocked. She opened the box, half expecting to find perhaps a random collection of collars. Instead, she found a pile of newspaper clippings. She unfolded the clipping that rested on top and read the headline.

"Body Found Believed to Be Victim Number 23 For Sioux City Slayer."

She looked for a date on the article. It came from the previous day's newspaper. Thumbing through the other clippings, she discovered they were all about the same thing. They came from different papers, different cities, but each one detailed the killing spree of a psychotic murderer who slaughtered men without an apparent motive or agenda.

Her stomach started to cramp.

Twenty-three separate murders, six occurring in the past five months. She sank onto the bed, reading each article, absorbing the details of the murders. The murders started two years earlier, with no rhyme or reason. Investigators couldn't profile the suspect because the only consistent clues were that all the victims were male. And all were found missing one shirt sleeve.

Copper is dead; Dr. Pift burned her body. So why did the murders continue? Was Copper an accomplice? Did the real murderer have access to Copper's apartment?

Now that she knew about them, would they come for her next?

Waves of nausea seized her, and she ran for the bathroom. Dropping in front of the commode, dry heaves wracked her abdomen. She rested her head on her arm and tried to clear her head.

And saw a puddle of bloody clothes in the bathtub.

An explosion in the living room pulled her away from the tub. Footsteps running through the apartment amid the shouts and commands of strange voices filled her first with fear, and then relief. She was saved!

Suddenly she was staring at the firing end of an automatic weapon, the man behind it screaming at her to lie on the floor.

"I don't understand! What do you want with me?" She couldn't make out exactly what he was saying because the bathroom quickly filled with officers, all angry, all barking orders that made no sense. She laid face down hoping someone would explain what was happening.

"Andrea Aimes, you are under the arrest for the murders of 23 people..."

"No no no! That's not me! I'm not Andrea Aimes, I don't even know her! You're making a big mistake. She's still here!" Alesha pleaded with her captors as they cuffed her hands behind her back and forced her to her feet.

A voice at her back snarled, "Save it, you bitch. We got you on video this time."

"No!"

"Someone tell Forensics we have some evidence in here."

Over her shoulder she could see a couple police officers leaning over the bathtub.

"I swear to you, I have no idea what's going on..."

They pushed her into the hallway, where a photographer busied himself with crime scene photos. A flash of light bounced off a passing mirror, drawing her attention. The woman in the glass that stared back wore a stranger's face.

To the Victor Goes the Soil

"Release the dogs!"

Forty-nine canines tore into the night, teeth bared, hackles raised in unison. Doug shook his fist in the air. "Tonight we will not be defeated! They'll pay for what they've done!"

The men stood back and watched the foxhounds disappear into dark fields, fearlessly pursuing their elusive prey. Their torches, held high, illuminated the vegetable garden for about fifty feet. Sheriff Moses tapped Doug on the shoulder.

"You know, we had plenty of them heavy duty flashlights back at the station. Don't you think you're overdoing it a bit? Drop just one of them torches and the whole damn harvest will be scorched."

Doug turned and flashed a shit-eating grin. "Sherriff, we done lost a dozen dogs to those demons. What happens if they get past our hounds? How we gonna protect ourselves with a bunch of Maglights? *Throw* 'em at their heads?"

The sheriff held up his hands and backed away. "Okay, okay. Whatever you say. You're in charge here."

"Damn right I am," Doug grumbled, and leaned to the man at his side. "Don't know what we do if this don't work, Tommy."

Tommy held a torch in one hand, and a hoe in the other. He was a hard worker, but not the brightest bulb in the box. Twice already he'd scorched his hair when he held his torch too low. The bitter smell of burnt follicles still lingered in the air. "It's gonna work this time. Barney Dog is the finest mutt I ever raised. If he don't get 'em, then I don't know what!"

Doug prayed he was right. The town was under siege, terrorized by an army straight from the bowels of hell. He manned the frontlines, determined to defeat Satan's legion before it took them all out. It came looking for food, ravaging people's crops while they slept. Radishes, tomatoes, pole beans... first it was heads of cabbage, then it was heads of babies. Well, not yet, but it *would* be if Doug didn't step in and take charge. So he rounded up all the farmers in the county and declared war on the monsters. So far, no luck. Them were some tricky bastards. A shrill yelp tore through the night, and everyone jumped except Tommy, who screamed, "Barney Dog, *nooo*!" Then he took off into the field, waving his torch in the air and stumbling several times over produce.

"Get back here, Tommy! It's too late!" But Doug's

command went unheeded. "Damn fool boy gonna get himself killed!"

He turned to the men and shouted, "Stay here and guard the home front! I'm goin' in after him!" With that, Doug tore through the rows of squash, following the fireball bouncing in the direction of a distant corn field.

Tommy was standing in a clearing when he caught up. They could hear the ruckus of growls and barks scattered throughout the stalks. Grabbing Tommy's elbow, he spun him about face. "He can't be saved, boy. Just let 'em go! He died in battle. There's honor in that." Releasing his arm, he said softly, "Come on back to the others now. You'll be safer there."

Tommy shrugged and mumbled, "Okay," his shoulders slumped in defeat as he dragged his feet. Doug could hear sniffling at his back.

Damn sissy, he thought. He saw them right as he got ready to enter the squash patch. Tiny pairs of red dots, glowing in between the butternuts, turning the field into a flickering sea of Nope. As he tried to formulate a plan of escape, more appeared. *Must be a hundred of them fuckers*, he realized. He'd left a load of dynamite back with the men, ready to be tossed if all else failed. Wouldn't do them no good from the other side of the field, though.

He whispered, "When I say go, you run like you've never run before."

From the corner of his eye he could see Tommy nod, his

Adam's apple punctuating his loud gulp.

Waiting a beat, he screamed, "*Go*! *Run*!"

Tommy shot ahead of him, squealing like a greased pig, but when Doug set to running, he tripped over some unruly vines and fell belly down in the soil. "Holy hellfire!" he screamed, as dozens of red–eyed rabbits slowly emerged from the vegetables.

"Leave me be, you spawns of Satan!" He covered the back of his head with his hands just as they leapt. Little teeth tore into his flesh. Them rabbits ate good that night.

But at least he died in battle.

There's honor in that.

Hell Does Not Bring Fire

She guards the shores
with closed eyes,
spire
of stone veiled
in black, since that night
the storm won, racing over rocks
without falling; bounding
across the slickest
of wet cliffs,
rattling
the
walls
of the chapel
where men offered
prayers to the wrong god.
Heaving their lives and their lies
into the belly of the churning
cataclysm, a prodigious
gateway to the
ocean

below the seas-

the Under underneath

her torch, saving the vessels,

but too weak to save the souls of men.

Their agony smothered in salt

water brine and the bite

of merciless

wrath,

punctuating each

wave with the copper tinge

of sangria—the opulent wine mortality

exsanguinates, delicate tender

lungs collapsing and

dulled orbs

staring

into the face

of the Unholy Almighty.

Stolen from her catwalk at the whim

of the sleeping god woken by their sacrilege,

pulling them into the endless depths

of infinite retribution, the

penance for a prayer—

for in the end

Hell

does not bring

fire… It brings the sea.

Dusk Droppings

The night melted.

Thick, tarry goo plummeted from the starless sky, landing first as fat drops, morphing into large globs that broke rooftops, downed tree branches, crushed newly sprouted blades of grass, and engulfed the citizens of Gulch. By night's end, the town was a featureless bed of tar, and everything that made Gulch was preserved within like fossils in amber. An entire history, generations that dated back to pre-Civil War, entombed in a pool of black.

They'd been warned.

Pastor Baynes stood aside his idling Caddy, his face lax. No shock or horror betrayed his stoic reserve. He prayed for Gulch's destruction, though. He'd paraphrased and spoke riddles in his church prayers, but he asked for their demise. Those fools prayed right along with him, throwing their faith into an untimely end they thought were just generalized pleas. *Serves them right*, he thought. Those ignorant lemmings.

Those *sinners*.

Baynes's fire and brimstone sermons were famed across the county. He rolled in with his tents and choir, and drained the small towns of their savings accounts through songs of sacrifice and salvation. He tossed a few fictitious prophecies in, a false miracle or two, then packed up and moved on. Once a year, he visited each town with the grandstanding of a glorious parade. The small-town mentality drank it in like moonshine. The money he made on his yearly revival tours kept him comfortable and lazy for the winter months ahead.

Until the local plastics plant closed operations.

Towns like Gulch couldn't survive such inevitable signs of the times. Most of the town worked at that plant. So when he rolled through, there were no savings accounts to drain. The townsfolk prayed desperately for a new factory. They prayed for new jobs. They prayed for lotteries, for winning horse races. Some of them prayed to leave. But those prayers fell short. The offering baskets returned empty. He left town with barely enough money for gas.

Pastor Baynes was outraged.

When their God turned a blind eye to their struggles, his god got creative.

Desperate people would make any plea deal with the great Almighty. So when they sought him out individually, asking what, if anything, they could offer, he told them any sign of faith would appeal to God's good graces. Small, temporary signs. Just as a show of trust. Something they could go back and undo after they received their blessings.

For some, it was an addendum on their homeowner's insurance policies. For others, it was a new beneficiary in their will. Notarized, temporary declarations of love and absolute, unwavering faith.

How could they possibly know they were about to encounter such abrupt catastrophes? Who could predict such horror? Not a lowly servant of the Lord who served these communities year after year with faithful guidance. Not a man of God.

He simply shrugged and said, "This was their ten percent."

Standing on the outskirts of town, he opened a flask of wine and poured it in the shape of a star around his feet. The wine was thick and coagulated and really the blood of a slaughtered farm animal, previously consecrated. He raised both arms and recited an incantation into the winds blowing from the west. He moved counterclockwise, repeating the call to the south, east, and north. He marked his forehead with a smudge of coppery blood and closed his eyes, arms outstretched, waiting for his god to answer.

That answer came within mere breaths. He kept his eyes squeezed shut until heat rolled over his skin and the heavy fumes that mirrored the burnt oil stench of truck exhaust flooded his nostrils. In the blurry scope of his squinted vision, he saw the black rain ooze, earthbound, and fill every crevice it seeped across. It pushed through door and window cracks until the barriers gave way. Anyone inside the homes would be glued in place before they could escape their beds. The tar would slide into their mouths and fill their ears, and they would suffocate comfortably.

Of course, he only assumed the latter. The tar was likely anything but comforting, with the steam rolling off it like a campfire's smoke. It probably hurt… exactly like Hell. He had no intention of finding out firsthand.

Satisfied with the complete burial of Gulch, Pastor Baynes slid into his Caddy and headed for the next town, where his crew already waited. It would take weeks, if not months, for the profits from Gulch to roll in.

Meanwhile, Cascade Falls looked to be green with donations…and the desire to live.

Even if he *were* the kind of guy to look back, he wouldn't see the thin figure of the boy in the black hoodie that watched him from the rise of a hill. He could not know that Anton Jones witnessed him calling the demons of hell to destroy the sleeping town where Anton's family lived. He had no idea that Anton also had family in Cascade Falls, as well as a scholarship to the state college for his impressive track record.

Anton took off his hoodie and tied it around his waist, his skin absorbing the night like polished mahogany, and set his pace for Cascade Falls.

Good thing he wore his running shoes.

* * *

Baynes looked across the sea of faces, red and splotched from the oppression of summer heat mixed with tears of grief. The news was flooded with the freak destruction of the small, nearby town, killing an entire population in just minutes. Baynes knew how to play the disaster. He'd done so in other places, and in the midst of their panic, most people remained completely oblivious to the other towns in other counties that disappeared overnight.

They cried out to him from their folding metal seats. They asked what they could do to avoid the wrath of God. Pastor Baynes answered them with the commanding consternation of a Holy man who received God's message just short of stepping behind the podium. "Repent of your sins!" he bellowed. "And give. Give everything you can give. Give even what you cannot give. And you will be spared!"

The offering plates circulated and returned overflowing with cash and checks. The town managed to pool just under twelve grand in repentance.

He smiled as he surveyed the annuals. While salvation wasn't cheap, it certainly was worth the investment. Cascade Falls would live to see another year.

Anton urged his cousins not to attend that tent revival, but being devout Pentecostals, they dismissed his warnings with a laugh. They were allowing him to sleep on their couch until he could move into dorm housing, but they didn't know that Anton already had a room at the university. After witnessing Bayne's clandestine ritual, he made a point to stick close to Cascade Falls. He didn't want the man to destroy what family he had left.

Baynes would still get to them, though. His aunt drained their entire savings account to tithe the pastor's service. She said God was truly working through that man, that everything they gave would be returned ten-fold. Anton didn't buy it, but what could he say without sounding completely unhinged?

He had to stop him. Before he bankrupted every small town he rolled through. Before he buried their existences under blankets of scalding tar. Pastor Baynes was an evangelical locust, destroying everything in his path. Leaving scorched earth and destitution in his wake.

Surely no god blesses such a vile creature?

Anton watched from shadows as the pastor oversaw his crews breaking down the tent and loading the sea of folded chairs onto a tractor trailer decorated in purple and gold glittered words that read, "Pastor Baynes' Traveling Miracle Ministry!" At the bottom of the trailer was a scripture, from the eleventh chapter of Proverbs. It read:

"A man may give freely, and still his wealth will be increased; and another may keep back more than is right, but only comes to be in need."

Anton couldn't believe how eagerly everyone bought into

the charlatan's show.

He moved closer, staying in the shadow of the nearby Arkansas Oaks that lined the fairgrounds. Perhaps he could overhear their conversations as they worked. He was curious about where they planned to go next. His gut told him Esthmarene, but he wanted to be sure.

Esthmarene was a small, impoverished community. They recently lost their grain mill, which was the town's livelihood. They would have no money to pay off Baynes. If Anton wanted to catch this murderous man red-handed, he needed to know where they were headed.

Two ragged hands were loading chairs onto a flatbed dolly as he slid over to the truck and pressed his back to the trailer, deliberately avoiding the side that would put him in clear view of the pastor. The men were laughing, cracking indecipherable jokes, but Anton clearly heard one of them mumble 'Esthmarene.' While that may not have been solid proof of anything, it was good enough to assume by.

Anton borrowed his cousin's car and used it to drive into Little Rock, where he found an apothecary, and sought out the store's owner. He withheld some of the crazier details, such as tar raining from the sky and a traveling evangelist and asked what he could do to stop someone in the process of casting harmful spells on innocent people. The older women smiled, her eyes suggesting she knew the details he'd left out, and led him to shelves heaped with various bottles and herbs.

"Anything you do is useless without faith," she said. "I will give you the tools. But you must provide the fertile ground for them to grow power. You must *believe* they will stop him. Otherwise, you will only manage to upset him further, and likely incur his wrath."

"So how do I do that?" Anton asked.

"Prayer and meditation," she said. She handed him bundles of sage, a velvet satchel full of coarse salt, white candles to destroy negative energies, and black candles for protection.

With his arms full of spiritual supplies, he said, "But I'm not religious."

She laughed and handed him a box of matchsticks. "This isn't about religion, dear. It's about *heart*. What color is your heart? Because anything done with a dark heart brings evil. Anything brought with a heart of light yields good."

He nodded and mumbled his thanks.

"Come see me afterwards," she said. "I sense you have powers you are unaware of, and I would be interested in helping you channel them. You could save your community with such power. You are the great one, young man."

Anton didn't know what to say. The shopkeeper's proclamation startled him. *Great one?* Was it possible that he possessed such power? Could he save anyone else, when most times, he barely saved himself?

He couldn't find the words, so he muttered something unintelligible and turned to leave.

She called after him to wait. When he turned, she placed a sheathed dagger in his armload of materials, and said, “Before the rain comes, pull him out of his star, and drive this into his heart. Throw salt in his face. Then *run*.”

Anton tried not to appear rattled as he replied, “Run? Why? Does he explode?”

She snorted. “Stand too close and you’ll find out...”

Her laughter followed him to his car.

The passenger’s seat held the supplies he’d been given, all ready for quick use. The shopkeeper contacted him later (which was unsettling because he hadn’t left his phone number) and told him the dagger needed to be rubbed with grapeseed oil. The blade of the dagger was carved abalone shell, and according to the shopkeeper, powerful because it harnesses the energy of the ocean. An ocean was the only water strong enough to stop the molten fires of the earth. It would be strong enough to cool the black tar rain.

As Anton expected, Esthmarene barely filled one collection plate with offerings at Bayne’s service. The pastor then preached his fire and brimstone warnings to a congregation of broken people who were terrified they’d angered their Lord. After the service, they all filed one by one to hand him deeds and titles and promissory notes. He soothed their worries as he pocketed their lives, assuring them that God was gracious and forgiving.

Esthmarene breathed a collective sigh of relief as they said their evening prayers. Then, one by one, the lights in the town went dark.

Anton parked on the outskirts of town behind a copse of trees that evening and sat in a clearing. He lit the black and white candles and meditated, lifting his face to the midnight moon. Eyes closed, he made up prayers and focused on the sound of his breathing. When he blew out the candles, he held them inside the car, and sat in the chamber of fragrant smoke, willing it to absorb into his black clothes and penetrate his pores. He tucked the satchel of salt and the abalone dagger into the front pockets of his hoodie and pulled the hood over his head. When the gold Caddy rolled by him in the dark, the Pastor couldn't see Anton or his car, lying in wait.

He slithered from the car and left the door open. Making his way towards the preacher's back, he noted the blood star the pastor poured around his feet. The shopkeeper's instructions came back to him.

He froze when the pastor turned to him, with his arms stretched apart, and bellowed a chant. Bayne's eyes were closed, fortunately, and Anton's dark skin and clothes cloaked him in nightfall. He held his breath as he waited for the man to complete his ritual.

Then Anton made his move.

He pretended he was competing in a 200-yard sprint, and bent down, bracing his body on his fingertips and the balls of his feet. Then he launched like a bullet, driving towards the pastor, an animal growl ripping from his throat.

The pastor's reflexes were slow, and Anton threw an arm around his throat and pulled him backwards, just enough for his feet to stumble outside the perimeter of his bloody barrier. Baynes struggled against him, but Anton was a strong athlete, and his sinewy muscles easily overpowered the pastor's weak appendages and gluttonous belly pudge.

He pulled the dagger from his pocket, and as he did, a prayer he'd never heard before fell from his lips. Bringing his arm around, he sank the small dagger into Bayne's chest. Though he stabbed blindly, his first strike was effective.

A ruby river flowed down the front of Bayne's shirt, as Anton circled him. He shoved his hand into the satchel and pulled out a fistful of salt, which he threw into the pastor's face. The man screamed in anguish, his voice deep and unfamiliar. It reminded Anton of a B-movie demon. He almost forgot the shopkeeper's last bit of advice, until he felt the earth rumbling beneath his feet.

He made for the safety of his car, putting yards between him and Baynes within seconds, when the sound of ripping overpowered the pounding in his chest. He turned and saw the sky above the pastor tear open, a giant rent in the nightscape that glowed fiery red. From the fire poured a heavy cascade of hot tar, steam rolling from it as it showered over Pastor Baynes, quickly smothering the man's demonic screams under a human-sized mountain of hardening pitch. Within seconds, the pastor was completely encapsulated.

All that was left was a mound in the middle of the road, still smoking, its malodourous fumes soiling the air.

The rent in the sky healed, leaving behind a cobalt blanket of stars that twinkled peacefully over the sleeping town.

Anton moved full-time into his dorm room after the small towns were compensated for all their offerings. His aunt received her savings back, plus ten percent, for her troubles. She found significance in that, and promised to tithe again, next time a traveling minister passed through Cascade Falls.

But Anton no longer worried about charlatans with nefarious intentions.

After all, he had a dagger for that.

While he couldn't bring back the lost lives of Gulch, Anton knew their souls were at peace. The shopkeeper assured him of it. She'd heard their voices the night he brought Baynes down.

From that night on, Anton kept his eyes on the horizon, in search of purple and gold tractor trailers and self-proclaimed Men of God who were *anything* but.

Small Claws, Small Guns

Those bastard eyes narrowed. They were the color of gasoline, but not the expensive premium-grade gasoline. I'm talking at least 20% ethanol-laced, the real cheap stuff. The kind that makes your engine sputter. The kind that screams for a quart of fuel additive at the pump. They were eyes you couldn't trust.

I thumbed the hammer of my .45 and tensed my finger around the trigger.

He snarled and stood taller. "I knew you didn't have the balls…"

His chest exploded the instant a deafening crack ripped the air. Red rained on the concrete slab as his body crashed on the garage floor. I was shocked still, frozen in place, trying to piece together what happened. Despite the tremble in my hands, I had the good sense not to drop my gun and accidentally discharge my bullet.

I mean, sure. This was what I came for. Argeno was dead. All I had to do was leave the coded message on the voicemail, and my assignment would be complete. I did not need to tell them it wasn't my gun that killed the mark. Probably.

But I needed to make sure I wasn't next.

I lifted my gun and inched to the left. The shot was fired from somewhere to the right, near a pile of used tires in a corner about twenty feet away. I didn't speak, I could barely breathe. Whoever hid in there could have easily taken me out with Argeno. Maybe they were intentionally avoiding me.

I coughed to clear my nervous throat, and said, "Hello?"

No response.

Even with my gun raised, I was an easy target. Clearly, they were studying me, weighing their options. I wasn't their mark. I lowered my gun but kept my finger on the trigger. "This guy," I said, pointing to Argeno. "What an asshole, am I right?"

I heard scuffling, and brought my pistol back up, ready to fire away, steeled for a fight against my stealthy opposition.

Two round eyes blinked from the shadows of bald Michelins. I could just barely make out an unusually long mustache. The figure stepped into a shaft of light.

I stood face to face with an otter. Standing on an otter that was standing on yet another otter. Three otters, wearing a beige trench coat. The top otter wore a dark fedora and held a Ruger

LCP between its front paws. Otters incognito. The trio eyed me like I was a delicious fish.

"Oh my god," I said, unable to stop myself. "You're adorable!"

Top Otter squealed twice. Maybe it thanked me. Either that or someone stepped on a squeaky dog toy. I never talked to an otter before, so I wasn't familiar with their vocalizations. Top Otter sounded like a cross between a rubber chicken and a Daily Bark toy newspaper.

I took a step toward the otters and extended my hand. Did otters greet strangers by sniffing hands like dogs?

A whistle shrilled from somewhere I couldn't see. The otters dismantled and scampered into the shadows, heading for an exit. Top Otter still wore the fedora and trench coat, which flapped behind like a bland cape. They were faster than me. By the time I emerged from the garage, I could see the otters climbing into a van at the curb. There were even more otters in the van with them. A veritable gang of dog-sized assassins packed into an Econoline. I waved at them—not sure why, just couldn't help it—but the door closed. As the van sped away, the ruckus of innumerable squeaky toys being squeezed filled the night air.

I waited until the taillights disappeared, then called my handler.

Orman's office sat in a perpetual blanket of sour smoke and

wood oil. It felt both grimy and pristine at the same time. Orman himself was the same irony personified. His expensive suit was tailored and immaculate, but his hair jutted from his scalp in unruly peppered gray gnarls, and he sported an around-the-clock five o'clock shadow on his jowled chin. I'd been doing contracts for him for a few years, and he never changed… the best-dressed slob I'd ever met. He took a couple puffs off his stubby cigar and studied me.

"So, Argeno is done?" His voice was as smooth as rocks tumbling in two fingers of bourbon.

"Yes."

"And *you* did him?"

"Yeah, I mean, yes." I avoided fidgeting with my sleeves. Orman could sense nervous a county away.

"Because I have video that says otherwise." *Puff-puff-puff.*

Shit! "What are you talking about?" How did he know? In my head, I could see my paycheck dissolving into nothingness.

Orman picked up his phone and swiped the screen, then turned it toward me. I could see the back of the costumed otter trio, with Argeno's backside in the distance, clearly distracted by me. Top Otter jerked back just a little as they fired off a bullet, which probably hit a few organs on its way through his chest. Whoever held the camera moved farther back as I became visible.

I realized "whoever" was probably the one driving the van. Why did it not occur to me that someone was with those otters?

Had I really convinced myself the otters were also responsible for their getaway vehicle?

I guess, after seeing an armed otter execute a perfect hit, I assumed those otters were special enough to also drive themselves home… wherever a gang of assassin otters might live. Full confession, I may or may not have been entertaining myself with visions of how that might've played out.

"Who gave that to you?" I said. I wished for something to soothe my tight throat, like a bottle of water or Maker's Mark.

"That would be the dispatcher who closed the contract." He rubbed the end of his cigar in an ashtray. "Look, Enno, you're a good hire. Someone just beat you to this one."

"I didn't know I was competing with an outside gun for the job," I said, calculating whether I had the funds in the bank to cover my rent without the job. Hint… I wouldn't.

"You weren't. But I tell you what. We have another contract. This one just came in. Some attorney representing that crazy activist group, PTARG. Worth about 17k if you can pull it off this week. Think you can take it?" He held a manilla envelope in his hand and waited for my answer.

"You mean People Treating Animals Real Good?" I'd never tangled with that organization before. They were frequently in the news with their protests and aggressive antics, and even as a hired gun, I found them intimidating. I could appreciate their love for animals, but honestly, I thought they were all just a little more than completely unhinged. That payload was one hell of an incentive, though, and there wasn't much unhinged that a .45 couldn't handle. I almost accepted, but paused to ask, "What about that other dispatcher?"

"They were already paid out before this contract came to us. If you act quickly, they won't even know about it." Orman fished a fresh cigar from a drawer and used a palm-sized cutter to trim one end.

It wasn't the answer I hoped for. Still, I took the envelope. I was more intimidated by my landlord than PTARG. No cute and talented otter would steal this job from me.

I squatted behind a bulbous boxwood hedge outside the PTARG headquarters and waited as all but two cars left the parking lot. The attorney, a man named O'Shea who had the ethics of a dinosaur but the backbone of an eel, was working late with one director, presumably on the upcoming court case. I didn't know why he was being scrubbed, and I didn't need to know. I didn't know who was paying for the hit. I only knew I had two nights left to complete the job. I was ready, in the event he left alone, to fire from the back of the bush, where security cameras couldn't see me hiding in the dark. Unless he was accompanied, or someone else showed up, it would be an easy kill.

The door opened, and my guy came strolling outside, his pace brisk but relaxed. He fumbled for his keys as I raised my gun and aimed. At this angle, I could either go for the heart or head. Either would be effective. Easiest 17k ever.

Squeak squeak.

"Dammit!" I whispered. "No!" I recognized it immediately. Fucking otters, man.

I pushed through the leaves to get a better look, without drawing attention. Four otters approached my mark and were squeaking and squealing at O'Shea's feet. He clearly didn't know how to react, but who would? How often do four chatty river otters approach anyone in a parking lot? Not *nearly* often enough, I say.

Everything happened so fast, I almost couldn't follow it. As he laughed and leaned over to scratch an otter on their head, one of the others—probably Top Otter—stood on their back feet and pulled a small handgun from a fanny pack strapped around their belly. Two quick shots and O'Shea went down … just as the door opened and a woman emerged. She screamed and rushed to O'Shea's side, crying frantically, smoothing back his hair, pleading with his lifeless body.

I suddenly realized why someone might have wanted him dead.

The otters retreated quickly, but not quickly enough to escape her notice. She catapulted after them with her jacket, and flung herself into the air, landing on an otter and smothering them in her coat. One otter circled back and picked something up from the grass, and I realized she must have captured Top Otter. Muffled otter cries faded as she struggled to carry the writhing creature inside the building. I slid back, further out of view of the cameras, and hid in shadows as I circled behind the fence surrounding the PTARG building, toward the parking lot.

By the time I got there, the van was already gone… presuming it was ever there. I needed to get away before the cops arrived. I made it to my car a block over and drove with the lights off for two more blocks, just to make sure they did not see me. I circled around a few blocks and passed by the PTARG building.

I can't say what surprised me more… that there were no police on the scene, or that O'Shea's body was gone. The sprinkler system sputtered to life as I drove away.

I sat in Orman's office and again watched surveillance of the hit I failed to orchestrate. The video cut off as soon as his body hit the ground, which I found both odd and frustrating.

Indeed, the whole situation frustrated me. I lost another contract. The otters beat me to another mark. But there was an added layer now, as the news said nothing about the dead attorney. Nothing about any incidents at the PTARG headquarters, either. The top story during last night's eleven o'clock news had been the fire that broke out at the Bushel's Bacon Beanies plant.

Also, what happened to that poor otter?

Orman said nothing about the otter. In fact, he eyed me

strangely when I asked if the otter was safe. I sort of half shrugged and smirked, and then quickly changed the subject. "Isn't it strange they did not call the police after finding his body?"

Puff puff. Orman studied the cigar smoke for what felt like too long and leaned back in his chair. "The dispatcher reported the hit went without incident. That certainly appears to be the case, by the video they provided."

"They mentioned nothing about PTARG taking their otter hostage?"

"How does someone take an otter hostage? It's an animal. Animals aren't hostages, they're just animals."

"That's not what PTARG would say," I muttered.

"What's that?"

"I mean, yeah, it's an otter. But it's an otter that kills."

"It's a carnivore," he said. "Of course it kills."

Orman was not concerned about the otters. Honestly, I shouldn't have been, either. Despite their incredibly endearing faces and those huge shiny eyeballs and their long, twitchy whiskers, these otters were trained marksmen.

They were also my biggest competition. And the reason I was short on my rent.

"Got anything else for me?"

Orman handed me another folder and another chance to avoid a pissed-off landlord.

* * *

The Manfred hit went without a hitch or interruption. I scored eight grand, which was considerably less than the last two contracts I lost, but more than enough to cover my rent. I figured I could give myself a week before I needed to find more work. Maybe I would switch it up. When I wasn't a hired gun, I alternated between headhunting and landscaping.

Maybe it was time to break out the weed eater.

I was enjoying a burger and catching up on some television when hard knocks shook my front door. I froze and held my breath. Were the police outside? If so, wouldn't they announce it? I checked my doorbell camera on my phone and discovered the lens was covered. Someone didn't want to be seen. I picked up a bat that I kept beside the door and leaned against it.

"Who are you?" I demanded, my mouth an inch away from the deadbolt.

I heard a soft murmur but couldn't pick up anything other than whoever was on my porch was human.

"If you don't at least give me a name, I ain't opening the door."

"Noreen."

I turned the deadbolt and opened the door two inches. A lady in a wide-brimmed hat stood on my porch, her hand pressed over the doorcam lens, her face pinched and impatient.

"Do I know you?" She appeared harmless enough, if not annoyed.

"Can I please come in, Mr. Enno? We have business to

discuss." Her voice was clipped. She glanced back over her shoulder, as if she feared being seen. At first, I thought maybe she was the woman at PTARG, O'Shea's mistress. But as she took off her hat, I realized she was someone else.

I opened the door wider and stepped aside. My revolver waited in a secret pocket of my recliner, so I knew if she pulled anything, I could protect myself. She went directly to my couch and sat down.

"Might I trouble you for a drink?" she said.

"Might I trouble you for an explanation?"

"Sure. Once I have that drink." She picked up my remote and began channel surfing.

I might not be the most gracious host, but Noreen was pretty rude for a guest. Even so, I was more curious than annoyed. I rummaged in my fridge and found a half bottle of Grey Goose and a few hard ciders. I opened a cider and offered it to her.

She blinked and stared at the bottle. She probably meant a glass of water. I was bad at socializing.

"Sorry, I assumed you wanted a real drink," I said.

"This is fine. Thank you." She took the bottle and had a long drink, downing almost half the bottle in one pull, and placed it on the coffee table.

So, she really likes cider. I sat back in my recliner, making sure I could access my pocket in case she got any ideas. "Now, what business do I have with you, Noreen?"

"Please, call me Ms. Kittery."

"Oh. Uh… okay?" I frowned. She might be even more socially awkward than I was. "Ms. Kittery."

"I need your help," she said, "to find Shoggoth."

"I beg your pardon?" I could not have heard correctly.

"*Shoggoth,*" she said, emphasizing each syllable. "My otter."

At that moment, I knew exactly who sat in my living room.

"You want *me* to help *you*?" I laughed, but not in amusement. "Do you have any idea how much money you've cost me?"

"Do you have any idea how much it costs to shelter and feed a half dozen Asian small-clawed otters?"

"I am gonna guess somewhere in the ballpark of 30 thousand."

"I apologize for moving in on your contracts, Mr. Enno. It was a dirty move…"

"Moves," I said.

"… but it has been hard for me to raise the money to care for them by honest means." She finished the cider, burped, and handed me the empty bottle. "Thanks."

"If you can't afford to take care of them, why do you have them?" I studied her as she crossed her legs and leaned against the sofa arm. She didn't seem like such a threat any longer.

"The otters were part of an aquarium show back in Florida. They were a popular attraction until activists started picketing the aquarium. Made a few bomb threats, even, which scared the public away. They were demanding to take the otters into custody and free them into the wild," she said. Her eyes teared just the right amount. "Thing is, these otters were rescued as pups. They were never wild. Releasing them would be a death sentence. So one night, I took them with me. I could not leave them like that. I was all they knew. I would never forgive myself if something happened to them."

"When you say activists…"

Noreen nodded. "PTARG. They harassed me for years over the otters."

I chewed over what she revealed. "So that hit on O'Shea was… revenge?"

"Oh no, that was just a wonderfully convenient hit," she said. "Nothing more. My otters are well-trained assassins. Before we started getting contracts from Orman, we worked for a contractor up north. We moved south because there were more prospects, and I figured we could find another aquarium show once I had enough money put away to build a sanctuary for them. Someplace permanent, where I could also be, to protect them." She smiled. "They are my babies."

"You know, some people just get a cat."

She scowled at me.

"Sorry," I said. I offered her another cider, which she accepted, and thought about the missing otter. "So PTARG has Shoggoth now. Do you think they know it's your otter?"

"Yes. I've been receiving threats from the local members. They said they were going to capture all the otters and drive them a few hundred miles off and leave them. Because they don't belong in captivity." We both made a face.

"Do you have a permit for them? They can't just take your pets from you."

"The aquarium held permits. I didn't have permission to take them. But demonstrators shut down the show. And, like I said, I wasn't about to leave them behind." She gripped the cider bottle so tight I worried she might break it.

"Why not just go to the police?"

She shot me a look.

"Oh yeah. Right." I cleared my throat, unsure of what to say. "I am sorry to hear about this. Of course, it would have been nice if you didn't bogart my marks… but I understand why you were so aggressive."

"That is why I am willing to offer you half of the money I made from those hits in exchange for Shoggoth."

"But I don't …"

"That's almost 15 thousand." She was not going to make this easy.

"Why ask me? I have no skills with animals. The only pets I had growing up were a rock and two goldfish. Animals don't like me."

"Shoggoth likes everyone," she said.

"You probably should have rethought that name."

She clenched the bottle with both hands, and, for that moment, she looked worried I was about to turn down the offer. In my head, I heard the frantic cries of the muffled otter being taken away. Even his distress was adorable.

"Dammit," I said.

What I didn't know at the time was that PTARG was looking for a groundskeeper, for both their headquarters and a second location just outside the city. Noreen, of course, knew that. Just as she knew I did landscaping as a side gig. It turned out to be stupid-easy gaining access to their buildings.

Noreen suspected if Shoggoth wasn't still in the headquarters, he would be caged somewhere on their second property. What scared Noreen was the possibility they might release Shoggoth before she could locate him. So my plan was to get in, figure out exactly where the otter was held, and then bust him out. I wasn't looking for an elaborate or complicated maneuver. While I didn't want to kill anyone while extracting Shoggoth, I would do whatever I needed to.

The headquarters comprised a nondescript office building, except for an enormous neon sign mounted on the rooftop that read PEOPLE TREATING ANIMALS REAL GOOD in orange block letters. The grounds were rather small, with just a few strips of grass to mow, and round boxwood hedges that would need regular pruning. I calculated how much time it would take me to finish the job before remembering I was only pretending to be the groundskeeper.

After picking up my badge key from the superintendent, I located the room where my equipment was stored. The door was outside, by the back entrance. I pretended to do my job, but after a few minutes, I returned to the building and searched for Shoggoth. I even searched the basement, which turned out to be nothing more than a makeshift recreational room that hadn't been used in a long time.

Damn. No otter.

I sent Noreen a text to give her the bad news before heading down a hall toward the front. I heard voices coming from a room, and they grew louder as I approached the doorway. I tucked myself around a corner in the hall and listened.

"They are in the silo," the woman said. "Next to security."

"Do I need a team for the extraction?" the man said.

"You can't lift 100 pounds?" she said. "The barrel is sealed, so you can use the forklift to put it on the truck. Take it to the landfill."

"And the other is a standard release, Liz?"

"God no," she said. "That beast killed Neil. Put a bullet in it. Dump it by the falls."

I recognized her voice. Liz was O'Shea's mistress. My blood chilled. This was worse than Noreen feared.

"Tonight," she said.

"I can't tonight," he said. "I have tickets to UFC On Ice."

"God, you're an idiot," she said. "Fine. Tomorrow night."

"Yes, ma'am."

I slid back down the hall before they came out and spotted me. Screw the hedges. I was taking the afternoon off.

"Thing is, which silo are they referring to?" Noreen and I agreed I needed to find Shoggoth tonight, before Muscles the Ice-Skating Freak got to him. We knew the otter had to be at either the second location or somewhere nearby. But according to the GPS, the area was all farmland. There were probably a lot of silos out there. And we were almost out of time.

It was growing dark. I'd met Noreen at a public playground, but her white Econoline drew more attention than we intended. We moved to a grocery store parking lot after a group of children pointed their fingers at us and chanted, "Stranger danger!" I suggested she consider painting her van another color.

"Wherever the silo is, it has to be somewhere on their property," I said. "She mentioned security."

"How will you get past them?"

"I will make up something about needing supplies. Grass seed maybe. Tell them I am just there to get an inventory since I couldn't be there earlier." I paused. "We need to dismantle the gate camera. That way, I can make sure you have a way in behind me."

We agreed it would be a wise idea if she parked nearby, in the event I needed help. Also, because an otter probably wouldn't fit in my car.

"Don't worry," she said. "I have it covered."

I decided not to ask what she meant. Noreen proved she possessed incredible cunning every time she upstaged my assassinations. The mission was already more complicated than I expected. Of all the hats I wore, animal rescuer was not one of them.

"In that case, I am headed over. I will see you there. Text me when you arrive." With a brief wave, I left. I could see her in my rearview, going into the grocery store.

PTARG's second property was located just outside the city line, not quite in farm country. I discovered the gate didn't appear to have a barrier preventing access. I spotted a camera on top of the chain-link fencing, but that was about it. The two-story building was lacking a garish sign, and instead had PTARG, Inc printed in simple white letters on the front door. I noticed, once inside, that most doors didn't even have locks. I was surprised. Based on their headquarters, I assumed this place would also be locked down.

I found one guy in an open office and knocked on the door jamb. He appeared startled by me, but not especially alarmed.

I introduced myself as the groundskeeper and asked where they kept the supplies. He gave me directions and turned back to his computer.

"So, what is it you do here? If I may ask," I said. I kept my questions casual.

"I'm just an intern. Name's Todd," he said. "This is mostly corporate and accounting over here. Some training. Boring stuff. I don't even think security is on duty tonight."

How could I have lucked out that big? "Is that usual?"

"Normally we have some security out here. Not a lot, though. Nothing important really happens out here. But our regular security guy has been out sick, and they've used temps here and there, but otherwise, it's just us."

"You mean, just the two of us?" Hell, I might not need to shoot anyone!

"There is someone who lives on the property. They are the general supervisor. But they're out for the night. UFC on Ice. I have tickets, myself, and I am about to head out there. I can remote lock up if you need me to."

I thanked the guy and told him I would let him know, leaving him to his computer. Around the corner, I stopped in a doorway and messaged Noreen to let her know about the gate camera and Todd. She promptly messaged back she was outside the gates and to let her know if I needed her to head inside.

I located the back exit and went outside. I found the closet and checked inside. Among the usual yard equipment, I also found a long-handled saw, an ax, a bolt cutter, and hedge shears. Useful. I shoved a tissue into the doorjamb so the door wouldn't latch and made my way around the grounds.

The property had more gravel than grass and almost no shrubbery. Heavy tree lines surrounded most of the perimeter. I thought about how odd it was that a company with so few actual groundskeeping needs would hire a full-time landscaper.

Even more peculiar was why the property had almost no security.

As I rounded a long building that appeared to include open parking bays, I found three other structures on the property. One was a small house, likely the supervisor's quarters. One was a modest brick structure, which I assumed was a security office.

The third appeared to be a short water tower, no taller than a three-story building, painted bright orange.

I messaged Noreen: I think I found the silo.

The house and security office were both dark. If the supervisor was inside, I preferred not to wake him. I pulled on the door on the silo's far side. It was unlocked.

This was too easy.

Inside, I discovered a hallway circling the building's perimeter. I walked down the hallway once, trying the doors as I passed. Two were empty rooms. The third door was the size of a garage bay, with another bay door the opened to the outside. I pulled the inner door up and flipped a light switch by the door.

The space was larger than I expected. A stairway was sitting on the opposite side of the room. There were shelves on one wall holding various tools and equipment. The room itself looked and smelled like an automotive shop.

In the middle of the floor sat a single white drum.

I didn't get too close to it. Probably because the label clearly warned the contents were acid. Sulfuric acid if I read it correctly. If this was the drum Muscles was supposed to pick up, did it contain O'Shea's body?

Why was PTARG covering up his murder? Maybe his mistress didn't want to be outed, but wouldn't murder override self-preservation?

None of that mattered, ultimately. I was there for Shoggoth. There were no signs of the otter in this room. I made for the stairs.

As I reached the second-floor landing, I heard something downstairs. The screech of metal. Someone had closed the bay door.

I unholstered my revolver and slid along the wall, looking for doors. I found a single door and turned the knob slowly, trying to listen for voices or footsteps. Someone had to know I was in there. I needed to find a spot to hide and message Noreen.

Inside the room, I discovered it was likely the only room on the second floor. The large space was a maze of aisles and shelves. This might take a while. I squatted below some shelves and sent Noreen a quick text: Upstairs in silo.

Someone downstairs in garage.

Almost immediately, she messaged back: Nyarlathotep killed the gate camera.

What? For a moment there, I worried she had a stroke.

I waited in place. There were no voices. No footsteps. Maybe someone thought the door was left open by mistake. After a few minutes, I stood up. I started searching the shelves.

Halfway into the room, somewhere near the center, I heard it. Faint, but unmistakable.

Squeak?

Yes, it sounded like a question.

I made my way around some other shelves, further into the labyrinth.

In the middle of the room was the cage.

A very defeated Shoggoth lay curled in one corner. A few bowls inside indicated he was fed. If the lady wanted him dead, why were they feeding him anyway?

"Hi, buddy," I whispered. This otter didn't know me. I had to let him know I was his friend. "Hi, Shog. Shoggy. Shoggs. How you doin', Shoggy?"

The otter just blinked.

"I am here to get you out, Shoggoth. Wanna go? Wanna go bye-bye?" Now I felt really dumb.

But Shoggoth understood. The otter slithered to me and whimpered, almost like he knew he had to keep his squeaks down. I looked at the latch on the cage and realized there was a padlock.

Made sense, I guess. Otherwise, Shoggoth could've let himself out.

I couldn't carry the whole cage, and I wasn't sure what to do. Shooting the lock would be noisy and would risk hurting the otter. But I didn't want to leave him. I remembered the door to the maintenance shed would be unlatched. I turned down the volume on my phone and dialed Noreen.

"I am upstairs in the silo. Shoggoth is here, but this cage is padlocked. I need the bolt cutters from the maintenance closet behind the main building. The door is open. Are you able …?"

"Sit tight," she said. "I am sending back up."

The call went dead before I could ask how she planned to reach me.

Ten minutes. Give or take. Ten minutes of me sitting on a cold floor staring at a cage holding an otter staring back at me. Aside from the occasional whimper, neither of us said anything. Yes, some of those whimpers were mine. Have *you* stared at an otter for ten minutes without whimpering? I bet not.

Squeak squeak.

I expected to see Noreen with the bolt cutters in hand. Instead, two otters wiggled toward me, one with the bolt cutter handle in its mouth. I was equally surprised and impressed. It dropped the tool in my hands and circled my legs. All three otters were excited, clearly eager to be reunited, so I worked quickly. I worried they might get noisy if I took too long.

Fortunately, the padlock snapped beneath the cutter, and the lock fell off the door.

Clattering loudly on the floor.

“Shit!” I ducked down. Whispering to the three otters, I said, “We need to get out of here quickly. No squeaking! You hear me?” I put my finger to my mouth.

One otter… no idea which one since there were three now, and they were all equally cute… put its paw to its mouth and raspberried. They blinked in unison.

Now was not the time to pet them. “Follow me,” I whispered.

We wove our way back through the maze and paused by the door. I shot Noreen another text: Have Shog. Is it clear?

To which she immediately answered: Sure

In retrospect, I should’ve proceeded a little more cautiously. By now, I had messaged her enough to know she rarely used replies like ‘sure.’ And she always punctuated. As I headed back down the stairs with three exuberant otters at my heels, all I could think about was getting them far away from PTARG. I wasn’t even thinking about the money at that point. I just wanted them free.

I should have known nothing is easy. An organization operating with high security does not leave a place open unless something else much worse is going down. As I crossed the floor, I saw Noreen waiting in front of the bay door.

And then I heard the hammer of a gun being cocked.

I froze.

A woman stepped out from behind a shelf. The woman from PTARG. O'Shea's mistress. She had a gun aimed at Noreen.

"You did me a huge favor," Liz said. "I thought I was going to track them down one by one, but you brought them all to me. Thank you."

"You're not welcome," I said.

Noreen didn't move. Didn't flinch. Not even so much as a blink. I bet she made quite the poker player. If she was scared, I couldn't tell.

"Don't you even think of hurting my otters, you bitch," she said, her voice as even as the night she showed up on my doorstep.

Liz laughed.

"Why would you waste your time on otters," I said. "Shouldn't you be more concerned about your dead lover?" I wanted to rattle her enough to weaken her guard.

"Lover? He wasn't my lover. He was my husband. And a real piece of shit, at that. I was the one who ordered the hit."

Holy. Shit. Confused, I said, "Then why are you trying to take her otters? They were doing what you paid them to do."

"Look, I couldn't care less about Neil. I knew Ms. Kittery here was doing hits for Orman. That's why I went to him. I was trying to lure them to me," she smirked. "Worked like a charm."

"But… why? Why should you care about one lady and six otters?"

"Because otters are wild animals and not pets! She has no business with them. Training them like circus animals to perform tricks for the public. All I wanted was to see them free, back where they belonged. Animals are not pets," she said.

"I still don't get it," I said. "You would murder people over *otters*?"

"An otter killed Mandy."

Noreen blinked. "The Manilow song?"

"My prized koi!" Liz snapped.

"You have pet koi?" I grunted. "Hypocritical much?"

Then a bang ripped the air, stunning everyone.

Well, stunning me, Noreen, and the three otters. Not Liz O'Shea.

She slumped to the floor, blood pooling beneath her.

An otter stood to the far left. It was standing on an otter standing on another otter. They were wearing a wizard's cloak. The Top Otter held a small Ruger LCP in its front paws. The otter squeaked a few times.

"Oh my god," I said without hesitating. "You're adorable." I seemed to say that a lot around these guys.

"Azothoth!" Noreen clapped. "Good boy!"

"You really need to reconsider those names." I shook my head.

The six otters squirmed around Noreen's feet as she pulled a can of sardines from her pocket and opened it, asking them, "Who is a good boy?" A cacophony of squeaky toys echoed in the garage, followed by the sloppy sounds of chewing.

You know, I rather dug those otters.

I refused to accept Noreen's payment after that night. Told her to buy the otters some fish and a river to eat it in.

So she did.

As luck would have it, she needed a landscaper for her property. Maybe I could talk her into naming the next otter something better. Something friendlier.

Mandy, maybe. Or Ruger.

Lucious

"I really wanna be a 10." A row of perfectly straight teeth gleamed between full lips. Bryce's eyes dropped from the botoxed smile to her taut calves, following their curve behind her knees and over her smooth bronzed thighs, to the cuff of her short shorts.

Damn. She's a ten already.

He pretended to look at the color swatch she held against her arm. "I think you've hit a plateau. That happens with regular beds. But our unique bed design will allow you to break through that wall and give you the deepest tan you've ever had. If you sign up for a platinum membership, the first 30 days are a trial offer."

His smile split his face in a calculated maneuver he'd perfected for his sales pitch. "We also have our own specially formulated line of lotions and serums to give you a deep bronze glow without turning you orange. And as a platinum member, you'll get them at a discounted price."

"I have my own lotion," she said, flipping straight black

hair over a coppery shoulder.

"I'm afraid you wouldn't be permitted to use them in our machines. Our lotions are designed to work with the bulbs we use, and other lotions will inhibit your results."

She frowned. "I dunno…"

"I've noticed you're starting to peel on the back of your shoulder." Bryce gently brushed her back—which didn't have so much as a flake of dead skin—and feigned concern.

Her eyes widened, registering immediate panic. "Okay, I'll do it!"

"Good girl," he said, steering her to the front desk, his hand on the small of her back. "Denise, please enroll Miss…"

"Candy."

"Of course. Enroll *Candy* in our platinum program. And give her a complimentary bottle of our starter serum." He winked at Candy before heading to his office, and she shot him a quick smile before giving the clerk her information.

Women spared no expense when it came to vanity, and twenty years taught Bryce Golden every trick in the book for securing their loyal patronage. There used to be a time when women were dissuaded from tanning due to harmful UV rays and the potential contraction of nasty melanomas, but Bryce broke that barrier with a cornucopia of lies that eased their minds and opened their wallets… and legs. At 53, Bryce had the physique of a man in his twenties, and the stamina to match.

The salon was a perfect remedy for his raging libido, which he assuaged on a daily basis with the various women that visited the beds. But only with the platinum members. A man had to have standards, after all.

He poured a glass of scotch and settled behind his desk, looking over the many applications of new platinum clientele. Opening his planner, he penciled different names into his schedule throughout the week. Before leaving the office, he knocked back the remnants of his beverage, and adjusted the rigid muscle in his slacks.

Membership wasn't the only thing on the rise.

Candy bounced on Bryce's lap, her back to his chest, the copper of her skin almost matching the deep bronze of his thighs. He reached around to squeeze handfuls of her round breasts and groaned. Candy, too caught up in the moment to notice it was a groan of disappointment, moaned and climaxed, leaning back against his chest as he emptied himself between her legs.

"That was so good," she gasped, still writhing.

But Bryce just grunted, waiting for her to move.

He'd explored her entire body with his mouth and hands, and stumbled across the repeated evidence of a surgeon's handiwork. There were two dark scars on the insides of her thighs as he'd peeled off her bathing suit. Two more scars hid in the bottom crease of her ass. Her breasts were a little stiff, the dark nipples perpetually erect, and two long scars could be felt on their undersides as he groped her.

Meanwhile, she whimpered and screamed, as helpless and eager as every other woman who danced on his lap. Five o'clock at Golden was packed; every bed in the facility was running. The women in the beds were blasted with the hum of the light bulbs, the blare of music from speakers positioned by their heads, and fans blowing cool air across their toasting bodies. Candy could have spoken in tongues and no one would've heard a sound.

She'd be good for an occasional wank, but nothing else. She was a life-sized posable action figure. All silicone, lipo, and Botox. Fake.

He ran his hands over her seemingly perfect thighs, wishing he could push her off his lap, but instead slid his fingers between her legs. Regardless of whether the clients met his physical standards, he tried to keep them all satisfied. Her moans followed him as he pulled the door closed and retreated to his office.

The last clients filled their appointments and left, leaving the staff to wipe down the equipment and gather the sweaty white towels for washing. New towels were folded and placed on the beds, the wastebaskets were all emptied, and the salon was ready for a new business day.

From his office doorway, Bryce spotted Denise checking a locked door in the back corner of the salon, and froze. He often worried he'd forget to lock it, and a towel girl would wander inside. But the knob held tight, and Denise walked away with not even a shrug.

"Everything is ready for tomorrow, Mr. Golden. I'm leaving now," she said, her smile polite but notably tired.

"Of course. Thank you. See you in the morning." He smiled, half waved, and watched as she disappeared down the hallway that led to the salon's front entrance. The front door closed, the hasp snapping in place as she locked up for the night.

Fishing for the key from his pocket, he opened the door and stepped inside. A pungent odor stung his nostrils. *I need to change the air filter.* Women turned their noses up at the idea of basking in someone else's aroma while they baked their skin to rawhide.

Bryce wiped down his customized creation and placed a folded gold towel on the plexi, readying it for the next client. He switched on the ventilation fan before heading back to his office for a well-deserved meal.

Mayor Teddy Andrews laughed too loudly at Bryce's joke, and offered him another scotch. After watching Sunday football in the mayor's luxurious theater room, they were sprawled on couches that lined a bar in the well-appointed recreational basement. Andrews was the spoiled trust fund baby of a local congressman, who tried only once to follow in his father's footsteps, and failed. Relegating himself as mayor was far less challenging than trying to be a real politician. But Teddy could rival any political figure with his self-indulgence, which made him a convenient choice as a friend. Bryce enjoyed the perks of being best friends with a man like Teddy.

"So, Bryce, how are the plans for the Anniversary Gala coming along? I'm looking forward to seeing how you outdo last year's soiree."

Bryce hosted a huge celebration every year for the city's most elite citizens, which was more anticipated than the Fourth of July fireworks or the yearly lighting of the Christmas Tree. The ball was practically a local holiday, and tickets always sold out almost immediately. Between the upscale celebrity studded guest list, elaborate menus, and fantastic decor, the gala raised a small fortune every year, much of which was donated to the city. It was a small price to pay for the immunity it afforded Bryce.

"Prepare to be amazed, my friend," he said, his speech slightly slurred by the top-shelf liquor. "This year's event will blow all past years out of the water."

Teddy laughed again. "I don't see how that's possible. Unless you managed to get topless Vegas showgirls to serve as waiters."

"Really, Teddy, can't you show a little class?" Aubrey

Andrews stood in the doorway, a scowl drawing together her perfectly arched eyebrows. Her arms were crossed over her chest as she leaned against the frame, honey ribbons of hair spilling over her shoulders.

Both men sat up, like a couple schoolboys caught looking at their father's dirty magazines. "I was just joking, sweetheart," Teddy said.

She strode to the bar and poured a glass of tonic. "Right. I'm sure you are." While her voice was light, her eyes were dark flashes.

"Looks like you're overdue for a visit to the salon," Bryce interrupted.

Aubrey froze, just for a moment, then chuckled. But her laugh sounded forced and too abbreviated. "My schedule has been really busy lately."

"You know all you have to do is call ahead. I will personally make sure there's a bed open for you." He finished his scotch, watching her flush over the rim of his glass.

"I don't know, Bryce. I will have to get back to you on that."

She left before he could respond, oblivious to his eyes starring daggers at her back.

Teddy slouched back down, tossing back the remnants of his scotch, and grinned. "So anyway, how about it? Topless waitresses? Whadaya think?"

Bryce trailed his lips over Aubrey's bronzed shoulder,

tightening his arms around her. She laid stiff against him, as she had for the past hour, never meeting his gaze. Usually she was passionate—reckless even—when they went at each other. But today she barely tolerated his ministrations, distracted by whatever was on her mind. Even her orgasm felt insincere.

She sat up and pulled on her clothes, leaving him sprawled naked on the couch in his office. He eyed her smooth calves, thighs… up to her hands, which trembled as she buttoned her blouse.

"What's going on?" He sat up and began dressing, stomach clenched in anticipation. "You've avoided me for weeks, and now you're in a hurry to leave. What's rattling around in that head of yours?"

Aubrey's eyes shimmered, her cheeks flushed. "This is it, Bryce. We have to stop."

Bryce never deluded himself that they were in love. Like all the others, she was just an object. They'd been doing this for years. Nonetheless, as she stood there, head bowed shamefully, his gut knotted and ached. His chest throbbed, and heat flooded his head. "What?"

"I can't do this anymore," she said, her voice wavering.

"What the hell are you talking about?" He shoved his balled fists into his pockets as he stood slowly, towering over her. "Are you fucking Teddy? Is that it?"

"He's my husband!" She stepped back, arms behind her as

she felt for the door. "Don't do this now. We both knew it wouldn't go anywhere."

"You told him." Bryce's voice was even, barely above a whisper. He took a step towards her.

"No!" The color drained from her face as she fumbled for the doorknob. "Of course not, but…"

"But?"

"I think he already suspects us." Grasping the knob, she pulled the door open just enough to slip out.

He raised his fist, ready to slam it through the door panel, enraged that she would lay such a bombshell on him before she ran away. His blood pumped furiously, the sound in his ears louder than a steam engine.

But then again, so what if Teddy knew? The man wasn't a saint to begin with. He'd had his share of affairs. Hell, Bryce knew enough to send Teddy and Aubrey straight to divorce court. Teddy would pay through the nose if Aubrey knew about her husband's infidelities, even in light of Bryce. So the chances of Teddy doing anything more than applauding Bryce for bedding his wife were nil.

But Aubrey didn't know that. She still operated under the illusion that the only malfunction in her marriage was the affair she'd been having with him. Perhaps if he told her about her husband, she'd stay.

He caught her before she made it to the lobby, pulling her into an empty restroom. "You never did use the beds. At least get in a last session. It'll be more suspicious if you go home as pale as you left."

She stood out of arm's reach, uncertainty flickering in her eyes. "I don't know… do you have any open beds right now?"

"The ultra bed is actually available. Usually its booked solid, but we had a cancellation today."

Her gaze narrowed. "I've been in all your beds. I didn't realize you had an ultra bed."

"Like I said, it's usually booked solid." He tried a casual smile, but his jaw was clenched, and he could feel the veins in his temple throbbing.

If she noticed, she chose not to mention it. After a brief hesitation, she relented. "It may take a while to find another salon. I suppose I should."

He led her down the hall with his hand on the small of her back, steering her wordlessly towards the locked door in the back. The door swung open slowly, but without so much as a squeak when he unlocked it. As he followed her into the room, he checked the doorknob to make sure it was still locked.

Aubrey stared at the stainless-steel monstrosity that ran the length of the far wall, and laughed, a nervous burst that almost sounded like a cough. "You call that thing a tanning bed?"

Bryce chuckled, and slid past her, opening the hood to reveal the bed inside. Like the other beds, a Plexiglas shield covered the rows of bulbs that would encapsulate her.

"I always thought they looked more like well-lit coffins,"

he joked.

"That's because they are," she said, her voice flat.

He waited, half expecting her to change her mind, or try to leave. The ultra bed always intimidated clients, but he managed to coax them in with his usual tactics. Of course, under the circumstances, those would only drive her out the door.

"You know what? I don't have my goggles or my lotion. I shouldn't do this."

He smiled. "No worries. I have extra oil and goggles right here." He opened a narrow cabinet that housed bottles of tanning elixirs, gold hand towels, and packages of tiny neon-colored specs. "Why don't you get undressed while I get the bed ready for you? If you want, I can apply your lotion."

She frowned, crossed her arms across her chest, and backed away. "I meant what I said, Bryce. No more sex..."

"What? I'm trying to help you, Aubrey. That's all. You know damn well you must use the proper oils for these beds to work correctly."

She nodded, dropping her arms. "Yeah, okay. Fine. Can't reach my back anyway, and I don't want to burn." She slide out of her shirt. "Just make sure you keep it in your pants."

As he pushed the proper buttons, the machine came to life, the lights whirring softly as they began to glow. The glow wasn't the usual bright blue-white, but a softer amber hue. He squirted a palm full of oil in his hand and spread it across her shoulder blades.

"Are the bulbs malfunctioning?" She studied the machine as he ran his hands across her, coating her tanned flesh with a generous layer of fragrant oil.

"No, they're supposed to look like that. That's why they work so well."

She was completely relaxed now, allowing his hands to reach every spot on her body as he massaged more oil into her skin. He relished the feel of her under his palms. Unlike most of his clientele, Aubrey possessed natural beauty. Her strict health regimen rewarded her with perfect skin and supple curves. No part of her body was enhanced, lifted, or tucked.

"That smells familiar. What's in it? It's wonderful." She leaned into his touch.

"Some herbs and oils, lots of nutrients. It's my own personal recipe. You're gonna love the results," he murmured. As he helped her slide onto the bed, his lips brushed her neck quickly. Placing the goggles over her eyes, he smoothed her blonde hair away from her face and whispered in her ear, *"Désolé, mon amour."*

"Hmm?"

Without reply, he lowered the heavy cover until it closed completely, and then buckled a hasp lock at either end of the bed. On the control panel, he entered a new temperature and set the timer. As the wire coils hidden behind a panel beneath the bulbs roared to life, he heard the faint sounds of her protests escalate to screams. He calculated she'd pipe down after, maybe, fifteen minutes.

After some time her screams died to whimpers, gurgles, then eventually a faint sizzle. He slid out of the room. The stillness of the hallway and the cool air conditioning revitalized him, like stepping into a swimming pool.

A towel girl passed with a customer in tow, and a customer exited one of the nearby tanning rooms. They smiled at him politely, murmuring shy hellos as they went about their business. He laughed softly as he headed for a glass of scotch.

Sound proofing. Best investment he ever made.

His cell phone buzzed in his pocket. He glanced at the screen before answering. "Teddy, my man. What's going on?"

"Can I talk to you?" Teddy's voice wavered.

"Sure you can. Shoot," Bryce said.

"It's about Aubrey. She's been acting weird lately. I think she might be seeing somebody." Teddy sniffled. "And I think I know who it is."

"That's rough, buddy. Why don't you meet me at the salon after closing time?" Bryce looked back at the locked door. "I'm having dinner here tonight."

Return by Fire

She died as a witch last life around,
Her body consumed by blazing fire,
History repeats itself, she found,
Staking her to another burning pyre.

Her body consumed by blazing fire,
Hemorrhaging magic from her veins,
Staking her to another burning pyre,
The familiar hell that leaves its stains.

Hemorrhaging magic from her veins,
Smothering her cries in the roar of flame,
The familiar hell that leaves its stains,
Brought back by fear, by ignorant blame.

Smothering her cries in the roar of flame,
Leaving her ashes to blacken the ground,
Brought back by fear, by ignorant blame,
She died as a witch last life around.

Love Me, Love My Alpaca

Jericho Flanders was not a hermit... he just didn't care much for socializing. He preferred to pass his time on the gravel shoulders of Highway 28, tossing dust and pebbles over the toes of his worn work boots and gnawing hay straws as he trailed the lengthening shadows. Every evening, once he finished tending his fields, he took a walk to Dixon, stopping at the corner store inside the town limits to purchase a cold pop. Savoring his carbonated treat, he headed home against the first glimmer of stars that danced across a deepening cobalt sky.

Just him, the wide country, and Josephine.

"We are the guardians of God's highway, girl," he declared, breathing in a lungful of fresh air as he stretched his arms to the horizon. Josephine hummed beside him in agreement, matching his stride. Occasionally she would wander away long enough to drop a pile of dung in the roadside grass, but she always came back, announcing her return with affectionate clicks. She nudged his ear, tickling him with her whiskers, and he showed his approval by scratching her hairy neck.

Teddy and Mary Sneedburger were on the way home from visiting family when they decided to stop in Dixon for pie. They needed a break from traveling. Highway 28 cut through the Midwestern plains without many worthy attractions, and they'd been on the road since breakfast. The country diner lured them in with windows framed in ruffled curtains of red and white eyelet, gingham covered picnic benches, and checkered tablecloths topped with daisies in white glass vases.

"Why, they're the most gorgeous little things I have ever seen!" Mary said, her voice bubbling over the twangs emitted from an old jukebox by the door. She plucked a daisy from its vase and shoved her nose in it. "Where'd they come from?"

A gum-popping waitress rolled her eyes at Mary's excitement as she sat them in a booth and readied her notepad for their order. "They grow wild for miles along Highway 28," she said. "You'll see them when you get out on the road. But if you happen to spot an old man and an alpaca, you better not stop to pick them."

"And why is that?" Mary pursed her lips.

The waitress ignored her question, instead scribbling down Teddy's order of ham sandwiches, coleslaw, slices of peach pie, and milks over ice.

"I'll be back with your food," the waitress replied, tucking her scratch pad in the pocket of her apron and retreating to the kitchen. Minutes later, she returned with a tray balanced on her palm.

Mary watched the young lady set the plates and glasses in front of them, and said, "What's an alpaca?"

The waitress busied herself with their napkins and straws to avoid eye contact with the pushy woman. "Jericho is a persnickety old coot, and he's got an ornery streak in him. Gets real bent out of shape if he catches folk picking the flowers or leaving garbage on the road." She placed their eating utensils on the table. "Take my advice: if you see them, it's best you just keep driving."

Leaving them to their meal, the waitress sauntered to a table in the far corner, where the only other customer in the diner sat, bent over a coffee mug. They watched her lean towards the gentleman, speaking too softly for them to hear.

He replied in a voice so loud they jumped in their seats. "What was that? I can't hear you!"

When he turned his head, the Sneedburgers spotted the small hole below his baseball cap where his ear should've been. He handed the waitress a bouquet of daisies, and she gave him a fistful of dollar bills.

"Thank you!" he shouted.

Mary leaned towards her husband and asked, "What's an

alpaca?"

He paused to think. "I believe it's a brand of lawnmower, dear." Taking a bite of his dessert first, his face lit up. "That's some good pie! Say, did you notice our waitress is missing two fingers?"

Mary giggled around a mouthful of sugar and peaches. "You're absolutely right—this *is* good pie!"

The setting sun highlighted the skyline neon orange as they turned onto Highway 28. They asked for directions back to the main road from a one-armed gas station attendant next to the diner. Leaving Dixon's town limits, Mary spotted the sea of daisies that raced along both sides of the road. She squealed with delight.

"There's so many of them!"

"Yes there are, dear," Teddy said. He eyed the endless acres of crop fields. "Look at all that unused land! That right there is some mighty fine real estate."

"Pumpkin?" Mary cooed, rubbing his arm. "Do you think we could pull over for one teeny, tiny second? I would love to pick some daisies to take home."

He blinked at her, the dollar signs in his eyes clouded with confusion. "What was that, dear?"

She leaned against his shoulder, walking her fingers up his chest. "You know what this place needs," she purred. "A shopping mall. I bet if we took a little walk, we'd find out who owns all this land."

He pulled the car onto the shoulder so fast the tires left streaks of black smoking rubber on the asphalt.

Jericho didn't like the looks of the sedan parked on the side of his highway, and Josephine's gravelly hums mirrored his distaste. He rested his hand on her back to calm her, but tension rippled under her thick fur. They watched a couple climb from the vehicle, a high-pitched shriek carrying on the wind as the woman bent to rip daisies from the earth.

"Damned city folk," he muttered under his breath.

Josephine, more vocal with her displeasure, emitted a bellow that mimicked a flattened French horn. The couple stopped and turned to face the road. Four pairs of eyes locked across the highway in a tense moment of silence.

Jericho and Josephine both winced as a feminine screech rattled their eardrums.

"Hold steady, girl," Jericho warned as the woman barreled towards them.

"Ain't she just precious? I've never seen a llama up close before!"

"She ain't no llama," Jericho spat, puffing out his chest.

The man approached, the swagger in his steps implying importance, and perhaps an unbeatable deal on a used automobile. He flashed a toothy smile. "No dear, that's not a llama. That's an emu."

"Oh Teddy, don't be silly! An emu is an ostrich!" She reached out to touch Josephine's nose, who *warked* and jumped away from her hand.

An ostrich is a bird, Mary, not an emu," Teddy replied. He scratched his chin. "Is she... a goat?"

"With that long neck, pumpkin?"

"Oh yeah. Good point. Maybe she's one of them miniature ponies," he said with a nod.

"Good God, what is wrong with you people?" Jericho groaned. "She's an alpaca, for Christ's sake!"

The couple didn't move, staring at the old man as if he spoke a foreign language. After a quiet second, Teddy replied. "Isn't that a lawnmower?"

"What are you, some kind of moron?" Jericho snapped.

Mary, distracted by the clusters of daisies waving in the evening breeze, bent over and tugged a few more blooms. As the delicate stems ripped, Josephine bellowed at her backside, stomping her feet in the dirt.

Mary cooed. "Would you like a snack, pretty girl?" She pushed a daisy against Josephine's mouth.

"You best not be doing that," Jericho warned. "Josephine don't take kindly to people defacing God's property."

Mary laughed, waving away his advice with her handful of already wilting flowers. "Don't be silly! She's just hungry. I can hear her belly growling!"

"That ain't her belly," Jericho said.

"Is this your land, sir?" Teddy interrupted. "Let me introduce myself. Teddy Sneedburger, real estate investor. You have the fine makings of condominium potential here. Let's talk numbers."

Mary was back to gathering daisies, pulling up as many as she could wrap her hands around. Josephine followed at her heels, her hums and shrieks ignored by the persistent woman, who bent to tear up fistful over fistful of flowers. With her attention diverted, Josephine took advantage of the moment and headbutted Mary's derriere.

But Mary, who wasn't exactly the sharpest needle in the pin cushion, just laughed. "You're a playful darling!"

Jericho cut off Teddy's sales pitch. "Sir, if you don't restrain your wife, Josephine's gonna get mighty ugly."

Teddy frowned. "Mary isn't hurting her." They watched Mary attempt to throw her arms around the alpaca's neck, only to fall off balance as Josephine sidestepped her embrace. "See? They're just playing."

Josephine's eyes bulged and a deep rumble erupted from her throat as Mary tried to feed her another broken flower.

"You're asking for it, ma'am," Jericho warned. "I'm telling you, she don't like that!"

Teddy pulled a pen and scrap paper from his pocket, and scribbled numbers on it before offering it to Jericho. "What if I told you I could get you *this* for your land?"

"It ain't for sale," he snapped, his attention on Mary, who

was trying her best to hug Josephine. The alpaca continued to growl and *wark*, pulling her head up in an unmistakable gesture of hostility. “Why don’t you two hop in your car and get on up the road before there’s trouble?”

“I don’t see why you’re so upset,” Teddy said. “My wife is just showing your llama some affection.”

“For the last time, she ain’t no llama! Now, take your wife and get outta here before she kills all the flowers!”

As if to emphasize Jericho’s outrage, Josephine jerked her head back and screeched, hurling a ball of green sludge at Mary’s outstretched hand.

Teddy gagged.

“That disgusting beast spit on me!” Shaking her hand wildly, she tried flinging the noxious spittle off her fingers, but it clung like tar. “What a horrible creat—”

A distinct sizzle stunned the couple silent for only a few seconds before Mary screamed. She flailed her arm about when smoke began billowing from her hand, but to no avail. The smell of burning flesh filled the air. Mary’s cries were deafening.

Teddy rushed to his wife’s side in time to see three of her fingers shrivel and fall off, landing in the dirt like overcooked cocktail sausages. They stared at the charred digits, unsure of what they should do next. Teddy pulled a handkerchief from his pocket and bent to retrieve them, but he was too slow. A turkey hawk swooped in front of them and snatched the fingers off the ground, flying off into the sunset with its snack.

Teddy's attempts to calm Mary were muffled by the rising timber of her screams. They huddled together, scrambling towards the car. Teddy's distant shouts were indecipherable over Mary's hysteria as he flung open her door and shoved her into the front seat.

Jericho shrugged and held out his hand, beckoning Josephine to his side. They watched the sedan fishtail onto the asphalt and disappear over the horizon. Clicking softly, she nuzzled his ear as he scratched her neck.

"I don't know about you," he said, as they resumed their walk to Dixon, "but I'm awful thirsty. Being the guardians of God's highway is hard work. How about I buy you a cold pop?"

Josephine hummed.

The Transmitter

Murky fingers of fog crawled towards the sleeping town of Dunn after midnight. Their grasp left the lines of the road barely visible. The outskirts were barren landscapes, nothing more than trees and narrow roads during the day. At night, they became tunnels burrowing into the void, even under ideal conditions.

Because of this, when the KBAM 99 signal dropped, Lottie was too distracted to notice.

Lottie hated the after-work commute. The bar made its last call at 1 AM, but by the time she cleared tables and mopped up beer-sticky floors, it was half past 2. The streets of Dunn sat empty after 11, and most of the bar patrons were truckers who were camping at the garish truck stop parking lot across the highway. Even on weekends, the town felt abandoned.

She kept the radio tuned to the local top 40 channel to keep the worst of her imagination at bay. She wasn't a fan of the music, but the upbeat hip-hop and dance songs were too vapid to unsettle her. On occasion she sang along, more to keep herself awake than out of enjoyment. Her mind, however, was almost always elsewhere.

Currently, her thoughts were on her bills, which she didn't have enough tips to cover. Her head cleared once she noticed the radio was dead air.

Ten minutes 'til three. Would anyone even be at the station that time of night? She was certain the overnight programming was run by computer. She spun the volume knob back and forth, hit the power button a few times, even punched the channel buttons. If the display wasn't lit, she might have assumed she had a blown fuse. Nothing she did broke the silence.

She almost tapped the power button again when static pervaded the quiet. It increased in volume, soft at first, then demanding, before the sharp grating alarm of an emergency alert filled the car. She turned the volume down, expecting to hear an automated message, most likely just a routine station signal test. She glared at the misty shroud obscuring the road. *Maybe a fog advisory.*

Instead, the alert preceded an inarticulate voice fading in and out of the static. The murmur was so buried, she couldn't determine if it was male or female, or what language it spoke. Lottie wondered if the station wasn't picking up two separate transmissions simultaneously.

Then the static stopped, along with the mumbling. The system's EMS had to be malfunctioning. She expected KBAM to cut back in behind the silence.

An abrupt, sharp voice caused her to jump. A woman with a distinct European accent recited random numbers, the sequence so clipped and precise, she might have been a computer. When she reached the end of the sequence, she started over, as if on a loop. Lottie didn't understand what she was listening to, or if it meant anything. It reminded her of a crime show episode she watched once involving short wave radio pirates. Or better yet, that weird Max Headroom broadcast hijack from the 80's. Lottie's skin crawled.

The recording cut off in the middle of a loop. A few seconds later, KBAM returned, amid their weekly top five countdown.

It was 3 AM sharp.

After almost four hours of troubled sleep, Lottie sat in bed with a mug of coffee and her television tuned to a local morning broadcast. She had a day of errands in front of her before work that evening, and she couldn't afford to sleep in. A deadpan anchor-woman delivered the news.

"Police this morning are investigating the discovery of a dead woman found outside 520 Main Street. Calls came in just after 3 this morning to 911 citing several loud screams from area residents, and authorities arrived to find the deceased body of a woman in the front yard. The house, which is currently uninhabited, did not show signs of forced entry, or

any connection to the victim. Due to the grotesque nature of her condition, photos are not being released, and citizens are urged to stay away from the crime scene. Police have no leads at this time, so if anyone has any information regarding this case, please contact the sheriff's department immediately."

"Holy shit." Lottie felt a chill, despite the hot coffee in her hands and the comforter wrapped around her body.

She rushed through her errands. Dunn was unsettled that morning, voices in hushed tones, nervous eyes barely making contact as folks navigated their Friday mornings without the usual gusto. Though the news stated that no photos would be released, one of the neighbours recounted a vivid eyewitness description to the customers waiting in line at the postal office, where Lottie was purchasing postage stamps.

"I've never seen anything like it. Her neck was bent completely under her back, like she had been dropped from the sky, and her arms and legs were shattered. You could see bits of bones poking through her skin." He shuddered. "Her head looked like a busted watermelon splattered on the sidewalk. Heard some cops say she was pouring smoke, too. Like she'd been on fire, but then was put out. She didn't look burnt, either. It was like she was on fire on the inside."

Patrons gasped, clasped their hands, shifted on their feet. Lottie's stomach churned and threatened to spill her morning coffee on the linoleum floor. She was grateful to be next in line.

Lottie had no choice but to put the dead lady out of mind as she pushed through her schedule. Her drive home Friday night was near unbearable. The fog returned, hinting at dark figures in the mist, malevolent shadows lurking on the outskirts of Dunn. She hit the gas harder than she would normally, swerving once with an exclamation at a branch laying in the road. When she reached her front steps, she could not lock the door behind her fast enough and burrowed under her covers without her usual bedtime preparations. Hiding in the blankets of her bed was not an option come Saturday morning, though.

Fortunately, business at the bar picked up, making that eerie drive worth the rattled nerves. She pocketed better tips over the weekend, managing to make enough to cover the rest of her bills for the month, with a little left over for gas and food. Her memory dismissed what happened that night as her exhausted, overactive imagination. She could breathe easier now.

The following Thursday night, the bar was crowded. By 1 AM, there were just a handful of truckers still left, chatting with the bartender, downing the last of the cheapest beer on tap. At last call, the last of them stumbled out. Lottie watched them cross the highway, headed to the silhouettes of tractor trailers on the far side of a fluorescently lighted parking lot.

By the time she mopped up and wiped down, the bar clock

read 2:40 in the morning. Lottie pocketed her share of the ample tips and locked up, eager to crawl into the warmth of her bed.

As another bank of heavy fog enveloped her car, Lottie slowed down, and turned up the radio. No matter how often she encountered them, the late-night fog banks tightened her grip on the steering wheel and tensed her nerves. She tried to ignore her growing apprehension by whistling along with what might be the happiest break-up song ever written. She wasn't scared, she just needed some sleep…she was in a great mood. Spooky roads be damned.

And then the music stopped.

The shrill of another emergency alert invaded her car, and she jumped, almost losing her grip on the wheel. The murmur was back, its accent as indistinct as whatever it was saying. She raised the volume, trying to focus on the noise behind the noise, without luck. The voice was a little louder this time, but still impossible to decipher. When the number lady cued up, her voice was sharp enough to rattle Lottie's speakers. This time, though, she heard something else, buried in the static behind the numbers.

Music. But not the usual music. *A music box*. The kind that got cranked by hand, and would eventually run flat as it wound down. As a child, she had a music box with a twirling pink ballerina inside, and the melody it played sounded like a harpsicord coming off a weekend bender. This music sounded just like that.

It gave her goosebumps.

KBAM resumed music abruptly. It was 3 AM... again.

She could not get home fast enough.

Another morning, another breaking news report. This time, it was the body was an elderly man, and a grocery store parking lot. He was found by an employee who worked in the bakery. Due to the condition of his body, police concluded that his death was connected to the previous victim. There were still no leads on her, either. The only information they released about her was her name…Marley James…and that she worked in a clothing outlet on the other side of Dunn.

The forensic team estimated time of death at roughly 3 AM. The same time Ms. James' died. No further details were released, other than the repeated appeal to report any information to the sheriff's office.

The weather report followed, and then sports, before a morning court show took over the channel. Lottie remembered the radio interruptions. Weird how she didn't hear anyone talking about them. Weird how they weren't even mentioned on the news. Funny how those signals seemed to show up at the same time on the same night, which coincided with the murders. Was she really the only one who was listening to the radio at 3 in the morning? Surely some insomniac somewhere had caught wind of the eerie broadcasts.

That Max Headroom incident back in the 80's drew a big investigation and plenty of coverage. Even with all that attention, they never did determine who was behind it. An almost forgotten unsolved mystery. Radio stations were monitored and regulated by the FCC. If they got involved, wouldn't that be a big news story for a small, quiet town? Nothing exciting ever happened in Dunn…

Until two people were mutilated in the middle of the night.

That broadcast, though. It haunted Lottie's head.

The people of Dunn were drowning their new fears in pitchers of Budweiser. In that uncomfortable way, the grisly murders were doing Lottie's wallet a huge favor. As long as she stayed busy serving bottles and glasses to a bar packed full of uneasy patrons, she stayed calm. It was good for tips. She charmed and reassured her customers, none who were in a hurry to walk out of those doors into the gloom of midnight.

She overheard a discussion by the pool table as she served a round to some locals who frequented the joint. A lady Lottie recognized from around town told her companions that her cousin worked at the county morgue, and they told her the bodies were in worse condition than the news let on. "They think their necks were broken *before* they hit the ground. And they were both completely cooked inside. There was smoke in their throats and coming from their ears and eyes, and all their organs? Burnt all the way through."

"So someone set them on fire? That how they died?" Lottie recognized the voice as the man from the post office.

"That's the thing," the lady said. "There were no burns on their skin. They looked normal on the outside...well, aside from being broken and mangled. Somehow, they were set on fire from the inside."

Someone else grunted. "Damndest thing I ever heard..."

Lottie hurried back to the bar. She couldn't stomach anymore eyewitness accounts. *What an absurd conversation. No one burns like that.* She could chalk that one up to nothing more than exaggerations and hysterics.

But the moment her shift ended and it was time to leave, Lottie was as nervous as the rest of them. She used to enjoy living outside of town. Now she wished she didn't have to drive so far to get home.

Les, the young bartender, stayed with her until she finished cleaning up. He'd only worked there a few months, since moving to town, but they'd become fast friends. After lock-up, he walked her to her car and waited until she was seat-belted in with her doors locked. That's when she remembered he didn't have a car. His apartment was only a few blocks from the bar, so he usually walked. Lottie knew it was not safe to walk the streets of Dunn anymore.

"Hey!" she called to his back, "Are you seriously walking home?"

"Yeah. I always do." He shrugged.

She pulled alongside him and unlocked the passenger door. "No. Get in. Are you crazy? It's dangerous out here."

He started to refuse, but she growled, reached across the seat, and opened the door.

"Okay, okay," he said. As he belted in, he admitted, "I am pretty beat, so I guess a ride would be nice."

After a minute of riding in silence, Lottie whispered, "I can't stop thinking about it, Les. Why would someone kill them?"

"Hell if I know. That's some fucked up shit." He shook his head. "I hope they catch the guy soon… *if* it's a guy. Or even human."

Lottie shot a frown at him. "You mean, like a bear or something?"

He barely mumbled. "Something."

She didn't say anything for a minute, mulling over the implication. It almost *had* to be an animal, didn't it? Either they were lifted high enough that the impact alone would pulverize them, or they were thrown at tremendous velocity. Like pulpy ragdolls flung to the ground. Either way, what animal could do that?

"Maybe a large raptor?" she offered.

"It would have to be Thunderbird sized," he said, "and I am not aware of any birds around here that are large enough to do that."

"Or aggressive enough," she added.

"I don't think it's something we know," Les said. His words froze between them, an ominous observation.

"Did you hear the people by the pool table tonight? That was a wild tale," she laughed, hoping Les would agree.

He grinned. "I swear I did not put anything in their beers."

At least he didn't buy into their bizarre theories. Last thing she needed was something else to make her drives scarier than they were already. She liked Les. He was… rational. In ways the townsfolk weren't. Probably because he was an outsider. Lottie bit her lip—a lifelong nervous habit—and then said, "I wonder if the radio is connected."

"What? Why the radio?" Les almost chuckled.

She realized he probably wasn't listening to the radio that time of night if he was walking home from work. Judging from his Rammstein t-shirt, he didn't strike her as much of a KBAM listener, either. She was probably going to sound silly, or paranoid. Or both.

"The radio has been acting up," she said, shrugging. She wished she hadn't mentioned it. He might think she was overreacting.

"I haven't heard anyone talking about the radio," he said. "But radio issues could be anything. Bad reception, loose wires…aliens tampering with electromagnetic fields."

"Ha. Ha." She snipped.

He did laugh, then. "Seriously, though, it might be something simple, like wiring. I can take a look at it for you one day this week if you want."

Lottie nodded, eager to drop the radio theory. "That would be great, thanks. I'll buy you lunch."

By then, they'd reached his apartment building. He thanked her for the ride and opened his door.

"Hey, Les?"

He paused. "Yeah?"

"Have you heard any screaming?"

His dark eyes were unreadable as he studied her, as if weighing his words. "No," he finally said. "This is a quiet neighborhood."

A few minutes later, she approached the outskirts of town, and her road home. The radio cut out again at ten 'til. The interruption ended at 3 AM. Just like before.

Lottie didn't sleep at all that night.

This time, it was a teenage boy at a playground. Screams were reported by nearby neighbors right before 3. The city council toyed with placing a curfew on the town, but as it was along a main trucking route, they knew such an ordinance would be futile. Too many strangers coming and going at all hours. Most of the residents didn't need an ordinance to tell them to stay inside, anyway. No one was going to be out that late at night now. Not until the authorities found their man.

Which would be an interesting trick, since there were still no leads or suspects, whatsoever. It was like those people were flinging themselves to the ground.

Lottie decided to stop by the police station and tell them about the radio interruptions. She may not know why or how they were happening, but she knew they had to be connected to the murders. They couldn't be just coincidence… not three times in a row.

The officers regarded her quizzically. They said they didn't know anything about the radio disruptions. One of the officers even mentioned that they listened to KBAM on their nightly patrols, but they had not heard any of the broadcast interruptions Lottie described. While they were polite enough, it became clear they thought she was grasping straws when another officer handed her the business card of a friend's audio shop and suggested she have her radio looked at. They weren't taking her seriously. She left embarrassed and frustrated.

The following Thursday, there was another interruption. Lottie still could not make out what was being said. The number sequences were the same, as was the eerie calliope music behind the recorded loop. And the next morning, there was another body.

This time, that body was the smoking, shattered remains of their cook.

Lottie was losing her mind. She knew she couldn't be imagining those transmissions, but no one else seemed to be hearing them. Les inspected her car, but didn't spot any loose or defective wires to account for what she experienced. What else could she say about it? What other details could she remember, other than it was always foggy when it happened?

Her own research told her that the second part of the transmissions matched descriptions of numbers stations. Such communications were usually broadcasted over short-wave radios. She was unaware of any such stations, or what their purpose could be. The numbers made no sense to her. Maybe they were coordinates of some kind. Maybe they were a code.

If they were a code… did it hold the answer to who was behind the murders? Also…

Why was she the only one who heard it?

The bar hired another cook, an older guy who looked like he spent an inordinate amount of time at the gym. He was nice enough, but he wasn't very conservational. Les was swamped mixing drink orders, so Lottie maintained a polite distance as she focused on the customers that wandered over from the truck stop.

She had no choice. While he'd been good natured about fixing her perfectly functional radio, she'd made herself look conspiratorial in the wake of a very real, very dangerous threat. She was mortified and thought it best to avoid him as much as possible. He still attempted small talk every time there was a window. He even asked her out a few times. She never gave him an answer.

Not to mention, the late-night drives were now taking their toll on her physically. Her nerves were shot, and every muscle in her body was a taut wire ready to snap. Her jaw ached continuously from clenching her teeth. She suffered perpetual headaches. Her stomach stayed tied in knots. She even took to praying as she'd start the car. "Please get me home safe. Don't let it get me."

She did not want to know what 'it' was anymore. She just wanted everything to go back to normal.

A cat crossing the road caught her off guard, and she panicked, swerving the wheel hard to the right and slamming the brakes with both feet. Her heart threatened to leap out of her chest. Forcing deep breaths into her lungs, she closed her eyes. *One…two…three…* She counted slowly to twenty. As her pulse calmed, she scolded herself. Tried to laugh. Put her car back in gear and headed towards home. She made it halfway when the radio cut out.

She didn't expect it.

Sure, it was that time of night.

Yes, it was Thursday.

But she'd changed the channel to a local country music station days ago. She no longer listened to KBAM 99.

The static filled her car, a sinister snake she couldn't see, but could feel slipping under her skin. Then came the murmuring. Followed by the piercing emergency signal. The woman with her clipped accent and robotic sequence of numbers. And that damned music…

A blanket of ice draped her. Her stomach lurched as she floored the gas.

Her car shuddered. "No. Nonono..." she pleaded.

The car sputtered and stopped.

The trees bowed over the road, illuminated in her dull headlights. Branches appeared to stretch and reach for the car. She wasn't out of gas, and the lights and radio continued to function, but the car itself froze in place. Lottie fumbled for her cell phone on the seat next to her, to call for help.

No bars.

One of the trees began to move. Only…

That was not a tree. It was a shadow emerging from the bank of trees, as tall as their tops. Its black, elongated body loomed in front of her, a tower of emptiness in her car beams. As it moved towards her, it bent down, keeping within the boundaries of the yellowed light. Its skin was smooth, almost featureless, and shiny like plastic. Arms like tree branches jutted forward, long and knobby, with hands that ended in pointed claws. The tips of each glinted in the light, and to Lottie, they looked like metal spikes.

The head resembled a giant vintage tube radio, complete with a bent antenna and two yellowed radio dials for eyes. Like an old Crosley come to life. As it drew closer, she could make out the gelatinous sheen that covered them. Whatever it was, it wasn't plastic. The closer it got, the more its plastic skin cracked open, oozing something that sizzled as it hit the ground in front of her in fat, oily globs.

Between the radio dial eyes was a yellowed coil speaker. It pulsed and throbbed as the radio broadcast got louder. Then it opened up.

The speaker became a mouth full of teeth that appeared to be broken, bloodied radio tubes, circling a gaping hole. The static was almost deafening now.

It hit her like a taser. The bizarre radio transmission was coming from this beast. It resonated from the gaping orifice mere feet from her bumper. The number sequences repeated, and the ground beneath her vehicle shuddered. Her windshield and windows cracked and shattered.

Lottie bit back a cry as she attempted to turn the key in the ignition. The engine screeched but did not move. That thing in the road continued to slouch toward her, its clawed fingers reaching for her window. Sparks flew from the tips of its fingers.

Electrodes. Its claws were tipped with electrodes. A jolt shot out from them and struck her driver's side front quarter panel, the blast jerking the vehicle like a gunshot.

She scrambled across the seat and fell out the passenger side door. She did not know how fast it was, but she had no choice but to run. She *would* get away from this thing. Then she would pack her belongings and move far away from Dunn.

Pushing to her feet, she sprinted forward, and saw bolts of argon blue voltage striking the ground near her feet. She lost her footing in a puddle of oily sludge.

"This morning, police discovered the body of a woman on Route 24, just outside of Dunn Proper. She was found crumpled in the middle of the road, next to an idling older model sedan they believe to be her car. A forensics team determined the time of death to be 3 AM, which coincides with the previous murders. This is the fifth death in what police believe is the work of a serial killer, but there are still no leads as to who might be responsible for these horrific attacks. Residents are urged to be alert and exercise caution. Police are asking everyone to stay inside their homes between midnight and sunrise. Anyone with information is asked to please contact the Sheriff's department immediately. And now, Friday's weather..."

Sanguinary

Many ways to stop a heart,
That pounds against a cage of bone,
To exsanguinate for lifeless art.

A needle's prick can play the part,
Of an embolism brusquely grown,
Many ways to stop a heart.

By hatchet for a craftless start,
If time be short, it's quickest shown,
To exsanguinate for lifeless art.

Pills bring fate if swallowed smart,
Delivery clandestine and consumed alone,
Many ways to stop a heart.

Toxic treats will easiest depart,
Candies laced with Death unknown,
To exsanguinate for lifeless art.

But a lover's blade is the poisoned dart,
That most oft carves forever into stone…
Many ways to stop a heart
To exsanguinate for lifeless art.

All Will Turn to Gray

Aaron saw red.

A single spot of it, splashed on gray linoleum, sat illuminated against a monochrome canvas. An alien intruder in his bland universe. He reasoned it must be blood, speckling the lab floor. Having never seen red before… or any other color, outside of white, black, and gray… he felt completely unprepared for such visual decadence. He never imagined such a tiny dot could engulf him so completely, but he could not tear his eyes away.

Damn Dr. Fredrick for wearing such pedestrian smocks.

The doctor droned in the background. "As your eyes adjust, you will start seeing a broader spectrum of color. Anything responsive to the L cones will start to take on different hues. If you fully acclimate to the implanted cones, we will begin treatment to introduce S cones into your retinas. Barring no complications, that is." He flashed the penlight briefly into Aaron's eyes, watched the corneas contract to near pinpoints, and slid the light into his pocket.

"How long do you think it will take for this to work?"

"We don't have conclusive data on that. This therapy is still in its experimental stage. There have been studies on small monkeys, but you are our first human monochromatic subject. If I had to speculate, I'd say each phase might run anywhere from a few weeks to a few months. It really depends on how effectively the virus delivers the pigments." He smiled, the gesture artificial and ineffective against his limestone features. "Monochromats are exceedingly rare. Your participation will go a long way to pioneer a cure for colorblindness, Mr. Denton."

"So happy to be of service," Aaron said, his mouth a lopsided sneer. "First, colorblindness… next, world hunger."

Dr. Fredrick's smile flickered. He cleared his throat and busied himself with the clipboard. "Well, one travesty at a time, I suppose."

Aaron regretted his snark. He didn't want to appear ungrateful. He'd never been bothered by his condition. There were worse things than a world of gray. But the attached paycheck was a handsome incentive, and Fredrick was a respected professional who simply lacked Aaron's smug sense of humor. They may not be curing world hunger, but his hunger would be sated.

"I do appreciate this. I'm looking forward to them colors," he said, his shrug intended as an apology.

"Of course," Dr. Fredrick said. "*If* this works, it will be a life changer."

The doctor's ashen smile did not reach his eyes, but the red spot on the linoleum danced in celebration.

"How did it go yesterday?" Margo caught his eye in the mirror, bent over the sink, stroking a mascara wand under her lashes.

"It was okay, I guess. No new revelations." Aaron shrugged, not interested in sharing the exciting development of red with her. She came in late last night, after he'd gone to bed, reeking of cigarette smoke, alcohol, and the faint traces of cheap aftershave.

She didn't smoke. Or wear Aqua Velva.

"No?" She frowned, using a small comb to prod her caked lashes apart. Leaning back, she appraised her efforts, and then dug a tube of lipstick out of her makeup bag. Catching his eye again, she said, "Did they give you a time frame, at least? How long before they give up, or try again?"

"Beats the hell outta me," he said. "And I don't care, as long as they pay me."

She sighed, eyes rolling skyward, before falling on the cosmetic in her hand. "So you're happy to be a glorified pin cushion?"

"*Paid* pin cushion," he corrected.

She pulled the cap from the tube and twisted it, and a bullet of red emerged, snagging his attention. It was deep. Visceral. Margo didn't notice his fascination. She smudged it across her lips, puckering them at her reflection, before patting the chiseled tip over her cupid's bow.

Mesmerized, Aaron took a step forward, grabbing her upper arm as he pulled her around. She cried out, protesting, caught off guard by his bizarre reaction. Her lips were full, lush. Coated in a thick stain that sat like putty on her soft flesh. He grunted, bringing his hand to her face to touch the swell on her lower lip with the pad of his thumb. The red felt like warm butter. He dragged his thumb to the corner of her mouth, and swept towards her cheek, smearing the red over her porcelain skin.

"Dammit, Aaron! I don't have time for this. I'm going to be late for work!"

But he didn't hear her. He was hypnotized by her full crimson mouth, by the streak that lay across her skin like a Gaussian flower petal. Seized by the primal need to consume her, he shoved her against the sink and yanked up her skirt.

She wasn't complaining any more.

Dr. Fredrick held up another inkblot, waiting for Aaron's answer. They did this every week, measuring the progress of his eyesight against random inkblots. For the first two weeks, it was all blacks and grays against plain white backgrounds. As Aaron's first treatment was to introduce L cones into the corneas of his eyes, Fredrick was using inkblots with splashes of red. To someone with Aaron's condition, reds appeared black.

"If you see something new, let me know," he instructed.

"There's a stripe on that car."

Dr. Fredrick flipped the card. Sure enough, the car shaped silhouette sported a thick red stripe down its side. Last week, Aaron only saw a black car. The doctor produced another card, this one bearing the hourglass shadow of a woman.

"Sexy red dress," Aaron said.

"It worked." Dr. Fredrick dropped the cards. "I'll be damned."

"Wasn't this the plan?"

"Of course. Best case scenario, obviously. You're my first subject to respond positively to the injection." He began scratching notes on his clipboard. "Roughly when would you say you started seeing reds?"

"Faintly here and there, maybe a few days before our last appointment. But I was here last week when I knew for certain what I was looking at." He pointed to the spot on the floor. "That is red, right?"

Dr. Fredrick looked at the linoleum. "Yes. Red latex paint, to be exact. The maintenance staff here is a bit sloppy, I'm afraid."

“I’m seeing changes in everything. There’s dense reds. Stoplights, cars, clothes. But I’m starting to see variations in people’s skin. Everyone looks a little different, now. Warmer, even.”

“Go on,” Dr. Fredrick did not look up as he urged Aaron to elaborate.

“For instance, my girlfriend’s nipples…”

Dr. Fredrick coughed. “Okay. That’s—I get it.”

“I mean, she’s a beautiful woman, but the red really brings out her…”

“Understood. Wonderful news.” Aaron noticed the faint tinge on Dr. Fredrick’s face. The doctor cleared his throat and made a few more notes. With a tight smile, he sat his clipboard on the table, dropping his pen in the process. “Next week we will begin the second stage.”

“Which means?”

“S cones. We will be introducing you to blue.”

“Nice. The color of Margo’s eyes.” Aaron’s smile split his face.

Dr. Fredrick did not return his smile. He met the beautiful Margo at the beginning of the study.

He must not like blue eyes, Aaron thought.

Aaron’s life transformed from newsprint to full colored magazine spreads. In six week’s time, he could see the world around him through the same eyes as everyone else. He’d never imagined just how vibrant the city was, with its dusky asphalt and sunbaked brick walls. The verdant grass in the park, as soft as shag carpet and bloated with patches of flowers so lively, he laughed as they danced in the wind. He stood in the paint aisle of the hardware store for an hour, transfixed by the wall of brilliant color swatches, shoving them into his pockets by the fistfuls before leaving. He watched *The Wizard of Oz,* and finally understood why it was considered such a cinematic achievement, with its remarkable Technicolor revelation.

It all felt like a celebration. Everywhere he looked, colors teemed and thrived, making every trip outside an adventure. Some of them were so easy to describe. The purple hat that mirrored the Tuscan merlot in his wineglass. The deep teal sports car that looked like it had been dipped in a pool of blue from the Mediterranean Sea. But other colors were more sensory, such as the sunlight that highlighted the shrubs, a shimmery white that looked like warm felt. Or the pink that flushed Margo's cheeks mid-orgasm that felt like discomfort, throbbing, and breathlessness.

He dragged her with him on every run to the grocery store or to the bookstore, trying to pull her into the kaleidoscope of his new vision. His excitement failed to fuel her, though, and her enthusiasm for his new vision waned. He could see the boredom in her unfortunate brown eyes.

And then, it stopped. Not the colors. Just the emotion. The

palpable joy that swelled in his chest as he took in every experience with his new and improved eyeballs. The colors were still there, but the world began to look stale. Unimpressed.

Ordinary.

He grew anxious. Would he wake up one morning to a world of gray?

Margo started staying out late again.

During his next routine follow-up appointment, he admitted his fear to Dr. Fredrick.

"Do you think I will lose the ability to see color? I mean, you used a carrier virus, right? Will I build a resistance to that?"

Dr. Fredrick aimed a pen light at Aaron's corneas, watching them contract, and expand. He glanced at the numbers on his charts, a frown furrowing his brow. "There is no source material to refer to. We are in uncharted territory with you. All the other participants either failed, or experienced adverse reactions to the experiment."

"What kind of adverse reactions?"

"Nothing you should be worried about," Dr. Fredrick said. "I think you are safely out of the danger zone. Regarding the effective longevity, we really do not know. This could be a permanent change. Or you could develop antibodies, and no longer experience the effects of the transplanted cones. The next couple weeks should give us that information."

"But I think the colors are starting to dull."

"Your eyes are still healing. It could be that what you've been seeing was intensified by inflammation. What you're beginning to see now might just be the average RGB spectrum."

"Doctor—" Aaron felt the twinges of panic return to his gut "—I don't want my vision to get dull. I want those colors back. You don't understand. It's like they were *alive*. Isn't there some way to enhance it further? Are there any other options?"

Dr. Fredrick's brow knotted and he shook his head. "Humans are trichromats. We've been harvesting human cones for this experiment. Locating a willing tetrachromat donor is an unlikely possibility."

"Tetrachromat?"

"Some humans actually have a fourth cone—the yellow cone—so they can see more colors than the average person. I personally do not have it, and I don't know how much difference you would experience if you did."

Aaron sagged. Duller days were on his horizon.

Dr. Fredrick stood a little straighter. "Humans are not the only tetrachromats, though. A number of animals are as well. And the squirrel monkeys were able to adapt to human L cones."

"So, do you think it is possible to get the yellow cones from a donor animal if you can't find a human?"

"I can't promise that. But give me some time to study this. Perhaps it's possible to take the research a step further."

Aaron shook the doctor's hand and smiled. "Whatever you come up with, count me in. I want to be the first. I want to see everything there is to see."

Dr. Fredrick faced Aaron from across a sleek rosewood desk. Not a scratch marred the brilliant red woodgrain. Aaron's face floated in the sheen. A disembodied head suspended in a pool of spilled cabernet.

"So," the doctor began, "here's where it gets tricky. I think we can help you. We've been working with hummingbirds, and we've managed to generate a fourth cone."

"Excellent! When do I get it?"

"First things first. Full disclosure here. This stage of the research has not been approved."

Aaron shrugged. "So I'll be a pioneer."

"Without approval, there's no funding. Which means no paycheck. Usually, that would translate as a billed medical procedure."

"Billed? Are you saying I'll have to pay?"

"Now…"

"You approached me. I was fine the way I was. But I listened to you, and you promised this would be a lucrative venture, and now you want me to pay for it?" His voice rose an octave and he realized he was leaning across the desk, shouting.

He'd have to stop. His growth would be over. Margo would never let him waste money, not for this. But he was so close.

No. He couldn't stop, not now.

Dr. Fredrick motioned to Aaron's seat and waited for him to sit back down. "I'm not saying you will be billed. What I'm saying is that without funding or revenue, I will no longer have the staff to assist me with this experiment. The university provided the grants to conduct experiments per subject to the level of completion that we achieved with you. Any further grants I obtain will only be approved if I already have data to justify a need for additional research."

"I don't understand," Aaron said. "What are you getting at?"

"If I have empirical data that confirms humans can adapt to cones harvested from donor animals, the innovations in this area of gene therapy would be unprecedented. This project could provide you with the ability to see colors humans have never before imagined, and it could provide me with the grants and funding to expand this research further—including a place in medical journals and history books. This could change the trajectory of my career. Because of that, I am willing to make you a deal."

"Which is?"

"Work with me on this. I will attempt to give you extraordinary vision, and in return, you will allow me to use your name and any pertinent personal details in all published papers, and articles. Possibly even an appearance on television."

"And as far as my money?"

Dr. Fredrick's eyes steeled. "I am not offering to pay you. What you are receiving in return is far beyond any monetary compensation. Not even I can imagine what this experience will be like for you."

Aaron deliberated. Margo would be angry when she found out about the money. But what had started as an easy paycheck for him was now an obsession. He wanted to see what colors were out there. *All* of them.

The doctor was right. It was not something that could be priced.

"I'm in." He leaned over the rosewood, offering a handshake.

The procedure started the same as before. Aaron received a sedative and laid back in a chair with a blinding light in his face. Dr. Fredrick used a small syringe with a two-inch-long needle so skinny it looked like fishing line to deliver a minute injection of virus into each cornea. The virus was wrapped around the foreign cones that would hopefully add a fourth cone to Aaron's eyes. If his body didn't reject it, of course.

He was given dark sunglasses and instructed to go straight home and rest in a dark room for the next two days, to give his eyes time to heal. But this time, the doctor also handed Aaron a laminated booklet full of small color swatches. "This is a thorough hexadecimal chart. I want you to study this. Get familiar with these colors. And then let me know if you spot anything new in your surroundings."

Aaron shrugged. "Sure, I guess. But what's this supposed to prove?"

"Very few people are tetrachromats, so you will be the only one who knows if you can see something new with them. I am relying completely on you to let me know if it's working. Your feedback will be charted and evaluated intensely."

"Yeah, okay," Aaron said after a brief hesitation.

"Will you do that, Mr. Denton?" Dr. Fredrick's gaze was as hard as his voice.

"Not like I can refuse," Aaron replied. He understood how important his cooperation was to the doctor's career. Just as important as the doctor was to his journey.

He paused to consider that. He didn't realize he'd been thinking of it as a journey. He wasn't going anywhere, yet still, he was nearing his destination. Someone else was piloting this evolution. Yes. *His evolution*. He would not stop until he had become.

Aaron wasn't sure what to look for. Was it a color that was absent from the charts Dr. Fredrick gave him? How would he know if he was seeing colors differently? They all looked the same to him. Maybe a little brighter, perhaps a little more complex. Even so, he knew these colors already.

Margo's eyes were still a dull brown. The same color as off brand chocolate. He felt a twinge of resentment when he looked at her now. Especially when he saw other women with blue eyes. He felt cheated, even more than he felt cheated on. He began to fantasize about the blue-eyed women when he fucked her. Conversely, she began complaining about how rough and impersonal he was in bed.

He left earlier that morning, three weeks after his last unremarkable visit to Dr. Fredrick, to run by the bank before he reported to work. Stepping off his porch, he squinted against the harsh glare of the sun, the white-hot heat immediately watering his eyes. He stopped to fish a pair of prescription sunglasses out of his pocket, keeping his eyes squeezed shut until the stinging in his corneas relented. They'd become overly sensitive to daylight, and he could not leave the house without saline drops anymore.

He looked at the sky, slightly shaken by his harsh reaction to the sunlight, which was usually burdensome more than uncomfortable. And froze.

The sky was streaked and swirled, not by clouds, but with colors. Mixed into the blue were discernable streams of yellow and red, eddied in patches and oozing around the puffy pink tinged clouds pushing by in the breeze. His mouth dropped, mesmerized by the pulsing fluidity of the expanse he'd always believed was simply blue. That's what he parroted as a child... the sky was *blue*. When, in fact, it wasn't blue at all. Especially not now.

He drove towards the riverfront, leaving his car at the docks. Heading to the piers, he studied the water. Its usual murky green-brown waved and peaked with caps of orange. He could see the undercurrent clearly, as it discolored the waters with a shimmering emerald green that reminded him of a snake slithering past the banks.

Everywhere he looked, he noticed more colors where there had been less before. They were colors he still recognized, just in unexpected places. The bright rainbows that sparkled in the feathers of sunning seagulls. The magenta crystals that twinkled in the ordinary black asphalt. The green threads in his blue blazer.

When Aaron contacted the doctor, he was ordered to come in straight away.

"So, what's next? Five cones?" Aaron blinked as Dr. Fredrick pulled the penlight away from his eyes. He'd recounted his morning as the doctor typed them into his charts, and waited as he inspected his eyes to gauge their reactions and light sensitivity. Both men were notably excited. This was completely unexpected, this successful fourth cone.

Aaron did not want to stop.

Dr. Fredrick admitted, "I'm not sure a fifth cone is

possible."

Aaron deflated. "So this is it? These are all the colors I can see?"

"You now see more colors than most of the human population. 'All the colors' is an unfair assessment. I consider you rather fortunate right now."

Aaron nodded. "Yeah, yeah. Look, I'm sorry. I didn't mean to imply that I'm not grateful. I just thought… well, I figured we were looking to break boundaries here."

Dr. Fredrick perched on a stool. "I appreciate your enthusiasm. But we'd have a challenging time finding donors that have five cones. Pigeons and butterflies are believed to be pentachromats, meaning they have six cones. So that would be the next step going forward."

Aaron stared at the ceiling tiles. The pale gray foam had lavender edges. He couldn't begin to imagine what two additional cones would reveal. And then the thought struck him. "Hey, doc? Which animal sees the most color?"

"Stomatopods are believed to have the most complex eyes of all living specimens."

"Oh yeah? We talking eight or nine cones?"

"Twelve cones," Dr. Fredrick corrected.

Aaron bolted upright. "You're shitting me?" He sat quiet for a moment, and then, "What is a *stomopod*?"

"Stomatopod," the doctor corrected. "For example, mantis shrimp. They see more colors than any other known creature."

Aaron had no idea what those were, and didn't care. All he knew was he wanted their eyes. "Okay."

Dr. Fredrick frowned. "Okay?"

"Let's do it. Give me mantis shrimp eyes. I don't want to waste any more time."

"No, Aaron, it's not that simple."

"You injected hummingbird cones into my eyes, right?"

"Technically speaking, yes, but…"

"So find some of those shrimp and give me their cones."

Dr. Fredrick shook his head. "It's more complicated than simply extracting the missing cones. Their eyes are completely different. They don't have twelve separate cones. It's a system of multiple dichromatic cones. Our eyes are much simpler."

"But what is the harm in just injecting a sample of their cones in there? Wrap them in a bug, shoot me up, and see what takes." Aaron grinned.

"This could really backfire. Worst case scenarios involve infection and complete blindness. And if that infection spreads, possible death."

"But think of the best-case scenario. I can see more colors than can ever be imagined. Hell, maybe even different dimensions…"

"You're getting carried away now." The doctor sighed.

"Couldn't you just check their eyes out? Maybe there's a way to make this work. We would both make history if it does. It goes beyond anything they've ever done before."

Dr. Fredrick stared at the degrees on his wall, lost in thought.

Aaron noticed the yellow in the gray hair peppering the doctor's temples.

The doctor cleared his throat. "This may take a great deal of time. I'm not even sure it's possible to do. But I will at least give this some consideration. In the meantime, protect your eyes. No sunlight without your sunglasses. Get at least nine hours of sleep in a completely dark room every night. The key is to keep your eyes rested and healthy. No eye strains. I need your word that you will take precautions."

"Of course," Aaron said. "I can't wait to see what you come up with. Get it? *See what you come up with*?"

Dr. Fredrick groaned.

Margo hadn't been home in a week. She came in while he was working and was gone before he got home, her excuses scribbled on the white board attached to the fridge.

'Business meeting in Tucson, will be back Wednesday.'

'Mom fell, took her to hospital, staying overnight.'

'Cousin having her baby, will be back once she's settled back home.'

Aaron wasn't interested in checking into her stories, especially after he spotted her heading into a bar across town with one of her male co-workers the night her mom went to the hospital. The guy looked like the kind of asshole who'd wear Aqua Velva. To be honest, Aaron wasn't particularly interested in what Margo was up to. As long as she paid her share of the bills, she could fuck the entire 8th floor of her office, and he wouldn't care.

He'd recently set his sights on a gorgeous young woman with thick black hair, deep rose lips, and eyes so blue he could see them glittering like polished sapphires from twenty feet away. She was new to the office, and according to rumors, newly single. He played it cool around her, pretending only slight interest when she'd initiate conversations with him. It made him seem more interesting. Eager men put off beautiful women. He could tell his casual approach was working.

Cheyenne agreed to dinner that Friday. As tempted as he was to bring his date home and give Margo a taste of her own cloying medicine, he decided to keep the evening loose. So they got acquainted over steak dinners and red wine, and shared a decadent chocolate dessert, before he escorted her back to her apartment.

When she leaned in to kiss him goodnight, her cleavage threatened to spill over the lacy trim of her top. He barely noticed. He could remember a time when all he cared about was the tactile experience of soft flesh in his hands. Now, he was too distracted by the allure of her lips. They were a startling shade of crimson, though she admitted earlier that she was terrible with makeup, and therefore chose to go without. Captivated by their natural color, he was still staring at them when she pressed them against his own.

They looked like two juicy slices of blood orange, glistening in the streetlight. Soft, inviting, and just slightly sweet. She was succulent. As she clung to him afterwards, he murmured, “So that’s what red tastes like.”

He bought a bag of blood oranges on the way home that night. As he placed each dripping wedge on his tongue, he imagined he was consuming her delectable mouth.

“I don’t know if this is a good idea,” Dr. Fredrick admitted. The needle hovered an inch above Aaron’s eye, prepared for insertion. He warned Aaron repeatedly that he believed the new cells would not only fail, but undo all the progress they’d made.

Aaron was not deterred. “We can start over if we need to.”

“Your eyes are not batteries, Mr. Denton. There is no evidence that they would recover enough to start over. I have no way of knowing what reactions you would have to this. Humans do not have multiple dichromatic cones, and there are no tests that reveal how they would interact with our own cones.” A light sheen of sweat speckled the doctor’s forehead. The drops of perspiration reflected tiny rainbows from the lamp positioned just above Aaron’s head.

“Do it,” Aaron growled.

The doctor shook his head, and brought the needle to his cornea, the tip piercing the thin barrier of the sclera and sliding into position in the macula of his retina. With a small push of the syringe, he injected only a few drops into Aaron's eye. Once the needle was pulled free, a cotton patch was positioned over the delicate orb before the procedure was repeated on his other eye.

Aaron sat under the light with the cotton protecting his eyes, and felt no different than he ever did. "I think it's going to be fine," he said. "Either nothing will happen, or I will soon have bionic vision."

Dr. Fredrick removed the cotton after turning off the lamp. "We've done the best we could with these, and your eyes have accepted more than any other. If it's ever going to work, it will now."

He gave Aaron a new bottle of eye drops, these specially formulated for his eyes alone. They included a heavy sunscreen. The doctor ordered more sleep, and prescriptions of strong anti-inflammatory pills to prevent a harsh reaction. Aaron had to affix a shield to his already dark sunglasses to keep the sunlight out.

"Be especially careful with sunlight now," the doctor warned. "Mantis shrimp see deep into the UV spectrum. Your eyes are not designed to. It would be similar to staring directly into an eclipse. The effects could be permanently damaging."

Aaron realized that the only way he'd truly know what his new eyes could see, meant forgoing the protection of his glasses. Who knew what he would find? New colors, certainly.

But what if there was more? Spaces and planes…possibly even beings. Men couldn't see them because their limited vision restricted them to three dimensions, but what if this was his game changer? What if he could see preternatural creatures?

What if he could see God?

He nodded, shook the doctor's hand, and agreed to meet in a week.

He woke from his nap with a slight headache. Considering he expected a headache that rivalled an anvil to the skull, it was a pleasant surprise. He reached for the lamp on his nightstand, casting the room in a faint glow as he rolled onto his back and opened his eyes.

The ceiling was a little blurry. Likely from sleep, he reasoned. Pulling himself from the bed, he stumbled to his bathroom, and reached for his eye drops. He tilted his head back and squeezed three medicated drops into each eye. The irritation began to dissipate as the cool liquid lubricated them. He blinked repeatedly, rolling his eyes behind their lids to make sure they coated evenly. Once they felt somewhat normal again, he flipped on the light.

The immediate sting was brutal, and he howled as he tripped out of the room, into the unlit hallway. He squinted. While a little sore, he could see much better. In fact, he could see clearly. The dark of the hallway did nothing to impede the vibrancy of the small paintings hanging on the opposite wall.

The light in his bedroom didn't cause his eyes pain. A single soft bulb beneath the dark vellum lampshade kept the space purposefully dim. It calmed the burning in his eyes, but caused his sight to go hazy. Even so, the colors in the room were dayglow. The teal linen of his comforter, the abstract Mediterranean blue curtains, the rainbow row of shirts in his closet… his bedroom was transformed into an art-pop still-life. He couldn't make out sharp edges or details, but the intensity of the different hues and shades were captivating, an impressionistic adaptation of the surreal.

Within a few minutes, his eyes were stinging again, and a growing throb in his temple had him pulling the cord on the lamp. He sat on the bed and felt the throbbing in his eyes ease as they readjusted to the darkness. Looking down at his hands, he noticed the highlights across the thinner skin of his knuckles and joints. The blue paths of veins beneath his skin were more visible than before. *I wonder what they look like in the daylight.* He squinted at the alarm clock under his lamp. Through the blur, he could make out the time. It was just before two in the afternoon.

He dressed, ran a comb through his hair, and tucked his sunglasses, wallet, keys, and eye drops into his pockets. Pausing briefly at his front door, he glanced over his shoulder. The living room wavered in the growing distance. These next steps would take him into a world no one could describe, or warn about. This was no longer a quest for more color. This was the search for the Tree of Knowledge. He had the keys to a kingdom all humans sought, but never realized.

He was Magellan. Drake. Vespucci. He was the Pied Piper, and his front door was the door into the mountain. He would lead them through.

He sat on his front steps, eyes squeezed shut, trying to adjust to the jagged bursts of electricity that shot all the way through his optic nerve anytime his lids even so much as shuddered. The sunlight was a white-hot spire that pierced through to his brain. Digging into his pockets, he located the sunglasses and fumbled to pull them free. They jumped from his fingers and clattered down the steps, out of his reach. He muttered a curse and covered his eyes with his palms, hoping he could adjust to the bright light at least long enough to find his glasses.

Cracking his eyes open a sliver, he attempted to peer through his lashes. That wouldn't work. A stream of tears slid down his face, an automated response he remembered from being submerged in an over-chlorinated swimming pool. Except as the minutes passed, the burning dulled to an ache, and then eventual numbness. He shadowed his eyes with his hands, took a staggered breath, and opened them.

The world glowed fluorescent around him. He'd stepped into a Dead Head diorama. But for all the brilliance and color, the clarity was muddy. When he held his hand up, he could make out the vague outline of its shape, but it lacked resolution. He could've been wearing a fleece glove. As he brought it to his face, the definition returned. He could make out every hair on each knuckle. The creases in his skin were almost blackened by their infinitesimal shadows. Every vein and capillary under the transparent veil of his skin coursed with the blood his heart was frenetically pumping. He stared at his arms, at the musculature woven around his bones. He was a wonton wrapper. A parchment husk. He pulled his shirt off, his eyes falling on his chest, and the faint edges of the organ palpitating behind his boney armor.

The world was fractured in jarring lights and kaleidoscope colors. Rather than seeing trees and sidewalks and bushes, he saw their pixilated impressions shimmer before him. Placing his hand on the bark of a tree, he saw the rough textile beneath the map work of his circulatory system. He could see all the colors, and then some… and he saw them all at once. But they didn't morph together in new, undiscovered colors. He saw them simultaneously *and* separately.

He recently went to a 3D screening at the theater. The dimensional effects his glasses provided were less enthralling than what happened when he removed them and stared at the screen, sans eyewear. The colors were splintered, misaligned. Two versions of every person…the same person, but in two separate planes. Cordial doppelgangers inhabiting their spaces in harmony.

Only that was 3D, and this is… 6D? Is that how this works? If time is the fourth dimension, can I see its passage? And what dimensions come after that?

He'd stripped off all his clothes by then, inspecting his abdomen and legs. He walked the yard stiffly, imagining himself an alien armature stripped of its human costume. He could hear voices in the distance, but they were as indistinct as his latent vision. "Hello?"

The mass appeared in his peripheral, a gelatinous slug in shades of reds, blacks, and blues, rushing at him. A piercing squeal deafened him as it charged, and he ducked under the shield of his arms and shouted a warning. The creature stopped, heaving breaths as it appeared to regard his threats.

"Aaron, what the hell are you doing?"

The squeal simmered into a familiar, if not caustic voice. He recognized her. Margo had returned. Although he never anticipated how different she would appear with his heightened vision.

Figures she'd be an ugly beast.

"Sorry, babe," he snarled. "I didn't recognize you for a minute. Did you do something new with your hair?"

The creature lurched forward and grabbed his arm, pulling him off balance. He hit the sidewalk in a skid, scraping his cheek and chest across the rough asphalt, an oversized hunk of Colby on a cheese grater. Yowling, he pushed himself up and sat on his haunches, tenderly brushing the chewed skin across his sternum.

His fingertips were blood dipped, glistening with viscera hued a velvet red, but he saw tiny brown and white discs dancing in the goo. The dichromatic pairs in his eyes had gone beyond extending his sensitivity to lights and colors. His head became a microscope. He chuckled at first, and then laughed, flicking gobs of blood onto the sidewalk before leaning in close, nose practically touching the ground, to marvel at the details of the blood cells and plasma that had, just moments ago, remained restrained inside blue channels.

"Get up! Have you lost your mind? The police are coming!" The voice was again at his ear, its animosity poorly disguised as hysteria. He felt the sharp brush of fingernails graze his shoulder before the vice of thin fingers gripped his bicep. She was pulling on him, trying to throw him off balance. Trying to get him back down. Just in time for the cops to take him.

"You'd love that, wouldn't ya, bitch?" He thrust his elbow back, hard, making contact with her ambiguous chest. He felt her grip pull free as she landed behind him, surprised by his reaction. Whirling around, he faced the creature laying on the sidewalk, her legs splayed open. Like the whore she was.

She was still too pixilated to see clearly, but he'd seen her a million times already. He memorized her dark hair, her brown eyes, her wide mouth. He imagined, too many times to count, how they must've looked beneath a body other than his.

She thought she was better than him. She thought she was too good for him! There she was, wearing an oversized pair of sunglasses to hide her traitorous eyes, anger twisting the seam that must've been her mouth. He straddled her and pulled back his fist, driving it directly between her eyes, breaking both her glasses and her nose with one punch.

She screamed, the high-pitched wail raising a commotion of shouts in the distance. He grabbed her head in his hands and lifted it off the sidewalk, before driving it into the concrete. Over and again, screaming above her cries of pain, "Do you think I didn't know about the men you've been fucking, you whore? Did you think you were smarter than me? I've already replaced you, bitch, and I can't wait until you fucking die!"

She was no longer screaming or thrashing beneath him. The back of her head caved in from the repeated blows as he pummeled her over and again into the concrete. When he released her, she fell with a splat. She was a Monet face in a puddle of broken bone, brains, and viscous fluids.

He threw his head back, searching out the sun in the argon sky, the ball of blaze pulsing above him. Black spots shot off its surface. They flew through the sky like javelins, aiming for the iridescent clouds scattering on an afternoon breeze.

He was looking at the portal of Heaven, the gates opened to him alone.

He was *God.*

He threw his arms up to the sky and roared, pushing his

voice from the depths of his belly into his skull. He ignored the twinge… and then pop… in his temple. He screamed long and loud, even as unseen hands seized his arms, and the world around him went completely white.

Something beeped. It was coming from somewhere over his left shoulder. A steady sound, like an electronic pulse. He could smell the antiseptic odor of alcohol mixed with urine. It stung his nostrils.

He tried to speak, but he had no voice. His eyes wouldn't open. He couldn't move as much as a finger.

Where am I?

Two voices grew louder, drowning out the beeping. They stood above him, to the side. Familiar voices.

"If he comes out of the coma, he will be taken into custody. If he's lucky, he'll die first. For what he's done, he doesn't want to find himself behind prison walls."

"Did the police mention who she was?" Her voice was bruised. Soft.

"A coworker. Cheyenne Mays. According to friends, they were dating."

NO.

"Oh god. What a bastard!" Her voice feigned horror, but he knew she was faking it. Margo was evil. She deceived him and ruined his life. He tried to move his arms. He needed to choke the last breath from her soulless body, but he was trapped in limbo.

NO.

"I'm so sorry. You are safe now, I promise."

"I don't understand what happened." She sobbed. Alligator tears.

"I tried to warn him the experiment could turn out wrong, but he refused to listen. I was concerned there could be complications that extended past his vision. Mantis shrimp are incredibly volatile, unnaturally strong. He took those last injections against my advice. When they apprehended him, his eyes were so infected, the inflammation caused them to bulge out of their sockets. He was a monster. So the doctors removed them."

"Jesus," she whispered.

No.

"He's on life support, and there's no medical directive. Does he have any family?"

"None living."

"They will ask if you'd like to keep him on life support in that case, if he doesn't wake up. Considering he's a murderer, I doubt the staff will be upset should you choose to cut it."

NO.

She laughed. "As far as I'm concerned, he can rot."

NO.

"I think that's a reasonable choice." Dr. Fredrick's voice was conciliatory. "I hope I'm not being too forward, but I've always thought you had stunning eyes, Margo. Perhaps you'd let me buy you a drink? You shouldn't be alone right now."

Her yes was a breath and a sigh. And then they were gone.

Beep!Beep!Beep! Beep…

NO.

War Dance

Murky dusk fades into early evening as a crisp breeze snakes through the tall grass, ruffling Fido's thick chocolate guard hairs, standing them tall on his backside. His whiskers twitch as he skips along the unmarked path. The scent of earth and something unidentifiable fills his nostrils… something *meaty*. His paws barely touch the ground as he follows his nose. It's there, right in front of him, a dark cavern tucked in the weeds.

He pokes his head in blackness, and his face feels a damp chill. His eyesight isn't great, but he's used to that. Sniffing the air, he searches for the scent of meatiness that lingers somewhere just beyond his vision. Squeezing into the hole, his bones compress to fit comfortably in the tiny space.

The meatiness moves! He can't see it, but the aroma shifts, swirls a little like dust in shafts of sunlight, and then recedes. Running towards a blurry dot of white, he snakes through the length of the tunnel. He's almost there. The meatiness will be his! He's so close now, he can see big eyes fixed on him. Two pointy ears perked at his approach, as he emerges from the tunnel and leaps…

Fido rolled on his back in a blind fury, gnawing first on his tail, then his backside, then his toes. He sprawled across the platform in his cage, bumping against the food dish and water bottle. Beyond the metal bars he could see blurry restless lumps. His people were still asleep. One snorted and shifted under the blankets. He shrugged and inspected the kibble in his food bowl.

Not meatiness. Sighing, he returned to his hammock, curling around Fifi, his cage mate. Although younger only by a year, she was nearly as small as a kit, and he almost completely encircled her dainty body. Her tongue poked out of her mouth as she slept and her whiskers twitched. *She must be dreaming of meatiness too*, he decided. He should go back to sleep and dream of meatiness with her.

Sudden movement in the room caught his attention. A beige blur fell off the bed and slipped through the door. It loped down the hallway, receding into darkness. He couldn't see it well enough to make out what it could be, but holy dook, it smelled delicious! Just thinking about it made his paws antsy. *I need to sleep,* he thought. *I will feel better in the morning. Fifi looks so cozy.*

I must lick her ears.

Three licks later, he was asleep again, tunneling through

grassy dreamland, searching for the elusive meatiness.

Fido stretched one leg in the air, yawned twice, then licked his paws and rubbed them across his eyes. Awake already, Fifi crunched kibble over their bowl. She looked tense, her white fur tufted and messy. Fido slowly stretched his lanky body onto the platform, sliding to her side on his belly.

He licked her cheek, and said, “What’s wrong?”

Fifi whispered, “Something bad happened last night. Mommy had a nasty mark on her leg this morning. Daddy said it was a bite!”

“Probably just a spider,” Fido said. “We’ll eat it later.”

Fifi’s bright red eyes were full of fear as she shook her head, and said, “It’s not a spider this time. Daddy took her to a doctor!” She whimpered softly, “What if they don’t come home?”

Fido frowned, remembering the weird blur from the night before. He sniffed the air but couldn’t detect the mystery meatiness. His stomach grumbled, not just because he really wanted to eat whatever that thing had been, but because somehow, he knew it meant to hurt their people. He didn’t know why, but… *It was on the bed last night, right?*

Fifi loved their people almost as much as she loved Fido, because she was separated from her mom and siblings too early. And she worried a lot... about everything. If he told Fifi about what he saw, she would panic. Panic gave her the hiccups.

He never slept well when Fifi had the hiccups. It was worse than having itchy butt!

Together, they curled up in the hammock, waiting for their people to return. Fido rested his head on Fifi's shoulder as she drifted to sleep. His eyes were locked on the hallway. The daylight illuminated the house, revealing the shadowy corners he couldn't see the night before.

So when the creature returned, he recognized it. *Rabbit!* Brown, furry, big footed… the only difference being the pointy things jutting out of its head, like mangled head teeth. *Head teeth?* Smelled like delicious meatiness, alright. But it looked… wrong. Mean. Moving toward their room with lopsided hops, its huge ears pricked in his direction.

Fido let out a long hiss. Leaping from the hammock, his tail fur standing on end like a bottle brush, he locked his masked eyes on the intruder and hissed again.

The rabbit loped back down the hall and disappeared.

The owners returned while the ferrets napped. Mommy woke them for their playtime as she did every day, giving them both kisses before releasing them. Fido and Fifi thanked her by arching their backs and erupting into spastic dances of joy at her feet. Fido even nibbled her big toe for good measure, dooking when she squealed and reached down to tickle his belly.

But Fido didn't feel especially playful. He'd barely napped as Fifi snuggled against him, his mind too busy concocting a plan that would save their people from the evil rabbit. He could smell the creature faintly, could feel its eyes watching him from its hidey spot. Fur bristling, he sniffed the floor, searching for his prey.

We are going to eat you tonight, rabbit.

Fido led Fifi to their dig box, and they played in the rice as Fido told her about the creature with the delicious aroma and the bizarre head teeth.

Fifi stopped digging, her eyes wide with fear. "A monster rabbit?" She chuffed, "Holy dook! Is it gonna eat us?"

"No!" Fido said, and pounced on her back, so Mommy would think they were wrestling. "It had that same smell, the smell that means *we* can eat *it*. We've eaten rabbit before, so I say kill it. Then we munch it all up while our people are sleeping. We get a big tasty treat, and they have no idea they were ever in danger. DANCE!"

They both leaped around the dig box, showering uncooked rice all over the floor, scrambling away as Mommy exclaimed over their mess.

"What was that for?" Fifi dooked softly, her tiny fangs latched onto the back of his neck.

"We need to be ready," he said. "It will be back tonight, I can feel it. Go play with Mommy so she won't see what I'm doing."

Fifi bounced across the room and latched onto Mommy's ankle, her impromptu ambush a successful diversion. Mommy was too busy tickling and chasing Fifi around the living room to notice Fido scampering back to the bedroom.

In the cage, Fido packed a few pieces of kibble into a hole below the door with his paw. *That will do.* When Mommy put them up for the night, she would close the bottom door, but the lock would not catch. Once their people were asleep, he would be able to push the door open.

He hopped out of the bedroom, dooking, *"It's time to practice my war dance!"*

Daddy's loud snores woke Fido. He'd eaten only a little kibble after playtime, curling up in the hammock to *dead sleep* as he waited for their people to retire. Dreams of delicious aromas circled nightmares of jutting head teeth and empty round eyes, leaving him both edgy and hungry as he stretched awake.

Fifi yawned and climbed from the hammock, red eyes glinting in a wayward shaft of moonlight. After a drink of water, she licked her lips, bouncing her head from side to side. "Do you think this will take long?" she whispered. "I was dreaming of pinky mice, and now I'm starving!"

Fido shook his head. "I haven't seen it yet, but I can smell it. Get a whiff."

Fifi lifted her head and sniffed. Her eyes widened and her

tail puffed, her fuzzy body poised to pounce. She chuffed, "I need to eat that!"

"Me too!" he replied, licking her ear before taking the lead. "Now, follow me and stay close."

They descended the ramps and paused at the cage door. Fido squinted into the dark. No sight of the rabbit. Paws on the cage bars, Fido gave them a shove.

The door hinges squealed as it swung open. Their people didn't stir.

But just past the dark of the hallway, something else did.

They crept along the wall, bodies low to the floor. Fido was tense, ready to attack… but he was not afraid. Squeezing under the scalloped trim of a sideboard, they peered into the gloomy dining room. A rabbit couldn't reach them there. The perfect command central for two slinky assassins.

"Okay," Fido whispered. "The plan is easy. Distract and attack. If I can get on his back, I can bring him down."

Fifi licked her lips again, bouncing her head, and said, "Hey! What if I poof on him? Will that distract him?"

Fido chattered. "Holy dook, that's a good idea! Give him a big poof in the face, then come back here. Do not come out until I tell you it's safe." Fido crawled into the open and sniffed the floor. "I'm gonna get him over by that chair, so I can leap on him from behind. Wait here until I bark. Then run out, poof like crazy, and come back. The evil bunny won't know what hit him!"

Fifi chuckled, her eyes twinkling in excitement, and said, "I bet he tastes like chicken!"

A long shadow fell across the floor, sending Fido scampering back under the sideboard in surprise. The shape jerked forward awkwardly, blocking the shaft of light that spilled from the kitchen. The biggest rabbit they'd ever seen followed, stumbling over its feet as it padded across the carpet.

Fido could see the head more clearly than before, and his tummy contracted when he realized the weird head teeth were large antlers.

Fifi clucked softly, every hair on her body standing on end. "What *is* that thing?"

Fido had never seen a rabbit with antlers before. It looked… ridiculous. "A rabbit suffering from an identity crisis?" He chuffed.

Fifi dooked, "It looks like an abdominal snowbunny!"

The smell wafted into their hiding place, the same wonderful aroma Fido hunted in his dreams. He hissed, "Abdominal or not, that's dinner!"

Fifi, overcome with excitement, darted from the hidey spot before Fido could hold her back. Her tiny white body bounced across the floor into the path of the evil horned rabbit, and spun around. Tail erect like a miniature skunk, she hopped up and down as she poofed, barking almost as loud as a dog.

"Get him, Fido!" she squealed. "Come on! He's right here!"

"Yeah, Fido, come and get me!" The rabbit's voice was a low growl meant to taunt, spittle dripping from his incisors as he turned towards the sideboard. "Ah, a smelly cat snake! I eat cat snakes like you for breakfast," the rabbit slurred at Fifi, and flashed his jagged teeth.

His eyes were red-rimmed, his fur mangy, and mud caked his oversized feet. Mixed in with the delicious aroma of raw rabbit was an unusual smell Fido didn't catch earlier. Vaguely familiar, sort of chemical… Fido sniffed the air, trying to identify the foreign odor, but he couldn't place it.

Meanwhile, the rabbit turned back quickly, head low, his antlers swinging to the right and lifting Fifi off the floor. She hissed and barked, wrapping her legs around a horn as he thrashed his head back and forth.

"Get off my horn, you overgrown weasel lice!"

Fido watched his beloved being tossed above the monster's head, and for the first time, he felt afraid. He needed to get Fifi back to the safety of their hidey spot where the rabbit couldn't hurt her. For a moment, he thought about waking their people to intervene, until he remembered the fat bandage on Mommy's leg.

No! Fido thought. *This is my plan, and I'm gonna bring down that oversized buffet, if it's the last thing I dook!*

The monster rabbit hit his horns against a chair leg, still

trying to dislodge Fifi. “Come here, you fur covered hors d’oeuvres. Let me eat you. It’s only going to hurt… A LOT!”

Puffing up his dark fur, Fido charged into the open, his banded eyes locked on their attacker. Just inches from the rabbit’s feet, he pushed off his paws and shot into the air, arcing, and twisting his body. Bouncing and hopping back and forth, he proceeded to war dance like never before, a streak of chocolate and musk that mesmerized the interloper. Jumping over the rabbit’s head, he catapulted across his backside. The rabbit staggered, struggling to stay upright.

“What are you doing? Stop that ridiculous jumping! Have you lost your mind?”

But Fido continued dancing, around the floor, up and over, cartwheeling and spinning faster. The rabbit swayed and stumbled, Fido’s crazed movements confusing his reflexes. He snapped at Fido as the ferret somersaulted across his nose, and Fido caught a whiff of that strange smell again. Only this time he recognized it. He smelled it on Daddy’s breath sometimes.

Whiskey!

Suddenly the rabbit roared, jerking his head forward and flinging Fifi to the floor.

“You farted in my eye! That is absolutely revolting! What is wrong with you?”

Fido did not stop moving, his dancing erratic. He pounced circles around the horned rabbit, who stumbled and fell like an inebriated old man. Seizing the moment, Fido leapt onto the rabbit's back and sunk his fangs into the back of his neck, the familiar taste of blood in his mouth. Digging his claws into the monster's fat haunches, he bit down once more, deeper this time, over and again. The rabbit screamed and flailed under his assault. Driven by the coppery flavor in his mouth and the metallic smell that flooded his nostrils, Fido ripped into the rabbit's flesh, severing the tough tendons of his spinal cord.

The rabbit collapsed, his movements reduced to involuntary twitches. Fido continued decimating his body until he went completely limp, arterial blood seeping into the carpet. The monster was gone, the remnants of life fading from his black marble eyes.

Fido scampered to Fifi's side, nudging her with his nose, licking her ears frantically. She did not move, her body lifeless as he tried to wake her. He tugged on her neck, blew on her whiskers… but she didn't respond.

Exhaustion won over, so he wrapped his body around hers, rested his chin over her face, and drifted to sleep.

The smell of meatiness filled his nostrils, wafting in circles around his head, and his stomach grumbled. Slowly opening his eyes, he looked over at the giant horned rabbit. He should've felt jubilant, satisfied… but he was weary. So very lonely. Rather than making a well-deserved meal of his kill, he decided to return to the bedroom and wait for his people to wake.

He whimpered, thinking, *I miss Fifi. Mommy is gonna be so sad when she finds her.*

A tiny white head popped up from behind the carcass, mouth as ruby red as her eyes. "Hey," Fifi chattered, "Where are you going? You gotta taste this! Abdominal snowbunnies are delicious!"

Fido, overwhelmed by joy and relief, danced again—but this was no war dance. He bounced around the dead rabbit and pounced on Fifi's back, covering her in licks and nuzzles as they wrestled, oblivious to the blood smeared all over their fur. They chased each other around the dining room, dooking their victory, leaving tiny crimson paw prints in their wake.

Then light flooded the room and they heard Mommy scream, "My carpet!" And then, "What on earth *is* that thing?"

Daddy, who followed the muddy monster tracks into the kitchen, shouted, "My expensive whisky!"

Despite their people's horror, Fido and Fifi were allowed to eat their fill of the giant rabbit before Daddy burnt the remains in the garden. The antlers were saved and mounted on the wall in the dining room above the sideboard.

After the night of the Jackalope, Mommy let Fido and Fifi inspect the house before bedtime to be sure more monsters hadn't found a way in. She would kiss them both on the noses, calling them her little *jackalope assassins*, and watch them drift to sleep.

In his dreams—night after night—Fido ate that giant monster bunny.

And *holy dook*, was it delicious!

Met Halfway

"There's something happening here... what it is ain't exactly clear..."

Avery huddled in Bark Winslow's tottering woodshed, draft card in trembling hand, listening to Buffalo Springfield through his earphones. Every few minutes he slid forward to peek through a cracked window at the Winslow's driveway, waiting for Craig to arrive in his cherry '66 Chevelle and carry them to freedom. They were Canada bound—they had no choice. It was that or die in a skirmish in some Vietnamese rice field.

"Shit guys, come on," he whispered. The sound of voices from the street carried on the fall breeze, and he ducked before he could be seen. At exactly 2:05 that afternoon he officially became a criminal.

The townsfolk weren't very approving of the 'hippies' that protested the violence and burned their cards. The adults had welcomed the draft with open arms, but why wouldn't they?

Uncle Sam had no use for them. Older, married... their duty to the war was fulfilled by paying their taxes and spitting out babies to be cultivated for the future fight against the Viet Cong.

It was nothing short of cruel irony that the lifelong friends were summoned to report to Knoxville for enlistment on Halloween. Only once a year the usually sedate little community transformed into a ruckus of brightly lit thrills and terrors.

Preparations for the biggest celebration to date had been underway since the New Year, and Avery especially looked forward to this year's spectacle. They were pulling out all the stops to make this Halloween the most memorable ever.

But while their friends and family celebrated Halloween with parades, masquerades, and fireworks, the boys would steal away from Harvest Hill and head north through the mountain back roads. They'd take the same route Dickie and Jonah took a year ago—the route all the deserters took.

Once they crossed the Canadian border they'd be safe, and after waiting out the war in Toronto, who knew? Maybe they'd never come back to Tennessee. Hell, didn't matter none to Avery. Or at least that was what he told the guys.

They pooled their money and coordinated a fool-proof plan to skip out while the town played dress-up. Packing sleeping bags and clothes into heavy canvas duffels, they stockpiled their belongings in the Winslow's shed, planning to shove it all in the trunk of the Chevelle and lay tracks just after sundown. They'd drive in shifts, take turns sleeping in the back seat, and live on water and jerky. No stops except to take a piss or refuel. They should make the border in a few days.

Avery was pacing the cluttered interior of the hideout when Bark emerged from the back door of his house, two bottles of pop in one hand and a paper bag in the other. He crossed the yard in seconds and ducked through the doorway. "Ham and cheese. You hungry?"

Avery accepted the sandwich and soda, muttering his thanks. His knotted stomach had been protesting for the past two hours, so he wasn't about to turn away food, no matter how nauseous he felt. He'd never eaten so fast in his entire life. After guzzling the last of his soda, he leaned back against an old kerosene heater and belched.

Bark crumpled the paper bag and tossed it on the floor. "I rode my bike into town and got some snacks for the road. Chips and Coca Colas. You bring anything to eat?"

"I grabbed Mama's cookies and some Sky Bars hidden in the cupboard."

Bark grinned and pulled a pack of Marlboros from his pocket, popping one into his mouth and lighting it with a silver Zippo. "Groovy. We'll have something for dessert. It's gonna be a helluva smooth ride."

"When you went to town, you think anybody noticed you?"

"Nah. Everyone's fussing over decorations and costumes.

Trick or treat starts in a couple hours, so I figure we can get going after Ma takes Sissy down the street."

"I ain't seen Craig yet. Something's gotta be wrong." He pinched a crimp in his earphone cord, then grimaced. *Best handle them more carefully.* He wouldn't have money to buy new ones anytime soon. Fastening his nervous hands in the waistband of his jeans, he tapped a drum roll on his leather belt.

Bark sighed and rolled his eyes. "Calm down, will you? Ain't nothing wrong. He ran by Swanky's to get our stash, but he should be here anytime. No worries."

He swallowed. "Yeah, you're probably right. Just that the bus left an hour ago and people might say something if they find out we weren't on it." In a small town like Harvest Hill, everyone knew each others' business.

They sat together for what seemed an eternity in the loudest silence Avery had ever heard. It whooshed in his ears like a washing machine, vying to drown out the crazy rhythm of his racing heart. He worried too much, sure. But his gut told him this was different. They were in deep, facing jail time if the law caught up to them.

A distant rattle heralded Craig's approach. With a painful grind of shifting gears, he backed the polished blue car close as he could to the shed. The door screeched as he pulled himself out, flipping his shaggy hair out of his eyes. Dangling from his hand was a baggie bulging with sticky buds of pot.

"We are officially ready to go," he drawled.

He swaggered into the hovel past Bark, wearing a lazy grin that the girls all swooned over. "Swanky gave me the directions and the weed, so we can head out soon as I stop in town to get some gas."

"What?" Avery's stomach dropped. "I thought you just said we were ready to go." His pulse tripled.

"We are, all except for that. I didn't realize I was so low on fuel. Won't do us no good flying outta here on fumes. Relax, brother." He offered the bag to Avery. "Wanna light up? That'll ease ya."

"No thanks," Avery mumbled. He preferred to keep his wits about him. "Let's just get this over with."

"Come on, man, let's book it." Avery's earphone fell in his lap as Bark tugged it loose and slid out the car. Craig was already in the gas station making his purchases, but the boys had been trapped in the car waiting for the crowds in the market to thin. He must have dozed off listening to his music.

The closest gas station was conveniently situated next to the grocery market. Unfortunately, so was the Sheriff's office. They hunched in the backseat, watching Ned Folsum, the deputy mayor, attempt to run off three men Avery recognized as Black Panthers. He wasn't very effective. They took one step towards him and he scurried back into his office like a red-faced rodent, huffing and hollering obscenities all the way.

"I ain't seen them round since King was shot. Folsum couldn't run them out then; he sure as hell don't stand a chance runnin' them out now. Wonder what they're doin' here?" Avery admired their strength, but was intimidated by the anger that fueled their cause.

"Ain't too many of them left to recruit in these parts. My guess is they're probably passing through from Atlanta. Bet there was another rally," Bark whispered. "It would be far out to go with them."

Avery snorted. "Far out? No thanks. I ain't tryin' to get lynched."

"Don't be such a candyass," he snapped.

Avery shoved the plastic buds into his ears and closed his eyes. Bark might be his best friend, but he'd become a real asshole since they decided to run, constantly knocking Avery for his severe anxiety. When they reached Toronto, Avery intended to find Jonah and ask to crash at his pad. Bark could take his attitude and shove it up his ass.

Next thing he knew, they were crossing the parking lot, Bark grumbling at his side to 'move it.' Across the street, Folsum and three armed officers were facing off against the Panthers. The escalating commotion provided a perfect diversion for the renegade boys. Avery ignored Bark's complaints, focusing all his attention on the store entrance doors instead. As they stepped inside, a small bell announced their arrival. His stomach somersaulted.

Bark wandered in search of snacks, but Avery made a beeline for the refrigerated section to grab a bottle of milk. If he didn't soothe his knotted stomach he'd be cramped up before they got past the town limits. Probably not a bad idea to grab some Alka Seltzer as well. He could just hear Bark's arrogant voice as he taunted him for being a panty waist again.

The bottles of milk were slick with condensation, but he hugged the wet glass against his chest, feeling the cold sink through his t-shirt. As he turned up the aisle to locate Bark, he bumped into Old Man Haverty.

"Boy, what you doing here? Wasn't you s'posed to be gone out on that bus earlier?" He glared with rheumy eyes, his jaw working on chew. A thin stream of tobacco spittle ran down his chin.

"N-No sir." Avery racked his brain for a quick excuse. "We're going to Knoxville in Craig's car so he can leave it with a cousin there. Headed out right now, in fact." Haverty planted his feet in Avery's path, blocking his escape. He gulped and felt the sheen of perspiration building on his face. The vile old man always made him particularly nervous, and he'd never been a good liar.

Haverty was silent except for a rumble in his throat, grinding tobacco with his gums and staring deep into Avery's eyes. The boy shifted from one foot to the other, fighting not to break the old timer's unflinching glare and give himself away. Finally he cleared his throat. "Well, I better get going, sir," he said.

"You don't fool me none, boy. You and them hippies gonna turn tail and run, aren't cha? Just like a bunch of dogs. Ain't got no balls, the lot of you."

"We can't be late for our physicals. Don't want to get in trouble." Avery squeezed past him and barely avoided colliding with a pyramid of dry oatmeal. He could hear Haverty's growled accusation trail him down the aisle.

"Go ahead and get t' runnin,' you sorry sack of shit. Ain't gonna do you no damn good, no ways. Ain't no dodger ever got away. Yer gonna fight, no matter if yer lookin' to or not."

Bark was scowling as a flushed Avery put his milk on the counter. "What took you so long?"

"Haverty saw me. Wouldn't let me pass. Mean fucker." He counted out his change and took the milk before the cashier could bag it. "Thanks," he stammered, looking back over his shoulder one last time. Haverty wasn't following them.

Finally out the door, he practically ran to the car with Bark close on his heels. "All you're doing is drawing attention," Bark hissed.

"He's gonna say something, Bark. He's gonna rat us out. We need to get the hell out of here before he gets to Folsum!"

Back at the car, Craig had the hood popped and was checking fluid levels, whistling as if he didn't have a care in the world. Avery rushed past him and just about dove into the car. He stuck his head out the window. "Hurry up, man!"

"Everything's copacetic, buddy. Take it easy, I'm almost done." He pulled free a dipstick and wiped it clean. "What's eating you, anyway? You all right?"

"Just got a bad feeling is all. Too many people can see us here."

Bark sauntered up behind Craig. "Never mind the melvin, Haverty's just bustin his chops. You know how scared he gets." He motioned to the small angry crowd across the street. Voices and tempers were rising, a sign of danger. "It's getting ugly over there real fast, though."

Craig observed the brawl without expression, then nodded at Avery. "What say we lay some tracks outta this dump now?" Finishing his checks, he dropped the hood and wiped his hands on a greasy rag. "Not a bad idea to beat feet from the heat."

Avery sighed and smiled, relieved that Craig hadn't joined Bark in his criticism. "The sooner, the better."

"I aim to please, mi amigo." Craig slid a pair of dark glasses over his pale blue eyes. "Let the journey commence."

The sun was sitting on the horizon as they passed the last houses and headed for the highway. Parents were already milling about the streets with their miniature demons, ghouls, and witches, all swinging bulging bags of candy and squealing like pint-sized banshees. After trick or treat everybody would head to Main Street for the annual parade and follow the procession to Town Hall, where there would be a party, dance, fireworks, and hayrides. By then they'd be two counties away and counting.

Avery bid the town a silent farewell as he thought of everything he'd be missing from then on. The future stretched ahead of him, clouded in dark uncertainty. But at least he had a future. If he'd gone to war he'd never make it out alive. *I'm a man now,* he thought. *Time to act like one.*

The sun was dropping below the trees, bathing the clouds in an eerie blood red hue. Avery had finished the half gallon of milk and was digging through the bags for a Sky Bar, his anxiety finally easing. There were no cars to be seen and they had plenty of gas to get them across the state line.

Craig and Bark were in the front seat passing a marijuana cigarette back and forth, but he had declined when they offered a drag. He could hear them over the music in his earphones, laughing and cracking jokes about the Canadians. Tossing them some jerky, he settled back and tried to relax. He'd be the next to drive and therefore the first to sleep. Craig whooped just as he was stretching his legs across the seat.

"Hell yeah! Crossing the county line, boys! We'll make the Canadian border in no time!"

Avery smiled and closed his eyes, lulled to sleep by the vibrations of a four-wheeled chariot.

The rattle of gravel under the tires shook Avery awake. Groggy and disoriented, he sat up halfway to see Bark roll down his window and lean out. "Hey buddy, where you headed this time of night?"

An unfamiliar man in a khaki jacket and ragged jeans approached the car. There was a guitar hooked over his shoulder and a small army duffle in one hand, the other shoved in his pocket. *Bet that's a knife,* Avery thought, fighting his growing panic.

The stranger leaned against the window. "Headed north, my friends. Things are getting too heavy in these parts."

"I don't remember seeing you around here before," Avery piped in. He knew he was probably overreacting, but something about the fellow made him uneasy.

"I'm coming out of Mississippi, so I ain't really a local. When I said 'these parts' I was referring to the whole country." When he grinned his teeth practically glowed. Craig and Bark seemed to like him right off the bat, but Avery didn't trust him.

"Right on, brother," Craig said. "It's a mighty long walk. You wanna lift? We're headed the same way."

"That would be far out if you got room on board for another traveler and his guitar."

"Plenty of space in the trunk for her. Climb on in." Craig killed the engine and pulled himself from the front seat, stretching slowly as he groaned. "Man, I haven't been driving very long, but it sure as hell feels like I've been going for days. Smoked too much, I think."

From the front seat, Bark laughed. "I could eat a cow's

worth of jerky right now."

"Fellows, I know the way north. If you like, I can do the driving for a while. Give you a chance to relax a bit."

"You're awesome, man. That sounds great," Craig agreed.

Avery leaned forward and whispered, "This is a bad idea, Bark. We don't know anything about this guy."

Bark turned halfway in his seat. "Damn Avery, quit freaking out! He's a runner just like us. We ain't just gonna leave him out here."

"What if he's undercover heat?"

"Can't you hang loose for once in your life? Pipe down and go back to your music."

Avery glared at Bark's back as Craig announced, "Let's make a switch. Bark and I will sit in the back, and Avery can keep this guy company in the front."

"Fine by me," Bark said.

"Not fine by me," Avery blurted as he scrambled out the backseat. "We don't know him."

Bark groaned, but the fellow just grinned and offered his hand. "Name's Dusty. Good to meet you, Ave."

Avery bristled but accepted the handshake, trying to settle his nerves. No point fighting when he was outnumbered. Besides, Dusty seemed way too laid back to be fuzz. "All right, I guess. I was taking next shift anyway."

"That's the spirit," Craig said, slapping Avery on the shoulder as he ducked into the backseat. Bark slid in the other side, leaving Avery alone on the road with Dusty.

His new companion cleared his throat. "It's all cool, man. I ain't a cop or nothing if that's what's got you bothered."

Avery's cheeks flamed, but Dusty didn't notice as he hopped in the driver's seat and cranked the engine. Avery sighed and trudged to the passenger's side and scooted in carefully, sitting as close to the door as possible.

The silence was awkward, but Avery was too nervous to drop his guard enough to enjoy his radio. He drummed his fingers on his thighs and attached his gaze to the dense masses of passing trees that flanked the dark mountain highway. Dusty fiddled with the radio as he held his cigarette and the steering wheel with one hand. Through the fuzzy station static the crunchy riffs of Hendrix could be heard.

He shot Dusty a sidelong glance but averted his eyes when Dusty tossed him a grin. "So Ave, you got any friends up north?"

"Couple friends went to Toronto last Halloween when they were drafted. Jonah and Dickie. We were gonna look for them when we got there." He debated over how much he should tell the stranger. "How about you? Meeting up with anybody when you cross the border?"

Dusty shoved the finished cigarette through the crack in the window. "Nah, I just travel around on my own. Been all over the country. I'm gonna pack as much into my life as I can while

I can. Cause you never know when your number's up."

"You're right about that," Avery said.

"And I sure as hell ain't lookin to go off and get shot in a hatemonger's war before my bill is due." He lit another cigarette, taking both hands off the wheel momentarily. Avery stiffened and held his breath until the wheel was in his hand again. "I've been from one coast to the other and everywhere in between. New York, Chicago, D.C., Detroit, Corpus Christie. But I was in Mississippi visiting my folks. Dull as hell, especially considering I'd just spent a year in San Fran..."

"You were at the Haight?" Avery blurted.

"You got it, man." He blew a puff of smoke on the roof. "It was a crazy time, all those people there loving each other, high on life. You could get just about anything you wanted for free. I went to a 'be in,' met up with some musicians. It was fucking beautiful, man. Transcendental explorations, dancing with the lightness of infinity. Know what I mean?"

Avery shook his head, envious of Dusty's free-spirited adventures. "Wish I did. I ain't ever been anywhere outside Harvest Hill. We're lucky we can even get marijuana here."

"You gotta be kidding me! Really?" He stared in disbelief. "That's mind blowin,' my friend!" He was quiet for a moment, then nodded and grinned. Reaching in his pocket (the same pocket his hand was shoved in when they picked him up) he pulled out a small bag.

"This is your lucky day, Ave. I just happen to be carrying

your ticket to the galaxy."

"Huh?"

He handed the bag to Avery. There were about a few dozen sugar cubes inside. He'd never seen them, but he recognized them immediately. "No way! You're shitting me!"

"Finest LSD you'll never find this side of the Rockies. Straight from the hands of the great Owsley himself." Owsley was the renowned acid king. Maybe not the creator, but a pioneer, none the less. Word was not even the government could match his quality. Avery was impressed.

"Is it... safe?" He opened the bag slowly.

"If you ain't sure, man, don't even touch 'em. Potent stuff. But that's the shit you want if you're looking for a wild ride."

Avery stared at the little white blocks in his hands, his excitement at war with his apprehension. He wanted the experience, but the idea of losing control scared him more than a little. Of course, when the guys found out Dusty was carrying, they'd want in on the fun, and Dusty struck him as a cool cat who didn't mind sharing.

He realized for some reason he desperately wanted to impress Dusty. So after just a moment's consideration, he selected a cube and placed it on his tongue.

"That's it, my friend," Dusty cheered. "Just close your eyes and get ready for the flight. You're gonna dig this!" He reached over and took two cubes for himself, then jerked his head towards the guys. "Pass it on back. The more, the merrier."

Avery turned in his seat and shaking the bag. "It's LSD," he told them. "You want any?"

"What a stupid question, Avery. Of course, we want it!" Bark reached for a cube and popped it in his mouth as Craig quietly took one for himself. He studied Avery as Craig munched on his treat and sneered. "So, you gonna try one or not, Yellow?"

Dusty came to his rescue, shouting over his shoulder, "Too late, man. My boy here beat you to it. Didn't even hesitate, he's that cool." He winked at Avery, and this time Avery smiled back. For once Bark was silent.

Dusty prattled on about spirituality and oneness, but his voice fought with the screaming white of the headlights bouncing off the road. Avery studied the trees that galloped toward them, the fall breezes playing their branches like electric guitars. They bent in laughter as he reached for them. Bark and Craig were laughing behind his head, but before he could join in, the blazing red trail of a menacing moon spoke low in Avery's ear.

"Do you see them, Avery? They're watching you."

Avery chuckled at Dusty. "How'd you do that with your voice, man? That's crazy!"

When Dusty looked at Avery, his eyes bulged and glowed, stars jumping through his retinas. "I wasn't sayin' anything,

Ave, I was listening to you."

"They're watching him, too." The voice was so deep it rubbed his eardrums with thick fingers.

"Huh?" Avery shook his head, trying to clear the trails of bloody color from his vision. A gnawing rat of panic started crawling in his belly. The voice dripped venom and malice, and didn't resemble the gentle symphony of colors Dusty promised he'd hear. He began shaking and tapped Dusty's arm.

"I think something's wrong with me."

"Don't fight, just go with it. Your mind is exploring the landscape." Dusty's eyes were half closed and he had one hand on the steering wheel, the other hand out the window, riding a wave of wind.

"I think maybe we pissed off the landscape." He shook the fuzziness from his head, and felt a cold wave of clarity brace him. The landscape was all wrong. Where were they? The landmarks they were told to look for were nowhere to be seen, and they hadn't passed a sign in what felt like hours. Certainly, they had to be near the state line.

He vaguely remembered a sharp turn onto an unmarked bypass. A wrong turn. He deeply regretted taking the acid; he should've been driving. Before he could say anything, the car coughed and sputtered, rolling to a stop. Silence smothered them as they sat motionless on the cracked asphalt.

Craig leaned forward and looked over Dusty's shoulder.

"Oh wow. We're outta gas."

"I don't remember seeing any gas stations back there. Does anyone know where we are?" Avery whispered.

"You were in the front seat, ding-bat, why don't you tell us?" Bark snapped. Seemed like everyone was coming down.

"I wasn't driving, asshole!" Avery shouted, every nerve in his body on edge.

Dusty exhaled loudly. "Don't sweat it, guys. I took a shortcut is all. If I'm not mistaken, the road bends to the left and there's a gas station about a mile up. We can cut through the trees and buy a couple gallons." He took the keys from the ignition and opened his door. "I'll buy the gas can, since this was my fault."

"That's cool, Dusty. The walk will clear our heads, anyway," Craig said completely unshaken by their circumstances. "Besides, I gotta take a serious piss." He started towards the trees with Bark in tow.

Avery caught Dusty's arm as he started to follow suit. "Why don't we just stay on the road? Someone might come by and offer us a ride."

"Ave, my friend, don't worry. We'll get to the station in a jiffy. Those woods are only a few hundred feet thick. I'll just grab some fuel and we'll be back on course before you know it. Stick by me."

Avery was nearly on Dusty's back, listening for every breaking branch that echoed in the dark. The moon broke through the tangle of bare trees above them, occasionally illuminating their surroundings, spotlighting wild underbrush and thorny bushes. Decaying leaves padded the narrow path they followed. Craig and Bark were already too far ahead to be seen or heard.

"How much further?" Avery whispered.

"We should be getting close now," Dusty replied. "There's a clearing up ahead."

They approached an opening in the trees, expecting a stretch of road and a distant station sign, but instead they emerged onto a field. The moon was as bright as a light bulb, and the landscape sprawled in front of them clear as day. An old barn stood on the horizon, a wooden fence circling around, fencing a horse pasture and further distant farmlands.

An invisible fist punched Avery hard in the gut.

"Oh fuck, Dusty! I know that farmhouse!" His eyes squinted into the darkness. Yes, there it was. Just past the farmhouse was a rusty pickup truck. "We're in deep shit!"

Dusty shrugged and shook his head. "It's just an old farm, Ave. They can't even see us from here. What's the commotion?"

"This is Old Man Haverty's farm. We're back in Harvest Hill!"

"That's impossible. We're at least two hours away. No way could we have circled back that far." He pulled a cigarette from his pocket and lit up, blowing a huge puff of smoke over his shoulder. "You see one farm, you've seen them all. I can never tell one from the other."

"Trust me Dusty, we're sitting on the backside of Haverty's property. Of all places in town to show up, this is the worst. He'll have the sheriff out looking in five minutes flat if he sees us. We gotta find the guys and get outta here!"

Dusty stayed on Avery's heels as they hurried back into the brush. Searching frantically, Avery tried to recall the familiar pathways of the woods, but nothing rang a bell. "Where the hell did they go?" He hissed. They stopped, listening for footsteps, but the only sounds Avery heard were their heavy pants and racing hearts.

"I think this is the way out," Avery whispered, hands grappling the trees for direction. Suddenly he felt a hand twine around his ankle and jerk him off his feet. He screamed as his wrist struck the sharp edge of a rock.

Prepared to fight he scrambled to his feet, but the culprit was nowhere to be seen. He swore, rattled and angry. "Son-of-a-bitch!"

Dusty was at his side holding him steady. "You okay? You went down so fast I thought you fell in a hole."

"I'm all right," he groaned, testing his weight on his foot. "Could have sworn someone grabbed me."

A nearby crunch alerted them. Avery stiffened, searching the dark shadows for his buddies without success. The snap of dead sticks underfoot couldn't have been more than a couple yards away, but Craig and Bark were nowhere to be seen.

He took two steps towards the noises when a black mass swooped down and shoved him off balance. "Fuck! What the..." he shouted. The large bulk swung slowly beside him, the branches above creaking from the strain of the heavy weight. Although the features were too dark to be discernable, he knew in his gut what was hanging from the tree. He damn near pissed himself.

"Oh god!"

"Shit man, what is it?" Dusty's voice was panicked.

"Panther."

"What?"

"Black Panther. There were Panthers in town today when we were leaving." Avery explained, his stomach threatening an upheaval. "Looks like Folsum got them this time."

"Damn!" Dusty fell silent as they stared openmouthed, the body swaying before them like a silent pendulum. Another loud rustling from nearby bushes warned that they were not alone. Both breathless, they froze like roadside deer. Their gazes drifted from the the dangling corpse to a shadow partially shielded by dead pines and twining ivy.

Avery could feel the weight of eyes heavy upon him as he watched for movements, but the shadow was dead still. If his instincts were right, they were in deep shit. He leaned slightly toward his friend and whispered, "I don't think they got all the Panthers. I think that might be a Panther in the bush."

Dusty relaxed. "Aww man, Panthers ain't gonna hurt us. They don't hold beef with dodgers. Maybe they'll help us out."

"No!" Avery seized his arm before he could move. "If they think we did it, they'll kill us where we stand. They ain't got no reason to trust a couple white boys hanging around the scene of a lynching."

The shadow in the bushes moved again, but this time Avery caught a glimpse of straight black hair and tattered khakis in the broken moonlight. The shape shifted, revealing a rail thin silhouette, oddly childlike.

Straining his eyes, he took a step forward to get a closer look. If there was a child lost in the woods, he should help them. "Hello?" They didn't budge.

It didn't look like a Panther, and definitely not like Craig and Bark. He ruled out the possibilities in his head, and the only one left was a stray child. He looked over at Dusty. "Wait here. I think it's just a kid."

He took only one step. Next thing he knew, he was flat on his back, lungs searing and ribs sore.

An explosion shook the earth, balls of fire raining around him, leaving craters in the ground. Burning skewers pierced his arms and legs, and the air scorched his nose and mouth. Rolling over and lifting up on his elbows, he looked for Dusty, but he was surrounded by a wall of smoldering flames. He crawled on his belly across the ground, his ribs pushing against his flesh, threatening to split him open.

He screamed for his friends, but the explosive roar of flames erupting around him drowned out his scratchy voice. As he blindly searched the ground he bumped into a log. It coughed and moaned at his touch. Struggling to sit upright, he discovered his friend convulsing in the dirt.

"Dusty! You okay?" His hands stumbled across Dusty's arms and legs, trying to pull him closer. Dusty's body was seizing in his arms, and he whimpered as he tried to hold him still. He hooked one arm over Dusty's shoulder and wrapped his other arm around his waist... and felt the lower half of his torso tear away.

Dusty's body from the abdomen down rolled across Avery's lap and splashed crimson red across dead brown leaves. A rope of intestine coiled from the severed halves like an umbilical cord. Bile rose in Avery's throat as he shoved Dusty onto the ground and started to scoot away.

His path was blocked by the heavy weight suspended from the tree. It crashed to the ground by Avery's side, and in the red glow he had a clear look at the victim.

Bark's scalp was pulled half off his skull, his matted hair still dripping coppery streams down his face, mouth frozen open in a grotesque scream. He was riddled with gun blasts, and both arms and legs were nearly severed from his body. A flash of silver around his neck caught Avery's eye.

Dog tags.

He jumped to his feet despite the knifing pain in his ribs

and started to run, but he didn't get far before he tripped over another obstruction. He was sprawled across Craig's faceless body. Around the mangled mess that was Craig's neck hung another set of dog tags.

His stomach heaved its contents, a combination of bile and ash. He saw the figure emerge from the bushes as he sat amidst the gore, immobilized by shock. It crawled towards him on all fours, its dark eyes shining in stark contrast to its pale almond complexion.

He'd never seen one in person. Only in the photographs of newspapers, or on the projector screens in school. The man wore an expressionless mask as he crawled on top of Avery, their faces only inches apart. Past his attacker, dozens more stepped out from the shadows.

Twisting from under the soldier, he shoved free and landed in a patch of weeds. Half concealed in the brush was what used to be a body. Now it wasn't much more than a decaying skeleton, leathery flesh draped off brittle bones, cloaked in the heavy stench of rot. A chain with dog tags was tangled in its rib cage. Avery wrestled the chain free and brought the tags to his face to read the inscription.

Last name: Franklin. First name: Jonah.

He screamed as a cold hand wrapped around his neck and pulled him about face. The menacing eyes of the Vietnamese soldier pierced his, emotionless and gleaming black in the sooty darkness. He barely caught a glimpse of the grenade as dirty fingers pried open his mouth and pulled his jaw apart. There was just enough time to feel his vocal cords stretch and shred as the detonated device was shoved down his throat.

Old Man Haverty spit the sludge in his mouth into a canning jar that served as his spittoon and shook his head. Across the room from where he sat, a window looked out over the rolling fields of his moon bathed pasture. Beyond the outline of his barn, vegetable garden, and wood post fences, flashes of white lights shot through the trees.

He glanced down at the warm crystal amulet glowing in his hand. It dimmed and cooled as the grandfather clock in the next room announced midnight. The twisted semblance of a smile crossed his face as a distant boom barely rattled the old walls.

Then everything was still. Again.

MOTHER

Told me about
Bats in my hair
Bees in my head
Butterflies in my belly
But she never told me that
The most delicious sensations
Came from thick copper blood
And the flesh in my hands.
The moans from a windpipe
Crushed under the pressure of
Fingers that know less of a caress
And more of the passionate fist.
Adventures highlighted at six
As I plan my next debacle…
Nightmare escapades
Under black cover
Detonation
By desire
Hovers
In the
Dark.
Shh!

Reap

Ollie saw movement in the stillness.

The swirl around the light fixture in the dining room danced in gentle waves, circling the ceiling. The dolls on her shelves indulged in wordless conversations as she stared, transfixed, at their own cracked plaster facades. The silver drapes in the living room never stopped shifting, hiding human sized shadows behind their faux satin sheen. Even the frost on the windowpane jeered as the moon illuminated its frigid moonlight face. In every corner of her still house, something pulsed behind a veneer of viscous invisibility that her eyes were trained to perceive.

She watched with the calm of a woman comfortably numbed by alcohol and opioids… even though she hated being inebriated and refused to waste money on pills. After thirty-eight years of living isolated in the house Ollie's father left her, she was immune to hysteria. Her family had long since abandoned her, with only the most obligatory of visits here and there.

Her mom, just once before she passed on.

Bethany, her sister, maybe five or six times total, until three springs ago when she sent her daughter in her place. Like Beth, Riley didn't understand the soft conversations Ollie had with her possessions, particularly the old spinet piano, chuckling as she rocked in her chair next to it.

When the spinet began to play itself, a lilting lullaby a child might learn in beginner piano classes, Riley left, and never returned to check on her aunt. Ollie didn't realize she'd gone. She was there one day, but the next day? Nowhere to be found.

As it turned out, the spinet was a gregarious jokester. It amused Ollie for hours. She particularly loved the one about the bow that went to the bar. No, that wasn't right. Was it a bow? Maybe it was a knot. It was scared of something, she remembered that much.

Without the family's presence, Ollie kept her own company. Every so often, a teenager dropped bags of groceries on her doorstep. A family executor overseeing her father's estate handled the expenses and upkeep on the early twentieth century farmhouse that had been in her family since, well, the early twentieth century. She avoided people at all costs, and they were skittish around her when she did try to socialize. She had a modest pittance that appeared in her personal bank account every month, but she hadn't left the front porch in at least three years. No reason to. She had enough food, money, and comfort… she could afford to be antisocial.

Ollie was like the safe tucked behind the Edward Padrow painting in her parlor. The painting was known to be rude, but Ollie didn't mind. An unwelcoming American Gothic knockoff, it was complete with the severe faces of tired but honest farmers with eyes so dark, they vibrated when Ollie stared at them. The safe hiding beyond the belligerent canvas housed the jewels she found in her mother's special lavender hatbox right before her mom died, and the asshole art did a fine job protecting her treasure.

Still, none of that really mattered. Not the money, not the jewels, not the body of the baby buried in the cellar that died without even crying on that cold evening many years back…

Ollie felt certain her cramps were the result of a gallon of bad buttermilk, so she ran a hot bath after she spilled her stomach into the toilet. Sinking into the steaming water, she closed her eyes momentarily before a vice squeezed her belly. Grasping the sides of the tub with rigid fingers, she bent forward with a cry and felt the entirety of her abdomen slide through her body and emerge between her legs. It floated to the surface of the water, bobbing in the lilac scented bubbles, a silent baby sized buoy. Turning it over, she saw the little face, alien blue and coated in slime. A rope of flesh wrapped around its neck tethered it to her body.

Well, just look at that!

Sure, she'd gained a few pounds. Just a few, though, not

many… certainly not baby-many. Other than that, she had no idea what was happening inside her. Didn't babies kick? Shouldn't she have been sick? Ollie didn't recall experiencing any of those sensations.

She could try to remember further back, but then she'd get to one of those black times she pushed from her mind. One of many when *he* came to stay. He was gone—for now—and it wasn't worth remembering again.

So she decided the baby was a trick. Something sent from the unseen to rattle her, a cruel joke from him. However, it was as cold and lifeless as the dolls on her shelves, and where was the fear in a lifeless doll? At least the dolls on her shelves talked. This child did not so much as shiver. In fact, it was the only object that didn't move in her house.

She dug a shallow grave in the dirt floor of her cellar and laid the bundle of blankets that swaddled the baby inside the hole. Rather than marking the grave with flowers or a cross, she laid her mom's lavender hatbox over the spot.

They were still down there in the damp dark, and she could feel them waiting for her, the box and the baby bones.

As Ollie sat in the rocker by her spinet, the phone shrilled from the kitchen. She smiled, a twist in one corner of her mouth which managed to push the rest of her face askew. It rang four times, before the answering machine engaged. Bethany's voice cut into the quiet.

"Ollie? Are you there? … Olivia, pick up, please. It's Beth." A sigh into the telephone receiver sounded like the winds outside that stirred the neglected fields around the farmhouse. "Look, tomorrow is the three-year memorial anniversary for Riley. Doctor Richt said it might be good for you to attend this time, since you blew off the last two. I can send someone to get you if you'll come. Around 5:30?"

The disembodied voice sighed again, frustration edging her words. "You know, I don't give a shit if you do or not. It's up to you. But Richt said if you don't show improvement, you're gonna be looking at the four walls of a white room. So come, or don't… I don't care." Her voice trailed off, growing softer and angrier. "Miserable piece of shit. I hope she rots. Dad spoiled her useless. She belongs in a fucking rubber room for the rest of her life, not getting a free ride in the house that was supposed to be my birthright."

The line clicked, and silence took over again.

Ollie chuckled and winked at the spinet. "Can you believe her? I don't know what she's going on about, the delusional cuss."

The spinet played *Mary Had a Little Lamb* in a minor key, and Ollie laughed. "You ain't kidding. Crazier than a hen stealing dog food. She needs to cut back on the shine, is what she needs to do."

Laughing, she leaned forward to stretch her stiff back, and shut her eyes. She saw her niece again, wearing the same denim jeans and faded sweatshirt she wore last time she visited. Riley looked just like her mom, especially with her hair pulled back. Ollie remembered thinking about how jealous she'd been of her older sister's looks. Those sapphire eyes, her cornsilk hair, such a contrast to Ollie's own drab hair and dirt brown eyes. In school, Bethany was the crush of every adolescent boy, and she was wallpaper. Ollie hadn't been glad when Beth finally left home… she'd been ecstatic.

Now, here stood Beth's young doppelganger, staring her down with the expression of a trapped rabbit.

The spinet played itself, and Riley shrieked, demanding to know how Ollie did it.

She'd chuckled. "Do what?"

"How are you playing the piano if you're not touching it?" The young girl looked ready to bolt.

"Why, dear, I'm not. That's Marcella you hear. She was a concert pianist before someone chopped off her head."

She roared as Riley swooped over the spinet and yanked up the lid, staring into the cabinet where the strings were stretched. They vibrated on their own, rattling the cherry wood instrument as it continued performing.

The moments that followed always played in Ollie's mind as if she were in the back row of a theater, watching a show. She couldn't say why this happened when she tried to recall this memory… it just did. She accepted the uneasiness it stirred in her stomach and the anxiety that beaded sweat on her flesh, but the gasping for air caused her alarm. She felt as if there was a hand inside her chest, squeezing on her windpipe just hard enough to make her think she was going to suffocate to death.

Nonetheless, like a car crash, she could not tear her eyes away from the oncoming disaster.

Riley didn't see Ollie slide behind her and grab the lid. She likely didn't feel the snap of her neck when Ollie brought the lid down so hard on her, it cracked the wood. She remembered being angry that Riley had damaged her piano, but she did not remember how she carried the ungrateful girl to her car, wedged the gas with a stick, and watched the car plunge into the work shed at the end of the gravel driveway. A small fire engulfed the garage by the time Ollie came to, standing with the phone in her hand as she reported to authorities that her niece just ran her car into the garage.

Now she kept a lace runner across the top of the spinet, to conceal the fractured wood. Marcella was deeply self-conscious over the nasty gash, even though Ollie repeatedly assured her that she was still as beautiful as a baby Grand. She needed to keep her spinet in good spirits. Who else did she have to keep her entertained?

A knock at the door interrupted Marcella's afternoon sonata, and Ollie was equally perturbed and confused. The knock came from the pantry door. No one would be in the pantry, so unless bad canning was pranking her… again… the knock made no sense. She flung open the door and searched the gloom for a visitor.

"Had I known you were going to be so obnoxious, I would've turned you into sweet gherkins," Ollie said to a shelf of dill pickles. The pickles sank in their brine but didn't argue back.

Another knock, this time coming from the coat closet. This was not the act of fermented food. She grabbed the broom when the cold air circled her.

He was back.

Ollie couldn't see him and couldn't hear him, but she knew he was there, by the slither of chill that slid over her bare arm, like a cold palm caressing her. Pulling her arm away, she straightened her back and searched the room. Empty silence met her. From the other room, she heard Marcella play frantic scales. Marcella reacted to him in this peculiar way, always excited by his visits. An emotional barometer. Ollie didn't get her infatuation. He was a terrible bully.

"What do you want? I have nothing for you," she said.

She was answered by an icy hand across her belly.

"It's not there, if that's what you're after," she said.

With that, the whole house shook, hard enough to crack the dancing plaster off the ceiling and shudder the drapes. Marcello's playing grew to a disconcerted crescendo, an irrational pounding on the ivories that threatened to break the spinet strings. Ollie ran to the upright and slammed the cover

over the keys, hoping to stop the banging. She could hear doors opening and closing throughout the house as he searched.

"Stop!" she called. "Please! It's in the basement. I buried it."

A rush of arctic wind blew past her, and she heard the cellar door bang the wall as it flew from its hinges. Following slowly, she heard an anguished wail descend the darkened stairway. The musty underbelly of the farmhouse waited for her. She flipped the light switch before slipping down the steps, back pressed to the far wall, trying not to draw his attention.

The ground was ripped open, a yawning cavern in the middle of the floor. Ollie noticed the lavender hat box was missing. The air, heavy with formidable rage, pressed against her sternum, making it hard to breathe.

He stood just on the other side of an empty hole, face darkened with a hatred so palpable, it threatened her. She hadn't seen him since that night she tried to forget, the first and last time he materialized, the night he left a piece of himself inside her.

Now he stood, corporeal, holding a black shadow that resembled a swarm of angry bees in his arms. The lifeless baby no longer laid silent in its grave. It vibrated and hummed. It radiated and pulsed.

It wanted her dead.

"The child was stillborn! That's why I buried it. I swear, I didn't hurt your baby!" Ollie pleaded with him as his eyes grew darker, larger, too big for his face. She never knew what he was, and in that moment, she did not want to know. So she ran.

Up, into the kitchen, through the hallway, into the living room where the spinet waited.

There, on the spinet bench, perched the wispy apparition of her mother.

Ollie remembered her mother's last visit. How she stood on the doorstep holding one small suitcase and the lavender hatbox. How she sat at the spinet and played Chopin, the way she used to when Ollie was young. She'd forgotten her mom gave piano lessons when she was little, just as she'd forgotten her mom gave her lessons, as well. Lessons that ended with bruised knuckles when she stumbled over scales or fumbled the pastorals she'd rehearsed. Heaven forbid she botch a recital.

Now her mother held the lavender hatbox in her lap, the look on her face, a mixture of disappointment… and regret. As her mother turned on the stool and began to play the Blue Danube in a minor key, Ollie recalled how she'd slipped into the bedroom and stole the hatbox. Once again, she couldn't remember pushing her mother down the stairs and spearing her with the fireplace poker, after her mom demanded she return the missing jewelry. One minute she'd been caught with the stolen treasures in hand, the next minute she was standing over her mom's bleeding body.

Ollie wasn't even sure why she did it. She hated jewelry.

She also hated her mother, and those years of painful piano lessons.

An icy puff at the back of her neck drew Ollie around, to come face to face with enormous black eyes, and a smile twisted around sharp teeth and a forked tongue. He no longer held their child. It stood to his left, holding his hand, still an indistinct mass of swarming bees.

Ollie looked back over her shoulder to the spinet. Its bench sat empty and covered in a thick blanket of dust. She nodded, turned back to him, and said, "I hope Beth takes care of her."

His eyes started to shrink when Ollie squatted down in front of the swarming child and reached to pull it into her arms. The bees stung her face, chest, arms, and knees, thousands of electrified jolts that shot through her body.

She was allergic to bee stings.

While she laid on the floor, throat swelling shut, she saw him… the dark and handsome stranger… pick up the small girl with sapphire eyes and cornsilk hair, before everything went black and still.

One Fantastic Bauble

"It's beautiful!"

"Yeah? 'Cause I can totally get it for you, if you want it." Rog saw the gleam in Jayne's eyes, the sheen that covered her baby browns whenever she got excited. He'd been looking for a way to seal the deal with her ever since they hooked up two months prior, but she remained reserved. Every date following their first ended with a cold shower.

He hated cold showers.

"I dunno, babe. That's a steep price tag. I couldn't possibly accept this." Her feathered hair brushed over her bare shoulders as she shook her head. She had a freckle at the base of her neck that he was dying to lick, and he had a clear view of it as she contemplated his offer.

He shrugged, and said with a crooked grin, "We can always work something out, if that makes you comfortable."

She knew what he meant, and he knew she knew. Her answering smile confirmed his suspicion.

"Well, if you don't mind…"

"Of course not! This will look perfect on you!" Rog turned and motioned for the young guy slouching behind the register before Jayne changed her mind. "We're gonna take this one, brother."

The teenager lurched in their direction, hitching up his jeans before digging into his pocket for the keys to the display case. His name tag, Rog discovered, read 'Brother.'

"Hey, how'd ya know my name?" He fumbled with the case lock.

"Just an unfortunate guess," Rog said. From the corner of his eye, he saw Jayne cover her mouth, hiding her laughter.

With clumsy hands, Brother placed the velvet panel on the counter. Jayne lifted the choker from its display and inspected the polished stone that hung suspended from a sterling silver ring in the center of a leather band. "Is this hematite?" Her eyes reflected in its glossed surface, and the stone's curvature distorted her pupils into thin slivers.

"No," the clerk said. "It's Mosturian. A rare gem, almost impossible to find, though I hear it's a common sediment on Saturn."

Rog snorted. "A space rock? Really?"

The boy shrugged. "Dunno. That's just what I was told. I ain't no rock guy." He reached under the display case and produced a black velvet pouch. "I do know you need this if you plan to wear it, though."

"What's this?" Jayne placed the choker back in its case and

picked up the bag.

"How MUCH is that?" Rog said, loud enough to warrant a sharp look from Jayne. *Dude, watch it!* He winced at his reckless outburst and clamped his mouth shut.

"It's free with the necklace," Brother said. "In fact, I'd get in trouble if I didn't insist you use it. It's in the rules."

"Why's that?" Jayne pulled a small glass jar from the pouch. She twisted the lid off and took a small sniff, before wrinkling her nose. "This reeks like men's deodorant."

"The balm is supposed to be spread over the stone ten minutes before you put it on. It's to protect your skin. If you leave the necklace on too long and you haven't coated it first, you will have an allergic reaction to the Mosturian."

"I really don't care for the smell. And I don't have any allergies. None. Not even peanuts." Jayne dropped the jar into the pouch and pushed it away.

"It's not that kind of allergy," the clerk said. "If you have skin, you're allergic."

"We will take that jar," Rog said, his impatience mounting, "and I will let *her* decide if she wants to use it."

"You have to sign this waiver," the boy produced a form from a nearby drawer. "Policy."

Rog didn't feel like reading the small print. Unless it included a clause that offered his money back following yet another cold shower, he had no interest in the mumbled warnings of the kid. He scribbled his name and the date on a line that followed the bloated disclaimer, and pushed it back at Brother, along with his credit card.

Jayne was stroking the stone, a soft purr rattling in her throat.

Brother slid two small receipts over the counter and asked Rog for his signature on one. After he tucked the signed copy into his cash drawer, he produced a small purple bag with the words 'FANTASTIC BAUBLES' printed on both sides, and placed the choker box and the velvet bag inside. Mumbling something about a good night, he handed Rog the bag and walked away. By the time Rog and Jayne reached the door, the boy was playing with his phone, oblivious to their departure.

Jayne tucked her arm into Rog's as they walked the few blocks back to his apartment. By the way she leaned into him, he knew his evening would not close in another cold shower. The choker would pay for itself before the night ended. He gave himself a mental fistbump as he led her up the steps to his building.

Once inside, she excused herself to his bathroom while he set to straightening his messy quarters. He thought about spraying some body spray on his bed sheets, but decided against it after he recalled her earlier comment in the store. He lit a bayberry candle, instead. The room smelled like a sexy tree.

By the time she emerged, he was sprawled across his bed stripped down to his boxers. She had also removed her clothes… everything except for the leather choker. The stone hovered just below her collarbone.

Not that he cared about the jewelry. He was too preoccupied appreciating the rest of her naked body.

Ten minutes later found him beneath her, bedsheets tangled around their legs. He'd forgotten how vocal she was, and he didn't remember her growling the first time, but it didn't matter. He was so caught up in the moment, he didn't notice when the stone began to glow.

Then it happened. He pushed up on his elbows to lick her freckle, and his cheek barely grazed the stone. It sizzled and smoked on contact.

"Ow! Holy shit! What the…?"

She purred, pushed on his shoulders, and proceeded to nibble his neck. Which started as pleasantly kinky, but then became more than a little painful. He grunted and slid from beneath her.

Tapping the base of his bedside lamp, he cupped his throat and glared at her in the dim light. "Look, babe…"

Rog froze.

Jayne perched on all fours, still purring, but he could see the distinct tips of four white fangs jutting from her lips. They grew longer as he stared, and he suspected she would've taken a chunk out of his throat had he not stopped her. Her usually groomed nails were longer now, ending in black spikes, the dark traveling up her hands and wrists. A row of black spikes emerged from her shoulders, and down her upper arms. Unexpected movement caught his attention, and he noticed the speared end of a tail flicking at the foot of his bed, its motion reminiscent of a cat about to attack.

He was beginning to feel like a catnip mouse.

"Did you forget to use the balm, babe?" He stammered, sliding off the bed and covering his little buddy with a pillow as he backed against a wall.

A smile curled her fanged, feline face. She leaned forward, the motion unnaturally slinky, as if she were preparing to pounce.

"I lost my collar years ago. Didn't think I'd ever find it again." Her voice was hardly more than a growl. "I'm not done thanking you for helping me, Rog. Come back to bed."

He shivered, searching for anything he could use as a weapon, but the only item within reach was his deodorant. It would make for a lousy weapon against an alien cat. The knockoff brand of Axe wasn't even good at battling his BO, so…

"I would really rather not be eaten," he whimpered. A manly whimper, but still…

Jayne stopped and sat back on her haunches. Genuine confusion clouded her yellow eyes. "Oh." She drummed her fingers on the mattress, her claws piercing the pillowtop and leaving little popcorn shaped puffs of stuffing across the bed. "So… maybe just sex then?"

Rog held his breath for a moment before he responded. "Um, yes?"

Jayne shrugged, her shoulder spikes brushing the ceiling. "Sure. What the hell. You did do me a big favor, after all."

That proved to be the best sex of his life. He still broke up with her the next day, after she'd taken off the choker and returned from his bathroom much less pointy. Admittedly, his pride was a bit wounded that she didn't appear at all upset by his decision.

Before she left, he had to ask. "Hey, Jayne? Why *didn't* you eat me?"

She smiled, and he could see the smaller tip of one of her fangs punctuate her ruby lip. "You wear Axe. I can't stand Axe." She winked as she opened the door. "I prefer my men in Old Spice."

Agnus Dei

October 30th

Randolph pulls the sheet back, revealing the body underneath, skin leather stiff and tinged blue. The man's brown hair is touched with silver at his temples, his hands smartened with the polished manicure of someone who never picked up anything heavier than an ink pen in his lifetime. There are no birthmarks, no scars, except for a small pale line bisecting one eyebrow. His eyes, clouded by the lack of oxygen, are flattening in their orifices. His tongue reminds Randolph of a slug stuck in the cracks of a sidewalk.

Perry Richards met an unexpected end, but at least he went well-groomed. Randolph makes an initial assessment: one massive, fatal heart attack. Also known as The Widow Maker.

"Dr. Brown, here is a copy of the official police report, and the photos." Eric Hayes, assistant to the head coroner, hands Randolph the manila folder.

"Thank you, Eric." He opens the file and scans the yellow page on top, his brow creasing. "Let's get him ready for x-ray, please. I need a moment to look this over."

Eric, brandishing a small camera, nods and begins photographing Mr. Richards' body. Dr. Randolph Brown carries the file to his office to review the police information.

Turns out his initial assessment is very wrong.

October 10th

"May her soul, and the souls of all the faithful departed, through the mercy of God, rest in peace. *Amen.*"

Flicking drops of tepid water across the mahogany veneer of the casket, Father Moore completes the last rites of the burial and watches, stone-faced, as attendants lower the coffin to its final occupation. He turns to the small sea of black clothed mourners, sobbing politely at the loss of their dear mom, aunt, and friend. Their sorrow barely touches him. He hardly knew Delores.

Still, he forces empathy as her friends and family depart the graveside service. A few stops to inquire if he'll be attending the following wake. He smiles thinly, assuring them all that he will be along shortly, and watches as they trudge weary footed to the parked sedans along the cemetery drive—a procession of wheeled sarcophaguses waiting to escort them to their next destination.

He doesn't notice him, not at first. He's watching the gravediggers heap clumsy mounds of crumbling earth on top of Delores' well-appointed casket. An insistent cough alerts him to the bespectacled man in the generic tan trench coat and black hat standing behind the rows of folding chairs.

"Father Moore?" His voice is crisp, unaffected by the afternoon 's chill. Puffs of condensation punctuate his words.

The gravediggers, busy with their shovels, never look up.

October 30th

In his office, Randolph reviews the contents of Perry Richards' file. A diagram demonstrates the position of Perry's body when he was found. An order for the toxicology screen has been included. He gives the papers a cursory glance before settling on the official report, which includes notes from the questioning of the deceased's wife.

On Monday afternoon, at 4:27 P.M., Mrs. Diane Richards found her husband unresponsive and slumped over his desk. Authorities arrived at the scene to find a tearful, albeit calm wife, and a very dead husband. They searched the office for any signs of struggles, attacks, or suspicious behavior, but encountered nothing out of the usual.

Being the one to find him, Diane was taken in and questioned as a formality. She called their attorney prior to the interview with the investigators, which raised dubious questions about her innocence. But no evidence was found in the home to contradict the information she gave the police.

At a quarter to one, Diane left Perry Richards in his home office so she could go shopping. New drapes, she explained. And a fresh French manicure, which she proudly displayed to the interrogators. When she returned almost four hours later, he sat dead in his chair. She called 911, and they instructed her not to move him. There were no obvious signs of pain or injuries. He didn't have preexisting conditions that might've precipitated a sudden death. But she did mention his complaint about a throat irritation that started at church the day before. She said he refused to eat anything, and swallowing food became difficult. So instead, he drank glass after glass of water. He insisted it felt like something was lodged in his throat but did not think he needed to visit his doctor.

Dr. Randolph Brown closes the file, sitting back in his chair. No evidence of suspicious chemicals in the house. Poison hasn't been ruled out, but the events don't point to it, either. Samples of spittle around his mouth were taken at the house, but the tox screens haven't returned. An esophageal laceration might cause discomfort… enough discomfort to put Perry off his food, even.

But that wouldn't kill a man.

A soft knock at the door startles him. Eric steps in halfway, silhouetted by the lights in the hall. His posture is too stiff, his scrubs too baggy for his thin frame. He looks awkward and uncomfortable right now. Much more than usual.

"I'm sorry to disturb you, Dr. Brown. But there's something you need to see…"

October 12th

The air is too cold for October.

Father Moore pulls his jacket tighter across his shoulders and waits for the street vendor to hand him the cup of black coffee he orders daily. Picking up the day's newspaper and scanning the headlines, his mouth twists. It's a joke so bad, even he has to laugh.

These are dark times, indeed.

As a vessel, he can only offer forgiveness and love. His parishioners seek him out for absolution and guidance, whispering their vile secrets from the shadows of an archaic confessional booth planted in the church's vestibule. He won't allow them in his office as his contemporaries often do, where their indiscretions stain the air like nicotine. Administering penances from a textbook rubric, he provides the community their peace of mind… but at the cost of his. No amount of *Hail Mary's* can instill sincere conviction into the hearts of modern abominations. True change will only follow cataclysm.

He finishes his coffee and heads back to the church. Eight A.M., and his appointment is waiting by the rectory gates. "Good morning, Father Moore," says the man in the black hat.

October 30th

Large films clipped to illuminator panels reveal the immaculate skeleton of a fifty-four-year-old male in perfect health. No injuries, either past or present, appear on the screens. While no obvious evidence of a stroke or heart attack appears on the films, the next step of the autopsy will give them a better idea of what possible event concluded Perry Richards' life.

"We need to get started. Call the investigator," Randolph says, drawing each syllable out slowly, still staring at the films, his brow furrowed. He spots something unusual, a vague abnormality. It is so slight, he could well be imagining it. "Wait a second, Eric…"

"Yes, Doctor?"

"Do you see that?" He points at a light cloud in the film.

Eric steps close to the screen, investigating the area beyond Randolph's finger.

Randolph feels pinpricks race up his arms and down his back. His intuition is kicking in. He always experiences chills right before—

"Check the ETA on the toxicology screen, please."

October 14th

Elections loom less than a month off, the fight for the thirteenth congressional district heating the region faster than a waking volcano. The state, traditionally blood red, turned a putrid shade of purple over the past term… the color of rancid meat. Father Moore reads his evening news with a glass of Scotch, but the sharp sting in his throat does little to calm the trepidation tying his gut in violent knots. He barely recognizes the world around him now. American society is flailing in a pool of hedonism and iniquity. Surely they will sink under waves of depravity so deep, they'll have to rename their country Gomorrah.

He pours another scotch and takes it to his office. The light from a small lamp casts the room in shadows as it spotlights the desk blotter's sole occupant. Settling in his office chair, he drinks the scotch in ambitious gulps. Resolve bolstered, he picks up the unmarked legal sized envelope, turning it slowly in his hands.

I should throw this in the fire.

He doesn't. He's not going to. He just spent two days trying to convince himself that he is above the vile proposition offered to him. If he didn't need the money so badly, he would've flatly refused the offer. But recent circumstances have thrust him into a predicament that prayer has not absolved.

Recently, the diocese paid him a visit to discuss closing his parish and moving him elsewhere. The parish has struggled financially for years. The congregation that fills the benches every week are tight fisted heathens who demand their faith with a discount. Seems the parish in the next county was more stable and could use another lay minister. The long of the short—he needs money if he wants to keep his church.

Almost thirty years serving these people, gently prodding them towards salvation... and they would let me be dismissed to work as a lowly assistant elsewhere. Where is the just reward in that?

The envelope contains only a single photograph. A glossy 8x10 black and white. The man in the photo is standing behind a podium, smiling at his audience. He wears a tailored suit and a generous smile. He is groomed to be magazine ready.

According to his recent caller...a gentleman who only identified himself as Mr. Brimm... the man is a parishioner in Father Moore's church. He doesn't remember seeing him at any of the services, but his face *does* seem familiar. He studies the photograph, the wide, oily smile dissecting a chiseled face, the classy suit that undoubtedly sported an Armani label. Bitter bubbles of bile rise in his throat. *Of course he smiles. He wears the church's money.*

Budget cutbacks were emasculating. The crew that maintains the church grounds have been downsized to one elderly man who cuts the grass twice a month. The ladies who keep the inside of the church pristine shrunk from five to two. The toiletries in the vestibule bathrooms are cheap bulk knock offs purchased from a restaurant outlet supplier.

And the social services provided to the community disappeared completely. No food pantry. No homeless outreach. The only counseling he can afford to offer is to the young couples that want to get married in the church. Not that he charges for the counseling… he just doesn't have the time now. He's too busy doing the menial chores he cannot pay others to do for him.

In addition to a dangerous drop in tithes, the other avenues of church income have also dwindled. Reserving the church for a wedding is now so cost prohibitive, wedding requests have dropped considerably. Organized fundraisers stopped a few years ago. Part of it resulted from the recession, of course. But much of it is simply the growing absence of God in the lives of his congregation.

Do I no longer inspire my flock to live holy? Are the words failing to reach them? Perhaps it is better if I step down and let holier vessels lead the way?

This sudden lack of confidence angers him. At himself, sure, but mostly at the parishioners. They have put him in this position.

HE has put him in this position.

Whoever this mark may be, he is, undoubtedly, a wicked

soul. That someone else would plaintively seek for the destruction of one so vile… certainly the world will not mourn such a decrepit person.

Maybe this is the answer to his prayers. Mr. Brimm's parting words resonate in his head.

"Consider this a mission of mercy, if it helps you sleep. You do not yet know the righteousness you are doing." He put on his hat. "But you will."

God placed me on this road. He will provide the transportation.

Father Moore picks up the telephone.

October 15th

He plans the services accordingly, executing each as per the usual. He offers Mass four nights a week, as well as two services on Sundays, but as he searches the faces of his flock, he does not spot his man amidst the throngs. *Perhaps Brimm is mistaken... maybe this man is not a parishioner.*

He tries at first to identify the familiar stranger, without success. It must be God's plan that it remains a mystery. Would he still be able to follow through if he knew who he was after? He put the questions of the man's identity out of his mind… ultimately, this is a sacramental lamb. His death will save them all. He no longer exists in Father Moore's mind as an innocent member of his congregation. It is him, or everyone else will suffer. He is a modern-day Abraham preparing to sacrifice his son.

The Father's conscience only balks at the modus operandi. At first, the questions of 'how' and 'when' kept him awake at night. He refused to acquire a firearm. Any manner of poison would be easily detected and immediately presentable. A public crucifixion would be poetic, but hardly feasible.

Too bad, as he favors that method most.

He needs a miracle. An event so perfectly sculpted, not one who witnesses it will ever dare question why it happened. Something that could even be used to bring his faithful back into the fold. Something beautiful and reverent… if death could ever be reverent.

By the following morning his sister has come to visit the parish, with his two nieces in tow. She comes to help with cleaning and preparation for the grand Liturgy of the Eucharist that he holds on the last Sunday of the month. Parishioners who do not attend weekly Mass services rarely ever miss the large once-a-month ceremony, complete with all the bells and whistles he usually leaves out. Another cutback due to poor finances. *Soon this will be a bad memory… nothing more.*

He attempts to focus on his work, despite the chaos that disorders the rectory as the children are settled in for their visit. A cacophony erupts the silence of his office. The squeals of excited little girls interrupts his brevity as they rush to his desk to show him the trinket toys his secretary gave them when they arrived. Fashion dolls, plastic beaded necklaces, sopping wet sponges shaped like various zoo creatures the size of their fists… he chuckles and teases, feigning interest for their benefit. One string of beads breaks and scatters across the floor, and a doll loses her head, casualties of their childish exuberance.

He engages them for a while, before their mom comes to his rescue. She chides the lively girls and apologizes as she shuffles them from the room, leaving a trail of water droplets in their wake. He smiles, shakes his head.

It is late at night, and he is in bed when the answer comes. Divine intervention, some might say. In the dark of his room, he laughs aloud, his chest constricted with joy, thanking God for his newfound wisdom.

Every good gift is from above…

October 18th

Father Moore preaches creationism, but harbors a secret fascination in science. In fact, one of his oldest friends is a professor at the state university. At first, he worried the professor would refuse his unusual request, but like yet another gift from God, he instinctively knew what spin to put on it.

"So you plan to sell these to the children?"

"It's perfect. Of course their parents will be happy to buy

these… the little ones love them. Both simple and Godly. And I can use the profits to bolster the church's coffers."

Professor Mark Taylor appears unconvinced.

"I got the idea from my nieces, truth be told," Father Moore continues. "Out of the mouth of babes."

"I know things have been rough for a while. That parish means everything to you, I get that." He sighs, rubbing his hand across his eyes. "Tell you what… let me work up a prototype. Give me a few days. Then you can test it for yourself to see if it is what you had in mind."

"Can you give me two?"

"Uh, sure. I guess two are just as easy as one."

Father Moore shakes his friend's hand a bit too enthusiastically. "You've no idea the good you're about to do… but you will."

Four days later, Professor Taylor delivers. The prototype works perfectly. Father Moore begins his planning. The end of the month is approaching.

It is time.

October 30th

The toxicology report indicates Perry Richards was not an avid pill popper, unless those pills were vitamins and fish oil. There's no alcohol in his system, no traces of prescription medications. He might be the healthiest dead man Randolph has ever examined. Which makes death by stroke or heart attack less likely. Blood work shows the chemistry of someone who took their doctor's advice to heart.

More importantly, there are no traces of foreign substances. Arsenic, Botulinum, Cyanide, Dimethyl mercury… Randolph considers the possibility of a more antiquarian method. Perhaps Aconite, which is typically untraceable, but causes arrhythmia and asphyxiation.

Yes. Definitely a possibility.

He studies the report intensely, looking for the smoking gun. The usual suspects are nowhere to be found. He starts pondering the question of an allergic reaction to something previously undetected.

A piercing throb above his brows interrupts his hypothesis, demanding his attention. Pressing his fingers deep into the corners of his eyes, he groans. He could use some hydrocodone.

Returning his attention to the toxicology screen, his bleary vision readjusts to the smeared typeface on the page, courtesy of an archaic fax machine.

Wait a minute…

And there it is. Out of place, though not a usual red flag. An unassuming brown spider lurking spider on a bookshelf.

Hydrogel.

October 28th

10 A.M., Sunday Mass.

The congregation mumbles The Lord's Prayer and observes in faux reverence as Father Moore recites the Agnus Dei, holding a round crisp above his head. He halves it, and then halves those pieces, repeating the steps until he has eight wedges in his hands. Distributing them among eight chalices, he says, "Lamb of God, you take away the sins of the world: grant us peace." He raises a chalice and brings it to his lips.

After issuing communion to his attendants, the congregation lines up to receive the Eucharist. They approach him solemnly, eyes appropriately supplicant. Holding skyward a small communion wafer, he softly says to each person, "The Body of Christ." As they whisper their 'amens,' he places the host on their tongues. The wafers dissolve just enough on contact that they can be swallowed without chewing. The supplicant then shuffles to the left where an assistant offers them a chalice of watered-down wine. As each parishioner receives the communion, they return to their seats to reflect and pray.

Administering Holy Communion to so many people dulls his reflexes, and his motions and words quickly become robotic. The faces are blurring together before him as he sets paper thin white discs on fat, impatient tongues. On days such as this, the Lord's Work is tedious, and unsanitary. He resists rolling his eyes at some of the lesser refined recipients who still manage to drop their hosts on the floor, or genuflect incorrectly as they approach. One lady drools on his sleeve. *Clumsy cows,* he scoffs.

He glances up, gauging the approximate number of people still in line to receive, when his eyes collide with a familiar face. Three people back. His hands remain steady, but his palms begin to sweat. His mark is waiting to receive.

It is time.

October 30th

"I'm not sure I understand, doctor." Eric hands the report back to Dr. Brown. "Hydrogel? He didn't have so much as a paper cut on him, and outside of a bandage, I don't see why that would come up in a tox screen."

Pointing again to the image on the x-ray film, Dr. Brown says, "We need to see what *that* is all about."

October 28th

"Father?"

He stands before Father Moore, his suit impeccable, shoes polished to a mirror's sheen, hair perfectly coifed… probably with designer mousse. His aftershave overpowers the Holy incense that fragrances the sanctuary. Even his only flaw—that slight scar cutting through his eyebrow—is pretentious. He has the whitest teeth Father Moore has ever seen, and he's getting an eyeful of those artificially brightened pearly whites. His heart pounds louder than the choir singing *'Ave Verum Corpus'* at his back.

"Father?" The mark seeks his attention, genuflects correctly—of course he does—and opens his mouth to receive the host.

Father Moore lifts a host from the silver bowl, before remembering his mission. With a jerk of his wrist, too subtle to be noticed by the man with eyes fixed skyward, he pushes the wafers aside and plucks up the one sitting on the very bottom of the bowl. It is slightly sticky to the touch, just barely shinier than the rest of the bowl's contents. He holds the wafer up and repeats, "The Body of Christ," then places it on the man's tongue.

The man swallows, a little slower than his counterparts, and replies, "Amen." Clearing his throat, he follows the procession of people to an assistant waiting with a wine chalice.

Father Moore forces his attention back to the task at hand, portioning out hosts until the communion line has passed through and all the patrons are back in their seats.

During prayer, he searches the crowd, but he has no idea where his mark is seated. He hears a soft cough from the left of the sanctuary. The congregation rises as he begins the concluding rite.

"The Lord be with you."

Cough, cough -

In unison, the congregation replies, "And also with you."

Cough, cough, cough, cough -

"May almighty God bless you…The Father, and the Son…"

Cough, cough, cough -

"And the Holy Spirit."

He sees him then, slipping out of a pew and quickly heading down the aisle towards the vestibule. A blonde woman attired in a conservative suit follows him out. He watches the door close behind them as the congregation ends the service with, "Amen."

As parishioners file out of the doors, he can hear faint coughing drifting in from the outer hall.

October 30th

Dr. Brown hovers over the prostrate form of Perry Richards, while Eric takes notes. A small voice recorder placed at the corpse's head is running as Randolph rattles off the subject's name, age, weight, and other pertinent information. Officer Thomas North, the crime scene investigator, has joined them, to take his own notes. This is standard procedure during a criminal investigation, everything done by the book. So even though Randolph knows where the answers he seeks will be found, he prepares to examine Mr. Richards' chest, abdomen, and head. Being the protocol for the industry-preferred *Virchow* method that most pathologists use, Randolph adheres to it closely.

He studies the face through a magnifying lens and lifts each eyelid back. "Presence of *cyanosis* on the skin. *Petechiae* in both eyes." He motions Officer North to his side so he can see. "Cyanosis is the purple you see in his skin. And petechiae is hemorrhaging that appears in the eyes commonly due to suffocation. See those red specks?" He lifts the eyelids again to show the officer.

"So we are looking at a probable homicide by strangulation?" Officer North is furiously writing as Dr. Brown continues his examination.

"No bruises on the neck. X-rays did not reveal a broken hyoid bone. So far, my guess *is* asphyxiation, but probably not by strangulation. Not enough physical evidence to support that."

Brandishing a scalpel, Randolph begins an incision at the right shoulder and pulls it towards the sternum, then makes another cut from the left shoulder in. He runs the blade down from the incision juncture to the pubic area. An additional assistant steps in to help him open the large 'Y' shaped incision to investigate the chest cavity and organs. Each organ is removed carefully and weighed. Eric records the stats as Randolph relays them. As he'd already surmised, all are in perfect condition.

Richards could have lived to one hundred.

After removing the skull cap with an oscillating saw, Dr. Brown repeats the process of weighing, measuring, and examining the brain. Once again, a flawless organ. Eric and Officer North continue note taking as Randolph makes another incision along the jawbone. Very carefully, he traces the curve with his knife, extending it from ear to ear. The skin is carefully pulled back to reveal the musculature of the neck.

His gloved fingers run the length of the throat. *Yes. Right there.* He uses a smaller scalpel to make a shallow, vertical incision. As the cut separates, he slides three fingers into the cavity that should have been empty… but isn't. He pulls the foreign body free.

Eric curses. The officer gasps.

Randolph is too shocked to speak.

October 29th

The soft drone of the television accompanies Father Moore's dinner. Alone in his small kitchen, he savors the stew that simmered in a crock pot for most of the afternoon. It tastes incredible. Another blessing from God. He is surprisingly calm, considering his machinations the previous morning. But there is no fear. No concern. He has done the Lord's work. Soon his parish will be saved.

He eschews the dire headlines of the evening paper for a light-hearted situational sitcom on television. He laughs like it's the first time. His spirits are so high, he indulges in a second bowl of dinner.

The program on the television is interrupted by a breaking news bulletin. He turns up the volume when the face of his mark appears on the screen.

"Republican Perry Richards was found dead at 4:37 this afternoon. He was discovered by his wife in their home. Authorities have not released a cause of death, but it is being ruled as suspicious. Richards was running for state representative of the thirteenth district against Democrat Aaron Grant, and with elections just weeks away, it is unclear at this time who will run on the Republican ticket in Richards' place. We will bring you more details as they are given to us."

Father Moore's stomach lurches as the stew threatens to make a comeback. He switches off the television and reaches for the bottle of scotch. He'd been instructed not to ask questions, and he didn't. The money was worth more than his curiosity. He didn't consider that the mark might be someone important.

But why not? Who offers that much money for the head of an average nobody, really? A politician, better yet, a *conservative* politician… he never would have agreed, had he known. He told himself the man must be inherently evil. A thief stealing from helpless women and children. A pedophile.

A rapist. An investment banker, maybe.

And a member of his parish. He should be flattered that such a public figure graced his services. But he disconnected from his flock years ago when they stopped providing. Was this God's punishment on him for being so bitter and detached?

He finishes the bottle quickly, and heads for his bedroom. He has a hell of a lot of Hail Mary's to say tonight.

Oh Lord, have mercy.

October 30th

"Jesus Christ!"

Randolph almost laughed at Eric's exclamation, despite the chill that snaked over him. "Yes. You are absolutely correct."

The mysterious intruder has to be carefully cleaned, it is covered in blood, saliva, and bile. A closer evaluation reveals that Richards vomited while he suffocated—normal during asphyxiation—but with the item lodged in his throat, the bile was trapped. It stained the bottom of the object, soaking into the porous foam.

But that is what sponges are supposed to do.

Eric whispers, "What is that thing?"

"It's… *Jesus*."

Randolph squeezes the figurine gently around the middle, and the head and feet bulge around his fist. It is five inches tall and roughly two and a half inches around.

And it *is* Jesus. Hands open at his sides. Broad smile on the bearded face. Halo on his head, sandals on his feet. Randolph could even make out dimples in the palms of his hands to signify nail holes. A miniature statue of Jesus Christ, sculpted in white rubbery foam.

"I don't understand," Eric says. "Why would anyone swallow a sponge?"

October 30th

His morning coffee scalds his tongue, numbing his taste buds. No matter. His appetite is gone, anyway. He meets with his secretary, the parish treasurer, and oversees the choir rehearsal, throwing himself at his priestly duties in an effort to forget the dark shadow that looms behind him.

The news that morning offers no new developments, except to announce that Richards' body was now at the county coroner's office. He is anxious, trapped in a surreal daydream. He needs to separate himself from the pall of death trailing him. He smiles at the old ladies that trail into light candles and say their prayers. Old school Catholics. Just the distraction he needs.

He listens to a grandmother's lament over her wayward grandson, who recently joined band of punk rockers and now worships Satan. He pats her shoulder and assures her that her grandson most likely is just going through a phase, and probably really doesn't worship Satan at all. The black fingernails are a fashion statement, not evidence of a rotting soul. She smiles at the priest like he is the Savior. He starts to feel more relaxed.

A movement in his peripheral distracts him. A man in the vestibule is shuffling past the sanctuary doors. His drab coat droops off his hunched shoulders as he uses a cane to hobble in the direction of the confessional booth. Gives grandma another word of encouragement, Father Moore excuses himself.

The door to the confessional has just latched shut, so Father Moore steps into his cubby and slides open the partition. The screen obscures the occupant's profile, but he can just make out a head of gray unruly hair.

"Do you seek to confess, my son?"

The response is soft. Muffled. Father Moore cannot hear anything more than a murmur. He leans closer to the screen.

"I'm terribly sorry. I'm afraid I can't understand what you are saying. Would you mind repeating that for me?"

"I said, thank you." The voice is raspy and doesn't sound particularly grateful.

"Thank you?"

A sudden zing, followed by a fiery punch to his abdomen, startles Father Moore. He is thrown against the side of the booth, disorientated. A small hole under the partition screen is smoking. He reaches for it, but his arm is suddenly too heavy to move from his side. He runs hot, feverish, but then abruptly feels cold. Weakly, he presses his side and feels hot sticky wetness soaking through his robes. His hand comes away covered in copper scented wine. Fresh warm blood is pooling in his lap.

The booth fades to black.

October 30th

"He didn't swallow this on purpose. The police report indicates the wife mentioned he'd been feeling ill at church the day before."

"Guilty conscious?" Eric snickers.

"It would be funny, under other circumstances," Randolph says. "He's Catholic, right?"

Officer North replies, "Yes. I believe his wife said they are members of Holy Trinity."

"Who is the priest?"

"Father Peter Moore." Officer North is reviewing the reports. "Yesterday was communion, in fact."

Randolph's mind races, staring at the squishy Jesus in his hand. "Do you know what this is?"

"It's Jesus," Eric says.

"Not who. *What.*" Randolph's eyes mirror his excitement, but his mouth is a grim line. "This is an ultra-absorbent polymer foam. Same material as those funny toy dinosaurs that grow from eggs. You submerge them in water, and a day later, the egg is a Tyrannosaurus Rex the size of your hand. It is a novelty toy."

"I don't think you should be saying that Jesus Christ is a novelty toy, Doctor..."

"I bet this Jesus didn't look like Jesus originally. Look at the color. Ivory white. You know what else is this color, don't you?"

Eric clears his throat, shifting uneasily. "Truth be told, I'm not much of a churchgoer."

Officer North, on the other hand, is. "Communion wafers."

The three men stare in horror at the toy Jesus in Randolph's hand.

"I think I'm going to visit Father Moore," Officer North says. "Maybe he has a sin of his own to confess."

October 30th

Father Moore is discovered by his secretary. The police arrived to question him concerning Mr. Richard's death, but she doesn't understand why it would be the Father's fault if a man chokes on a communion wafer. Seems to her, God metes out His own judgment on unrepentants who partake lightly in Holy Communion with sin on their souls.

After all, the Body of Christ is nothing to toy around with.

Unfortunate Victim

The car in the bog
is rusted and broken,
Leather bloated with
mud and leeches.
Engine turned reef,
covered in murky moss.
An unfortunate victim
of unknown fortune.

The trunk of the bog car
is packed with ropes,
        hatchets,
        knives,
        zip-ties,

and a chipped machete.

And a stray left foot

        Where
        the spare tire
        should be.

Branching Out

Holly chose not to be an artist. She chose instead to be a protector of art.

Thanks to many years spent honing her profession in a variety of shops, she wielded knowledge and technique like a deluxe set of gold-plated Craftsman tools. She had an eye for color that Mantis shrimp envied, and carpentry skills that could put Jesus to shame. Her expertise and precision guaranteed every client left with an impeccable work of museum-worthy art.

Oh yes. She could *really* frame a picture.

The print now bogarting her table, however. was sun-bleached and bland. Against her advice, the customer requested it simply cleaned and reassembled in its dated barn wood frame. *Probably not even real barn wood*, she thought. They should've upgraded to a walnut veneer. C'est le vie. It was their dime, after all.

She reached for the old frame, leaning against her table.

That damn frame, frayed and dry-rotted… it bit her.

Sharp pain in Holly's hand preceded a string of curses. She dropped her awl and rubbed the pad of her thumb over the tender area, studying the throbbing heel of her palm.

A splinter lay just beneath the dermis, still visible, but too deep to be removed without a painful and dramatic production. In the bathroom, she found a pair of tweezers in the first aid kit and waited until the tap water ran hot. Shoving her hand into the steaming stream, she watched her skin change from pink to a puffy red. She dug her nail into the skin at the base of the splinter and pushed, trying to edge the splinter out. It hurt like a bee sting. Sliding the tongs of the tweezers over her skin, she searched for the tip of the splinter, but found not even the slightest bump. If anything, the splinter now seemed to be lodged deeper.

So she shrugged it off and returned to work. Splinters usually saw themselves out, eventually. In a few days, the discomfort would be a vague memory.

She woke the next morning with an intense pain in her wrist that rivaled a muscle sprain. She pulled her legs over the edge of the bed and sat up, inspecting her injury with bleary eyes. The bones and joints all looked to be in the correct spots. Nothing appeared to be swollen. Still, she could barely move it. She went to the bathroom and flipped on the lights.

Illuminated by the glaring brightness of 60-watt fluorescents, she saw the splinter still embedded in her hand.

She could also see strange swirling patterns offshoot the tiny piece of wood. They covered the base of her palm and extended towards her wrist. She scrubbed the inflamed area with alcohol, ignoring the sharp sting of astringent as she tried to dislodge the offender. As she dried off, more threads wound through her fingers and curled around her wrist. She really couldn't feel any discomfort, until she tried to make a fist. Felt like every bone shattered, and it sounded like a bundle of twigs being snapped.

She felt somewhat inconvenienced by this development, although her hand looked like it had been decorated with henna scrollwork. It was actually rather pretty. Most attractive splinter she ever sported, in fact.

Work proved more ambitious, as she attempted to complete all her tasks left-handed. The job was challenging enough to do with both mitts on board, and she was far from ambidextrous. She'd occasionally forget her temporary disability and grab a tool with her bad hand. Always, with stabbing pain and the sound of ripping wood. As the minutes crept past, she noticed, while it grew stiffer and less wieldy, it also hurt less. A few hours into her shift, it went completely numb.

Forgetting herself, she grabbed her hammer, and swung. She pounded the nail only once, however, before the air groaned with the sound of a felled invisible tree. A disembodied lumberjack cried, "Timber!"

Well, that might not be normal, she thought.

The day progressed the same…slow and stiff. Her hand grew rigid and brown, the embedded imposter trailing further up her arm. In its wake, her skin became uncomfortably dry and coarse. By the time her work concluded, her arm was solidified up to her elbow in dirt-brown callouses. Her right palm erupted in a twisting vine that hardened and began to sprout curling green hairs.

The warnings of her youth sprang to mind. She snorted, recalling the ridiculous predictions with a touch of irony. No one ever warned her about this. She should have stuck to masturbating.

Bad jokes about bushes and hands sprang to mind, to which she cackled. It surprised her to discover her laugh sounded like the twitter of robin chirps. She couldn't whistle to save her life, yet there she was, singing the song of the songbird's peop—er, birds.

In fact, three followed her home. Using her good hand, she gave them a respectful fist-to-chest thump before leaving them on the porch. Sounded like knocking on wood.

Well. She definitely needed to see her doctor about this.

Her mood the next morning was much less chirper. She struggled to get ready for work. Bending at the waist was impossible, and her right leg was stiffening where it met her hip. She obliterated her deodorant trying to apply it to her scaly brown armpits, which was challenging enough to do left-handed. She didn't hate the way the shower left her smelling like a forest after the rain, but the greens sprouting from her right hand had now grown perfect little leaves up to her wrist. As she attempted to comb her wet hair, she noticed suspicious strands at her temple…and they were green.

But green was still better than gray. She pulled one green hair free and watched five more appear. Heck nope! She wasn't going to pull those. She would just rock that look.

On her way to work, she felt the eyes of passers-by watching her. Perhaps they noticed her awkward, lumbering gait. Maybe they envied her headful of shiny, well-groomed foliage. Or, maybe it was when she passed by the huge oak on the corner. She fondled its bark as she leaned in, and purred, "Damn, baby, you're looking fine!" Then she whistled. Suggestively. Like some creepy tree weirdo.

By the time she arrived at her job, four finches tried to nest on her head. A confused squirrel chased her for two blocks. A stray mutt almost lifted his leg on her ankle. In addition, judging by her shadow, she'd grown a foot of leaves on her scalp.

Buying shampoo would be a lot trickier now.

Work became damn near impossible. Her right hand was completely useless. Her left began stiffening early in the day. The brown curlicues crept over her bicep, around her elbow, and reached for her free wrist.

Her boss, a mousy spectacled brunette by the name of Agnes Patch, asked, “Did you do something new with your hair?”

Before Holly could reply, an irrational blue jay shot out from the leaves behind her ear and attacked Agnes’ nose. The air filled with shrieks and bird profanities. Holly managed to lure the feathered fowl terrorist outdoors with handfuls of bird seed, and whistled platitudes. “Wow,” she said, watching the bird skip off on the wind, “I wish I knew what I just said.”

To find some purpose for her in the shop, Agnes placed her by the door. She could still greet customers, at least. The first few were caught off-guard by the new hostess, and one little old lady smacked her with her purse. By the day’s end, Holly wanted nothing more than a warm nap in the sun and a refreshing drizzle.

Agnes followed her out of the shop, knotting her fingers, her artificial smile shaking across her pasty face. That typically signaled bad news.

“What’s going on, Holly?” She cleared her throat. “You look… well, you look like a maple. Is it drugs? Do you need money?”

Holly tried to shrug, which now resembled an awkward hiccup. “It’s nothing. I got a little splinter, that’s all. I should be okay in a few days.”

The boss looked her up and down. “Did this happen in the shop?”

"I think so," Holly said. "But it's not a big deal."

Agnes blinked with owl eyes, and said, "Because I'm just not sure workman's comp will cover… *tree*."

Holly chuckled. Well, she tried to chuckle. It came out more like a low creak. The sound one hears out in the woods when the wind blows through the tall, spindly pines...

Then for a moment, she felt an insane rush of relief. Yes, at least she wasn't a pine! Pines were gangly and sticky. Maples were *so* much prettier. Shapelier. Better leaves.

Just then she realized she was thinking like a crazy person. What the hell? Where was her internal alarm? She was a warm blooded, hot and feisty female. *Not* a dowdy shrub. She needed to get her head out of the leaves and think clearly.

"I understand," she said. "I'm going straight to the clinic, Ms. Patch. I'll be back on my game tomorrow."

Agnes Patch did not look convinced, but she nodded. "Good to hear. Go get that splinter removed." She gave Holly one last hard appraisal. "And maybe take a shower."

Holly lifted her arm to wave goodbye, but the action required so much effort, she didn't bother to lower it. Odd that she felt more comfortable this way. She lumbered down the street, appreciating the gentle breezes rustling her foliage, the way the sunlight seemed to soak into every cell of each flat green surface sprouting from her hands, and the warmth on her bare bark… *BACK*. The warmth on her *bare back*. Which also happened to be covered in bark.

From the corner of her eye, she could make out a small, brown, fur covered head on her shoulder. A squirrel clung to her neck. She couldn't feel its claws digging into her rough exterior, so she wasn't alarmed. Though when she greeted the small animal, its eyes grew big, and it froze for a second before ranting in its undecipherable dialect and leapt to the ground.

As she passed a neighborhood park, small squealing children playing freeze tag circled her trunk. She stopped, observing their youthful shenanigans with a twinge of longing, remembering her own childhood. Always the outsider, she spent countless hours watching the other children play their games, never inviting her to join in. She'd witness the fun over the spine of the book in her lap, sitting beneath the shade of an old poplar as her peers created memories.

Much like these children. Except, now, she was a part of their memories. So she allowed them to use her as their base, and they played with her for the stretch of the afternoon, until her shadow reached past the bordering fences, and the sun fell below the horizon. The laughter and cheers faded as she closed her eyes and dozed.

She woke abruptly, disoriented. Where was she? The sun showered her in a gentle glow that signaled sunrise. She struggled with her memory, trying to understand the panic buried deep in her trunk.

No, wait… chest. She was a woman. She had a chest. Or at

least used to. She couldn't look down to verify she had cleavage. She couldn't move her head. At all. She couldn't even open her mouth to speak.

Or scream.

Well, that's a setback, she thought.

Holly then recalled the children, faces lit with joy as they ran circles around her. Oh, I'm still at the park, she remembered. Waving her limbs, she felt a refreshing coat of dew on her leaves. Satisfied with Mother Nature's gentle shower, she decided to head straight to work. She smelled fresh as a spring day.

Unfortunately, she couldn't move her legs. Her feet were cemented to the ground. She pulled up with each foot, struggling to lift them, realizing they'd become buried in the park dirt. With a hard tug, she wrenched one leg out of the ground, and then the other. Her toes had sprouted roots, and as she pulled each foot free, she felt the searing burn of severed nerve endings shoot up her trunk.

Every time she took a step, her feet tried to root themselves in place. Her journey back to the shop was now slow and arduous. She left a path of churned earth in her wake, and even managed to reduce the sidewalks and asphalt to rubble. By the time she arrived at the parking lot. She was completely spent. As she reached for the shop doorhandle, she felt the warmth of the sun bake her back. Her foliage thickened and gleamed in the golden glow. She closed her eyes, relishing the resplendent warmth washing over her.

When she opened her eyes again, she stood a foot away from the shop door, planted in the sidewalk. She saw Agnes watching her through the plate glass, eyes brimming, mouth turned down at the corners.

Uh oh, Holly thought, *I bet I'm late for work.*

Agnes pressed a palm to the glass door, and mouthed something, one tear escaping her misty brown eyes. It took Holly a moment to realize that Agnes was saying, "I'm sorry."

The sudden rumble of an engine interrupted Holly's thoughts. It was a familiar sound. But only when she felt white-hot teeth grind into the bark on her legs did she realize what that engine belonged to.

A chainsaw.

This time, the "TIMBER" came from a face she could see. She fell on her back, her weight quaking the ground. The man used his chainsaw to sever her arms, carrying them off before returning with his weapon. He studied what Holly presumed was her stump… weird tree creep… and told Agnes, who stepped onto the sidewalk, that the tree was roughly 32 years old. How was it that Agnes had a 32-year-old maple planted in front of her business door?

Agnes just shrugged, half-smiled, and shook her head.

He fired up his chainsaw again and tore through the branches that emerged from Holly's head. Had she a mouth to scream, her cries would've stopped the city. Instead, she laid on the concrete, the fibers of her mouth wielded forever shut as the man cut away her appendages, reducing her to a long, featureless trunk. As she considered the face of her executioner, she recognized him. He was a recent customer.

The owner of the ugly barn wood frame.

She hoped he was satisfied with his order.

She came to in the bed of a truck, on top of a pile of desiccated trees. As she was carried into a huge warehouse, she noticed the thin rails stacked against far walls. Skinny pieces, some 10 to 12 feet long, bunched in groups, arranged by colors and styles, stacked and bundled and awaiting shipment.

Picture frame molding.

Oh, I hope I get leafed, she thought. Or lacquered. Something in a shiny green, to match my eyes. Except shiny green lacquer was so 1992!

No. She needed to be a glossy black. Everyone wanted shiny black frames, these days. She could be both contemporary and traditional. She could lovingly encase just about any artist as a black lacquer. Even a priceless Chagall!

Then again…

She thought about the barnwood frame that did this to her. It was just protecting its artwork, after all. Far more effectively than any smooth, glossy frame could ever manage, at that. Not many frames had the ability to attack. But rough, splintery barnwood? One would have to handle such a frame… plus whatever was in it… with delicacy and caution.

Yessss!

She was right where she needed to be.

Now she finally would be THE protector of art.

Fellow

When her car puttered to a stop on the side of 95 north, Ana mumbled a curse and checked her dashboard. Not a single warning light flashed. She was no mechanic, but she knew batteries did not die while the engine ran. She swiped the screen on her smartphone to discover her battery power at one percent. Then the phone powered off.

She frowned and tapped the plexiglass cover behind the steering wheel, as if the nudge would kick start her car into action. The little Corolla gave a shudder and a sigh just as a rumble of thunder shook the car. After the rough day she had at work, the last thing she needed was to be stranded on the side of the highway in the pouring rain. Of course, she wouldn't need such a bad stroke of luck even on a good day, but this had been an especially terrible end to her work week.

Unexpected break-ups made for missed deadlines. Missed deadlines made for mad bosses. She spent a half hour in the ladies' room before lunch time, trying to cauterize the flow of tears after she received Josh's text.

A text message? Who the hell breaks up in a text message?

She saw it coming, really, but it still was a punch to the gut. She couldn't get her act together after that and dropped the ball on half the edits that were due that day. It meant she would be working into the night and sending them into the company email.

At least now she had the night free to work.

This night, and every other night, from here on out...

Josh was a loser, anyway. Too into his friends and his boy's nights to make her a priority. She considered dumping him on several occasions. Why hadn't she? Would have saved her the bathroom water works. It was the humiliation of realizing she was not enough for him that stung. He was lucky she ever gave him the time of day. Especially after seeing him out with his ex, Lara, on a date night he cancelled due to a 'work emergency.'

He changed oil at a local automotive shop for a living. She should have recognized the lie for what it was.

She sighed. She wasn't getting any closer to home just sitting on the side of a road. Maybe the problem was simple. She palmed her car keys, popped the release for the hood, and stepped into the growing twilight.

There were no visible cars in either direction. Rather unusual, for a Friday night. She walked around to the front of her car and lifted the hood. She pulled dipsticks from their receptacles and checked the fluid levels. She wiggled the battery cables. She looked for anything that might appear amiss, but the engine looked like the fastidiously maintained engine it was.

A crunch of gravel raised her hackles. She turned slowly, but she couldn't see anyone on the shoulders. She was completely alone. The sign for a truck stop jutted out over a distant bank of trees, at least a mile down the road.

If she wasn't alone, it was unlikely she could reach the truck stop before they reached her.

She remembered the mag light she kept in her trunk, and hit the trunk button on her key fob, afraid to take her eyes off the landscape. She still couldn't see anyone, but night was fast approaching, and it would not be so tricky for someone to hide in the tall grass beside the road without her seeing them. She kept her back to her car as she circled to the trunk and fetched the heavy metal lantern from her roadside emergency kit. There was a small gas can in there as well, which she grabbed.

The only recourse she had now was to hoof it to the truck stop.

"I gave a guy a concussion with this flashlight!" she announced, aiming her declaration at the grass. It rippled, but most likely due to the evening breezes, rather than abject fear.

She shut the trunk, circled back to the front and closed the hood. The car chirped as she set the locks. Then she squared her shoulders and set off in the direction of the truck stop.

Her modest heels may as well have been stilettos on the

roadside gravel. She winced. Her feet were going to hurt like hell tonight.

She wished there were things to see other than tall grass and empty highways. The highway was a main artery that bisected the eastern side of the country, and she had driven it a million times as she commuted to and from work. It was typically riddled with cars, motorcycles, and tractor trailers. She couldn't recall a time when there was no traffic at all. At least the truck stop promised respite. Its planet shaped sign spilled orange light across the tops of tall trees and reached for her through the descending darkness. She could get gas and food there. She could call her dad. He could call a tow truck with his emergency roadside service plan and come get her.

She would be fine.

The gravel crunched out of sync with her footsteps. She stopped and searched the shadows around her.

"Hello?"

Still no response. She couldn't make out the silhouette of any company she might be keeping. She took a step onto the asphalt, creating a wider berth between her and the grass.

"I'm not afraid to use this!" She held up the light like a pistol and aimed it at the tall weeds. With a tap of the button, a spotlight of yellow hit the grasses, highlighting the straw texture of dying blades of foliage. She swung the beam to the left, and to the right, but she didn't see anyone hiding.

The beam sputtered and she trained it again on the patch

directly in front of her. Something was off, but she couldn't put her finger on what it was. There was something there, even if she could not see it. She could feel it. It ran up her arms like gooseflesh and lifted her hair from her face.

"Hello?" She whispered.

Two yellow lights caught in the beam flashed off, then back on. Not as much like distant lights, as the reflection of eyes that blinked at her.

A black shape hunched behind the grass, staring back.

She yelped and stumbled towards the truck stop, too scared to scream for help. Who would even hear her? Whatever it was watching her was keeping pace on the other side of the barrier, tracing her deliberately, its breathing even and shallow. It made too much noise to be on two feet, and she wondered if she had simply attracted a stray dog or a deer with her flashlight. She was not typically afraid of dogs. But something told her that was not what found her.

In her peripheral vision, she could see the black shadow of something large, something that was taller than the grass, yet managed to stay just out of sight. She knew she would trip over her feet if she tried to look directly at it. She also knew if she stopped, it would attack her. She felt menace in the air that weighed against her like a blanket of humidity, slowing her down. She bit her lip and choked back frantic cries.

By now, all traces of daylight were gone, leaving only the sallow yellow of occasional highway lights and the neon moon reaching towards her from her refuge.

Then she saw it. Coming down the center of the highway. The distinct shadow of a person. Even at a distance, she could tell it was a man. A man headed straight towards her.

A rescuer. A good Samaritan. She raised her arms and waved, shouting for help, shouting for his attention.

The man moved faster in her direction. She knew she would be okay. The night made his features impossible to distinguish, though if she squinted hard enough, she could make out dark pants, a light shirt under a dark jacket, and the outline of a fedora on his head. She gulped the chilled air, gratitude filling her chest as she stumbled towards him.

She was almost close enough to see his face when she noticed the blade he was holding at his side.

She froze, just a moment, just enough to give him a chance to close the space between them. This was not her salvation. Her blood turned to ice as he lifted the blade.

A preternatural growl ripped through the night and stunned Ana and the man, enveloping everything in its domineering vibrato. She could feel it physically penetrate her skin and wrap around her bones. A black shape lunged from the barrier of dead grass and catapulted through the dark.

She cried out, her scream loud enough to certainly alert the truck stop to trouble.

It took a few seconds for her confusion to clear. The air rippled with the deep screams of a man in agony, mixed with the growls and roars of something she could not quite see. She backed away, realizing that whatever it was would be after her when it finished with her attacker. Still, she could not bring herself to run away. She was as fascinated as she was horrified.

The man's blood spilled to the asphalt like wine, his blade glistening ruby red in the streetlight. The monster ripped shreds of skin from the man's frame and swallowed them without chewing, its growls mixed with the wet sounds of carnivorous ecstasy. The air, which moments ago smelled of grass and worn asphalt, was permeated with the thick stench of copper and rot.

Ana watched, frozen in place, as the man disappeared into the beast's belly. All that remained were his clothes, his fedora, and the blade.

Then the creature turned.

Yellow eyes fell on her. But they were not hardened or narrowed in anger. They blinked, their giant pupils contracting and dilating, adjusting to the beam of her flashlight. The growls had transformed into the soft anxious whimpers that she had heard a thousand times in her life.

The beast stepped forward into the beam, and Ana nearly dropped the mag.

A brown wolf stood in front of her. Apart from the blood on its muzzle, it showed no signs of malice or aggression. It sat in front of her, as if waiting for a command.

"Were you following me just now?" Ana said.

The wolf chuffed and lowered its head slightly.

"Are you... are you going to hurt me?"

She knew she sounded idiotic. The wolf was not likely going to answer. She was not sure why it hadn't lunged at her yet, but there would not be anything she could do if it was so inclined to make her dessert.

The wolf whined, just briefly, and then stood. It was taller than the wolves she had seen in places like Yellowstone. This wolf could be twice as large as they were supposed to be. Wolves were not exactly native to Virginian highways, as it was. There were no tales of strange, oversized wolf cryptids... at least, not any that she could recall.

It took a step towards her, and she pushed her mag light forward, hoping to scare it off. "Stay back," she stuttered. "I don't taste good."

The wolf whined again and tilted its head.

She took a deep breath. The wolf could have attacked her already. If it meant to, it would've already done so.

But this wolf watched her from the grass. This wolf trailed her to the truck stop.

This wolf killed the man that meant to kill her.

This wolf protected her.

She slowly lifted her free hand, palm turned upwards, and waited.

The wolf took a few small steps forward and sniffed her outstretched hand. It chuffed again, then nudged her palm with its cold, wet nose. She jumped when she first felt the contact.

The creature circled her, sniffing the hemline of her skirt and shoes, like a curious dog greeting her in the park, checking out her scent. When it finished, it sat in front of her, resting its yellow eyes on hers, a calm expression falling over its face.

With slow, steady movements, she placed her hand on the canine's muzzle, and then on its head, stroking the rough fur between its ears. The wolf closed its eyes as if it relished her touch and sighed. She cupped its face in her hands and scratched its neck, and behind its ears, and it rewarded her with a small lick on the inside of her wrist.

Her eyes stung with tears she did not realize were coming. "Thank you," she said, squatting in front of the beast and wrapping her arms around its neck. She felt its breath puff across her shoulder as she hugged it gently.

"Miss? Are you okay?"

She turned to see a man standing beside a tow truck, his flashlight trained on her. He had flares in his other hand.

"Oh," she started, trying to think up a ready excuse for the monster sized wolf and the pools of blood all over the highway.

She looked over her shoulder. Her wolf was gone.

So was the blood, torn clothes, and discarded blade.

Vertigo struck her and she wobbled on her feet. The tow truck driver reached out and steadied her arm, giving her the leverage to right herself. Confusion muddied her ability to speak.

"I noticed your car back there. I know you didn't call, but... do you need a tow somewhere?"

She nodded and mumbled, "My cell phone died."

"Not a problem. I can get you hitched up in a jiffy and you can just tell me where to take you. I'm off the clock, so I won't charge you. It's not safe to be out here alone on a night like tonight." He led her to the truck cab and asked for her car keys. She searched the darkness for her wolf but saw no signs of anything in the shadows beyond the streetlights as she handed him the fob.

The twist in her chest caused her eyes to sting again. She could not believe she imagined the wolf, or the attacker. But all she saw ahead was an empty road. The sound of crickets and invisible birds filled the night.

The driver hooked her car up to the wench and pulled it onto the truck's flatbed. She was grateful to discover he was headed in her direction already. "I don't know how to repay you, Mr..."

"Mr. Wolf," he said, with a smile. "And it's no problem at all. I'm glad to help."

As the truck pulled off the shoulder onto the highway, Ana could make out the outline of hills that ran alongside the highway, beyond the grass.

On the top of one hill was the silhouette of a giant wolf.

Ana placed her palm to the window as the shadow

disappeared in the distance.

Erin did not blink as the keyless entry identifier scanned her cornea before it unlocked Nana Ana's front door. After being unable to reach her on the phone, and not seeing her for more than a week, Erin decided she needed to make sure her grandmother was okay. They shared a particularly close relationship, and after her grandfather died, Erin took it upon herself to make sure her grandmother was looked after. She brought her groceries and medications and took her to her doctor's appointments. It was unusual not to hear from her for so long.

The house was still, the only sound being the soft, steady beep of the air control system that kept Ana's environment sterilized and fragrant. She poked her head in the kitchen, but the counters were clear. The visual wall in her living room was off. Something must be wrong, she thought, because her grandmother usually watched the news around this time. She headed down the hall towards the bedroom.

"Nana?" she called. There was no answer.

But underneath the soft swoosh of air, she heard the faintest whimper.

She knew what she would see on the other side of the door. She nudged it open, revealing Ana's room.

Her grandmother lay in bed, still snuggled under her comforter. But she was not alone.

An enormous wolf lay beside her, its head resting over hers, one paw covering her stomach, as if it were protecting her. Her arms were loosely wrapped around the wolf's neck.

Had Ana never confided in Erin about the giant wolf that showed up on occasion to help her, Erin would have been terrified. Instead, she approached the wolf, and laid a hand on the wolf's back. It let out a whimper and a sigh as it laid against Ana and closed its eyes.

Ana never spoke about her wolf to friends or family, not even her daughter. But she told her granddaughter at a young age, because she wanted Erin to know that the world, even at its darkest, was full of magic and love. It sent her a guardian and a dear companion disguised as a gigantic wolf. And one day, she said, it would send her a guardian, too. Just when she needed it most.

So far, Erin waited for a companion that had yet to appear. But she had faith in what her grandmother said. She could feel it out there, waiting for the moment Erin could not help herself, to step in and save her.

"Thank you for watching over her, Fellow," Erin whispered, giving the wolf gentle scratches. "You are such a good boy." She leaned forward and kissed the back of the wolf's head.

Fellow sighed, licked her hand, then disappeared like vapor into the air around them. Erin exhaled a breath she did not realize she'd held, sat on the bed next to her grandmother, then hit the call button on her watch to contact emergency services. She smoothed Ana's silver hair from her face and took a stiff hand into hers. The faintest trace of warmth in her palm told Erin she had just missed her. She leaned over and placed a kiss on her grandmother's cheek. As she took in the peaceful look on her dear grandmother's face, her heart squeezed.

Ana had been smiling as she drifted to sleep that final time, her arms wrapped around her wolf.

Erin hoped her companion would be a giant wolf with gentle, yellow eyes.

Love, Betrayal, and Jackalopes

Dr. Bamma studied the screen, concern wrinkling his forehead.

No, that can't be right.

"What's the matter, doctor? Is something wrong with my baby?" Marilou's voice teetered on the edge of hysteria.

Dr. Bamma usually had a ready explanation to calm the nervous mothers, but what appeared in the sonogram would not be so simple to rationalize. It took a moment to find his voice. "I'm not quite sure how to tell you this, Mrs. Frank, but it appears that your baby is... a jackalope."

"You wench!" A red-faced Mr. Frank jumped from his seat so fast it tipped over. "That's not my baby!"

"Oh my," Dr. Bamma mumbled, "this is awkward."

Marilou Frank sobbed, reaching for her husband's arm. "I swear it's yours, teddy bear! I haven't been with anyone else!"

"We don't got no antelopes in my family!"

"Jackalopes," Dr. Bamma said.

"Well," Franklin Frank grumbled, "we ain't got none of them either. What have you been doing while I been workin,' you trollop?"

"Nothing, Pooh bear! I promise! There must be some mistake. Doctor?" Marilou locked her soupy eyes on the obstetrician. Now would be a good time to offer a plausible diagnosis.

"Maybe your baby is just really ugly?"

The couple erupted into screams and accusations again, as Dr. Bamma dropped his head in his hands.

Ingrid Lasso, head RN at Bamma and Bamma OB/GYN, recognized the look on Dr. Bamma's face as an enraged couple left his office. She slipped in with a mug of black coffee and placed it on the desk blotter.

His hair, which usually resembled a salt and pepper helmet, sat askew on his head. He should've skipped the toupee today, she thought, amused despite his frustration. As he sipped his coffee, she awaited his instructions.

Instead, he just groaned and thumped his head on the desk.

"I don't get it," he said. "That's the THIRD jackalope this week. What the sam devil is wrong with these freaks? You don't fornicate with rabbits. You *just don't*. That's bestiality right there. It's illegal. Plus, it's pretty gross."

Ingrid shrugged, half smiled, and shifted her weight from one foot to the other. She pondered the curious case of the Franks. Yesterday, the Berns. Two days ago, the Jacksons. She joked at the time that perhaps the Jacksons had an ancestral 'rabbit' in their tree. They didn't get the reference. Admittedly, it was a terrible joke.

"It's pretty weird," she agreed. "I can't say we prepared for this in school. I've been under the impression that interspecies insemination is impossible. This negates some of my training."

He sighed. "Those poor people," he moaned. "They had the hardest time conceiving, too. I honestly thought her clock batteries were shot. We were about to discuss other options when she'd finally turned up positive. We were so relieved. And now… jackalope. There's got to be a mistake!"

He chewed the end of his pen, lost in thought. Maybe lost in theories, although Ingrid couldn't tell the difference. Dr. Bamma had a perpetually confused look on his face at any given time. He gave his pen a good chomp, and blue ink trickled down his chin.

"Um, doctor?"

He tapped the busted pen against his cheek, leaving blue splotches on his flushed skin. "Come to think of it, both Mrs. Bern and Mrs. Jackson were also a bit long in the tooth. I think I discussed artificial insemination with Berns. And then she showed up already expecting." A spray of ink peppered his desk. His white coat was also spattered.

Ingrid handed him a Kleenex and motioned to his chin. It took a second for him to realize he'd cannibalized his Bic, and then he dropped it on the floor. He managed to smear ink across his chin as he dabbed it with the tissue. She retrieved the inked coffee from his desk, and said, "Why don't you freshen up while I get you another cup of coffee, sir? The next appointment will be here in a half hour, and you look as if you'd tortured a smurf."

Dr. Bamma looked down and saw the mess on his lab coat. "Oh. Oh my. Yes. Thank you, Nurse Lasso. Good idea."

She turned to leave, when he added, "Pull the charts for Mrs. Berns and Jackson as well. I want to check something."

The charts for all three women showed nothing out of the ordinary, aside from their ages. They were all childless, in their early forties, and had unsuccessfully attempted to get pregnant for decades. Dr. Bamma looked up their family medical histories for various illnesses or red flags. He ruled out Achondroplasia, Spina Bifida, and even Tay Sachs. Not so much as a potential Sickle Cell carrier in the lot. Not that any of those defects resulted in *jackalope...*

So he turned his attention to potential environmental causes. Were any of the patients exposed to radiation? Had any of them opened a meth lab? Were they caught streaking through the waste management treatment facility? Did they eat a suspicious amount of carrots?

He still came up empty handed.

He looked at their most recent lab results, and then the sonogram results. They each consistently described bunny shaped fetuses with antlers. That definitely was not a hallucination. His nurse could corroborate that he wasn't experiencing a mental break, even though she did watch him eviscerate a writing utensil.

His patients, though a bit soft headed and gullible, weren't risk assessments. They took care of themselves. They had great blood pressure, healthy cholesterol, and decent weight. They exercised, ate right, and took multi-vitamins. By reason, they should all be experiencing textbook pregnancies.

Then again, maybe they were. He'd never dealt with jackalopes before. Their babies might be fantastic. Just a little furry. He could be worrying for nothing.

Henrietta Smith could not believe her ears when her best friend, Yolanda Berns, told her she was finally pregnant. Both women struggled for years to get a baby out of their husbands, with no luck. So when Yolanda showed up on her doorstep, cheeks flushed and face glowing, Henrietta just knew something amazing had happened.

"I can't believe it! That's just incredible! What did you do?" she asked her friend.

Yolanda replied, "Have you not had the birds and bees talk,

dear?"

She laughed. "Yes, silly! I mean, how did you finally get pregnant? I've tried everything I could think of, and I'm still coming up dry. Was it a new position?"

"No," Henrietta said, "it was easy, in fact. I just started taking these new multi-vitamins my friend Marilou told me about. They have some extra hormones in them, that kinda jump start your baby oven. I took them for a month, and then BOOM! Instant baby. They ain't cheap, but if you can afford them, I suggest you try some."

Yolanda squealed. "Oh yes! Please, tell me where you get them."

Henrietta fished a pink business card from her purse and pressed it into Yolanda's hand. "He'll fix you up. Ask for Peter."

"Yes. Yes. I accept Amex, absolutely! Okay, great. I'll see you in a half hour, Yolanda."

Peter tossed his cellphone on the bed and punched the sky in victory. Yolanda would be the fifth new client in as many days. He'd be ready to move on to the next town in no time, he considered, as he downed the last of his aged whiskey. Desert women were an easy sell.

In the mirror he gave himself a wink, before settling a Stetson over his antlers and tucking his long ears into its crown.

Those Of Us Who Eat Brambles

They offered us fruit soft with rot ⸵
Flesh rancid and stuck in our teeth ·
The worms fat with spoil were worth
This pain in our bellies ‘
As we became what we craved –
Blood blooms on bare branches ‘
Bowls of bricks and bones
Under our ribs ·

Yet

We lived for the thick of hot copper ⸵
Searing trails through our larynxes ·
Daggers in our throats savoring
Songs from lacerations ‘
Slicing paths through our bodies–
Splinters searing our sweet sinew ‘
Wood in our mouths and
Under our breasts ·

A Grim Fairy Tale

The blood pooling around my body is starting to congeal, the putrid rusty odor mixing with the stench of recently expelled stomach acid. I scream repeatedly to turn off the oxygen, but they merely nod, observing my evisceration with morbid fascination. Asphyxiation would be a kinder fate, but now I can only hope my blood runs dry quickly.

Amanda squealed with excitement when she received the job offer from The Institute. A foot in the biological engineering door meant a six-figure income within just a few years. Of course I was happy for my best friend, but I was jealous, too. She had direction; I had generous aberrations. She had a burgeoning career in the field of her choice; my destiny involved wearing a manager's nametag at the local burger joint.

Two weeks before spring semester ended, she cornered me. "What gives, Margo? You've been quiet lately. Have your summer plans fallen through?" She sipped a cold chai and offered me half a raisin scone, which I declined.

"No. Didn't have any to begin with." I grimaced as I sipped my tepid mocha.

"So, what are you going to do?"

"I dunno. I'll stick around, I guess." I finished the last of my beverage and chucked the cup into a nearby wastebasket. "Besides, my parents are touring Europe for the summer. It's not like they care if I come home or not."

Her eyes narrowed as she studied my face, and murmured, "Sorry to hear that."

The beginning of summer found me working at the Farmer's Market, selling the squash and zucchini Old Man Harris harvested in his backyard. Amanda called occasionally to check on me, and I'd insist I never had more fun. "All the sunshine and fresh watermelon I could ever want. *I* should be worried about *you*."

I didn't mention how much it sucked, how I'd already nursed two nasty sunburns and had to constantly deflect Mr. Harris' advances. The last time she called, I felt a little more vulnerable, more tired than usual. "Yeah, I'm doing great. Fun, fun, fun."

"You don't sound like you're having fun. Are you sure you're okay, Margo?"

"All right. I'm miserable. I haven't seen anyone under the

age of sixty-five in the past couple of weeks. Last night I went to the movies... alone. This is unbearable!"

"Sounds like it." She slurped on a drink. "Guess you'd do just about anything to get away, huh?"

"You know it. Hell, if I had the money I'd go back home. I'd rather be alone there than in geriatric limbo here."

"Then I caught you at the right time. Yesterday the doctor told me he needs somebody for menial jobs. Nothing difficult. Sweeping the floors. Taking out the trash."

"I believe that's called a 'janitor.' Sounds fantastic," I said, my voice flat.

"I know it's a grunt job, and only pays twelve dollars an hour, but I need a roomie. Mine up and left last week." She added provocatively, "Did I mention the free room and board?"

It took all of ten seconds to make my decision. "Where'd you say this place is?"

A five-hour cab ride north brought me to the steps of The Institute, huddled in the shadow of a looming stone mountain. From a distance it looked clinically bland, an expanse of white plaster with only a small mirrored sign by the entrance. Inside wasn't much better, but I didn't care. I zipped my jacket against the polar air conditioning, glad to see not a single watermelon in sight.

Amanda sat at a table in a small break room with a

conservatively dressed man. Neither smiled as I entered.

"You must be Margo." He rose as he offered his hand, back as straight as a broom handle. His grip was firm, his palm cold and dry. "My name is Dr. Andrew Banks. It's good of you to come on such short notice. Amanda tells me you're a very diligent worker."

"Yes sir. I'm majoring in janitorial science." I could tell by the look on Amanda's face that my usually beloved sarcasm would not be appreciated. Dr. Banks pointed to a chair across the table from them. I sat. "What I mean, sir, is that I am looking forward to working for you."

"Margo is what you might call a jack of all trades. She's studied some of just about everything at school." Amanda appeared uncomfortable; her face so pinched I barely recognized her.

Dr. Banks studied me like a specimen through his glasses. "Still looking for your calling?"

I shrugged, trying not to squirm. "Just weighing all my options."

Dr. Banks responded with a thin, artificial smile. "Yes, well, let's get you situated, why don't we?"

Lights glared overhead, humming an ominous drone as I followed them through the maze of hallways. Trudging behind, I imagined we were trapped in a fluorescent labyrinth, home to some fearsome scientific Minotaur. Three semesters of Mythology will do that to a girl.

We passed a set of double doors with tiny mirrored windows over which a foreboding sign in large black letters declared 'RESTRICTED.' I stopped, studied the keypad, and peered through the window. But I could only make out a dimly lit hallway.

Then, without warning, a loud keening echoed from the locked corridor. Shaken by the shrieking, I nearly ran into the back of my new employer as I scrambled to catch up.

"Here we are." Dr. Banks turned to me and smiled again. It didn't warm his pasty features. "This is the supply closet. Take a cart with you when you make your rounds, so you can empty the trash and clean any spills as you find them. You'll be needing this." He pulled a hand radio from his pocket and offered it to me like the sword of Excalibur. "We'll call you if you're needed for any extra duties. Any questions?"

"Sure," I said. *Let's cut to the chase.* "What are my hours, and when do I get paid?" I saw Amanda cringe from the corner of my eye and could already hear her scolding.

Don't be so immature, Margo.

Dr. Banks didn't seem to notice. "Your first check will arrive next Thursday. Since you're already acquainted, Amanda will get you acclimated."

I nodded. "No problem. Sounds great." For an awkward minute no one spoke. I cleared my throat. "Am I on the clock now?"

"You start tomorrow. I'll take you to your room now so you

can get settled in," Amanda said. Dr. Banks excused himself and whisked off in the opposite direction as we exited the janitor's station.

With the doctor out of sight she relaxed and smiled. "This place is amazing! I know you'll love it here. I wouldn't be surprised if you switched to a science major come fall."

"I don't know that I'd go that far. But I am looking forward to doing something different for a change. Are the hours long?"

"Well, yeah. They are pretty long." She touched my shoulder. "But time flies when you're working in the lab."

"That's great," I said, "but I'm a janitor, not a lab rat."

She leaned in and lowered her voice. "I couldn't say it in front of Dr. Banks, but I was thinking once you've gotten the hang of things, I could get you promoted to my assistant. More privileges... more money."

"Sign me up for some of that!"

We took several turns and emerged on the back stoop of The Institute. Across an expanse of emerald green lawn, a sprawling structure appeared to jut out of the stone mountain. Its wooden exterior blended with the trees and rocks.

"This is where everyone calls home," Amanda announced.

"Everyone?"

"Absolutely! There's more sleep and less stress to be had if there are no bills or travel expenses to worry over. And if there's an emergency, everyone's already here. It's a huge win-

win. The Institute pays for everything, and in return they get a more productive staff."

Sounded like a cult to me. "So, you're saying no one ever leaves the compound?"

"The what?" She blinked.

"The Institute...no one leaves here?"

"It's not necessary," she replied, oblivious to my jab. "Deliveries are made several times a week. And there's a list for individual requests in the kitchen. Anything you want. It's on the house."

"Seems a little weird to me." I followed her across the lawn. "Have you ever been to town?"

"Not since I arrived, and you wouldn't believe the money I've saved! They provide everything we could possibly want—satellite television in all the bedrooms, swimming pool, club house, gym, sauna... hot tub. What's in town that we don't already have here?" She led me through the entrance and down the hall, stopping long enough to point out the large kitchen, small coffee lounge, and vending machine cubby.

Our bedrooms took my breath away. A large sitting room filled the space between the two rooms complete with their own full-sized baths and walk-in closets. My luggage sat on the bed of the room to my left. Adjacent to the bed, a large picture window overlooked a drop from the mountainside. I stared out over a sloping sea of green treetops in awe. Amanda's voice broke my reverie.

"Brenda comes in every morning to clean while we're working. She's good about keeping the towels stocked, but if you happen to need extra, leave a note for her on your bathroom vanity."

"We have a cleaning lady?" I was being paid to live in a resort, and all I had to do in return was a little mopping? Perhaps the car crashed on the way here and I'm in heaven, I mused. "I just decided I won't be returning for classes in the fall."

Amanda wasn't kidding; I worked insane hours. I didn't have the time to enjoy the luxurious living accommodations. The first few days, I worked from seven am to nine pm. Amanda's days ran even longer, but I never heard her complain.

I didn't see Dr. Banks again after my initial interview. Four days in, I asked Amanda about him over lunch.

"The doctor works in RAL."

"RAL?"

"Restricted Access Laboratories. He's in charge of all the big projects."

I recalled the bizarre scream I'd heard from inside the locked doors. "What's back there, anyway? The whole facility is already under lock and key."

"You must have special clearance to be permitted access to that area."

"Do you have access?"

"Yes, but I'm not allowed to bring in visitors." She touched my hand. "Give it a week, work really hard, and I'll try to get you assigned there."

"RAL has its own janitor?"

"Used to, but not now. My last roommate Carrie was doing it, but I think she had troubles back home. She took off unannounced and left us shorthanded. You were hired as her replacement." She added with emphasis, "If you do a good job, you'll get her clearance."

"That's not gonna be a problem," I mumbled through a mouth full of food. I had devoured my lunch in record time and contemplated going back for seconds. So far, every meal they served happened to be one of my favorite dishes, and I couldn't seem to get enough. I'd already gained six pounds.

"I need to go on a diet," I moaned.

Amanda teased, "Does that mean you're skipping dinner tonight?"

"Depends...what's on the menu?"

"Lasagna, bruschetta, and chocolate chip cheesecake."

I groaned.

When Sunday finally arrived, I toyed with the idea of staying in bed all day and vegging out on the free satellite, but I longed for a swim. Donning a modest bikini, I grabbed my beach towel and tanning lotion, and emerged from my room to see Amanda slipping into her lab coat.

"Hey, what gives?" I dropped my stuff onto the sofa and leaned on its arm. "You're working today? I was gonna see if you wanted to go swimming."

"I'm going to RAL for a while. We're about to start a new phase of experiments and I'm still getting everything set up."

"Really? What are they doing?"

"I was thinking," she began slowly, "it's just going to be me there today. If you promise not to fool with anything, you could come with." She waved her hand in the air and added quickly, "But I know you want to go swimming. Never mind."

"Gimme two minutes! I'll go change. That pool ain't going anywhere." I ran to my room and threw a pair of jeans and a t-shirt over my bathing suit.

She handed me a lab coat as we exited our room. "Remember, don't touch anything. No buttons, no levers... and more importantly, don't tap on the glass. It is imperative we keep all noises down to a minimum." Amanda rattled instructions to me as if I were a five-year-old about to enter a toy store.

As she slid her card through the groove on the keypad, a nearly indiscernible buzz indicated the doors had unlocked. They latched shut behind us silently. We walked briskly down the dim hallway, the soles of our tennis shoes a slight scuffle across the immaculate floor.

RAL was a tight maze of identical white hallways, a real

labyrinth behind locked doors. I paid attention to the turns we were making. *Left, right, left, right, right.* I committed the passage to memory as I followed.

We stopped at a windowless door with another keypad lock. Amanda swiped her card again, but this time she also punched a sequence of numbers. I peeked over her shoulder. Nine, Fourteen, Eighty-Five. I recognized the numbers.

My birthday.

What an odd coincidence.

A single red bulb and the blue glow of a row of computer monitors lit the room. A steel door stood to our left, next to an expanse of dark glass that ran waist-high to ceiling. An observatory? As Amanda took a seat behind one of the computers and began a whirlwind of typing, I approached the glass and strained my eyes to peer inside.

I could barely make out the darkened interior, but it looked almost like a zoo exhibit with a couple large tree trunks and foliage scattered about. Judging by the spaciousness I concluded whatever was inside must have been a large animal. After examining the quarters, I spotted a pink blanket puddled under one of the trees.

An ordinary house cat lay curled, sleeping, on the blanket. A seemingly average blonde feline, its fur neither long or short, but noticeably soft and fluffy. Speakers amplified its faint rumbled purring.

The situation confused me. Amanda once told me The

Institute produced synthetic insulin for the treatment of diabetes, so why would they be studying a cat? *Unless they're testing their insulin on it...*

My blood boiled as I watched the innocent creature dozing, unaware of whatever fate awaited it. I hated any type of animal testing, and Amanda knew that. The truth dawned on me... she conned me into applying for a job I would normally refuse so she could kiss up to her boss. "I can't believe you didn't tell me about this! You know how I feel..."

I turned and stopped short. I was alone in the room. Just me and the cat.

Angry at Amanda's deception and frustrated by my lack of insight, I wanted to know what tests they were performing. Sitting at the computer, I tapped the keyboard and the screen came to life. Crap, password protected. I entered my birthday into the password field. Denied. I entered Amanda's birth date, her last name, and any other word I thought might be a likely password. No luck.

My annoyance grew as I sat at each of the computers and tried to access their files. Other than glass and steel and computers, there wasn't anything else in the room. No file cabinets or signs indicating purpose or protocol. Pacing the room, I looked for clues, stopping occasionally at the window to watch the sleeping animal.

"What are you doing?" Amanda appeared as quickly as she had vanished.

My hand was caught in the proverbial cookie jar—or trash can, as it were. Half of its contents scattered on the floor as I rummaged through the only wastepaper basket in the room. I bristled and stood. "How can you be a part of this? What gives any of you the right?"

She glared at me. "What the hell are you talking about?"

"You forgot to mention this was an animal testing facility."

"What? Animal..." She shook her head slowly, placing a folder tucked under her arm onto the table and opening it. "It's not what you think Margo, I promise. We're studying Cally, sure, but we aren't harming her in any way."

"Cally?"

She handed me a page she pulled from the folder. "I thought maybe you'd like to see what we're doing here."

The paper was a chart covered in scribbled notes as difficult to read as a doctor's prescription and peppered with dates, checkmarks, and initials. It looked like gibberish to me. Across the top was the bold title:

Caligo Mediocris Imperium Project Objective.

Directly below was a list of basic stats, including the gender, height, and weight. But I didn't understand what kind of animal she was. Underneath 'breed' it read:

Specimen is a member of the Viscus Edo Caligo Mediocris family.

I shrugged and handed her the paper. "I don't know what that means."

"Cally is not a cat, Margo."

"So what is she?"

She looked me in the eyes and said, "Cally is a fairy."

I must have stared at her for five minutes before I could find my voice. "Bullshit!"

Amanda laughed. She took the paper and slid it into the folder, then took her seat behind the computer again. "Do you really think we'd keep it such a secret if we were running tests on a cat? Cally comes from a rare species long believed to be extinct. The Institute is studying the possibility of repopulation, but since she is the only one we've managed to capture, we still don't understand much of her biology." Amanda sat at a computer, absorbed in her work, the racket of typing vying with the purrs pouring from the speakers.

When she finished, she shut down the computers and picked up the folder. "Okay, I'm done. Let me put this away and we can go. But do me a favor and don't wake her? It's important she get as much rest as possible."

After Amanda left, I stood in front of the window and stared at the furry blonde back, now curious as to what the rest of her looked like. Despite Amanda's request, I lightly tapped the glass, hoping she'd move at least enough for me to glimpse her face. But all I saw was the outline of a knobby spine as she stretched slowly and switched sleeping positions.

Amanda returned and waved me toward the door. I walked into the hall, disappointed. She dimmed the observatory lights and we slipped out quietly. I waited for her to reset the lock with my birthday code, then followed her through RAL. "Remember, Margo, don't tell anyone you were back there. It would cost me my job."

"Of course not," I agreed, looking back over my shoulder at the dark corridor.

Amanda was quiet the next few days, and although I dropped several hints, she never mentioned my new potential job assignment. Knowing what I now knew was buried inside the halls of RAL, I was fiending to get back there worse than a cigarette deprived chain smoker.

On Wednesday afternoon Amanda spotted me at lunch, wolfing down my third plate of fried chicken. She slid into the seat across from me, a triumphant glow lighting her features. "Who's your best friend in the whole world?"

"Santa Claus?"

"You owe me big time for this." She pulled a plastic card from her pocket. "Your new key. From three to six every day, you're cleaning RAL."

Grinning like a fool, I took the pass and ran a finger over the smooth, shiny surface like I held a fifty-carat diamond. "That's awesome, Amanda! Thanks!" Excited, I pushed aside my empty tray. "I thought maybe you changed your mind after Sunday."

"I can appreciate why you'd be curious. I would be, too.

You'll start tomorrow. Report to the first door on the right when you get there." She stood to leave. "By the way, I might have forgotten to mention it, but RAL pays an additional five dollars an hour. I hope that's okay."

"Oh well," I grinned, "I guess that will have to do."

I sat in front of my closet, bemoaning my dilemma. I had put on so much weight in the brief time that I'd been there that all my pants were becoming uncomfortably tight. Within a week, nothing I owned would snap or zip. Even my sweatpants were stretched to capacity.

"When Carrie left, she forgot to take most of her things. Maybe she left something you can wear," Amanda said.

"I don't know. Was she a size fifty?" I fingered my favorite jeans and tossed them onto the closet floor, wiping away tears before Amanda saw them.

"Don't be silly," she said. "You look fine. If anything, you look healthier than ever."

Brenda showed up fifteen minutes later with a large cardboard carton labeled 'Carrie Burnes.' Packing tape crisscrossed the top and bottom, and as she dumped it in my arms, I understood why. I grunted my thanks and carried the box to my room.

A tangle of clothes and personal effects tumbled onto the bed as soon as I ripped the tape from the top seam. I unknotted a web of slacks and jeans, all size fours. I'd never been smaller than a six. Discouraged, I yanked on the sleeve of a light jacket, and something thumped to the floor, jabbing my foot. I winced but otherwise ignored the object as I continued to dig through the box. At the bottom was a ratty pair of sweatpants and three pairs of jeans, all size tens.

Tens? *Damn, she must've had one helluva problem with water weight!*

I scooped up the rest of the clothes and tossed them back into the box, but stopped before I resealed the tape. Bending over, I searched for the item that had fallen on my foot.

The photo album was thin, the kind you'd get for free at a one-hour photo lab. A snapshot of a beaming brunette peeked out from the first cellophane page, her slender arms thrown over the shoulders of other young women. The next two shots were also of her, one taken with her arms around the shoulders of a handsome man. The other was a Polaroid of her and Amanda sitting in the cafeteria. There were other various pictures of her with whom I assumed were friends and family, and in every shot she wore a wide smile.

The last photo showed a plump girl sitting by the pool. Her hair was unkempt, and she looked uncomfortably self-conscious. My stomach knotted as I realized it was Carrie. But how could someone change so drastically in just a few weeks?

"Did you leave out of embarrassment, Carrie?" I whispered to the girl in the picture. As I caught a glimpse of my reflection in the mirror, I thought I knew her answer.

* * *

Sliding my card through the groove on the keypad, my pulse raced as the muffled buzz granted me permission to enter the silent corridor. RAL was as deserted Thursday afternoon as it had been Sunday. I knocked before entering the door to the right, disappointed by the mundane interior.

A stiff woman with a sour face sat behind the grey metal desk, shuffling through a stack of papers. She barely looked me over before directing her attention back to her task.

"Margo, right?" She didn't wait for my confirmation or look up. "The closet next to you has your supplies. Start in the A corridor and work counterclockwise. Take a copy of the floor plan with you so you don't get lost. After you're finished you can return your supplies to the closet, but take the trash to the disposal receptacle in the D corridor before you leave. Once you check in you may not leave RAL until you are finished for the day. You may take one 15-minute break in the lounge next door while making your daily rounds. And try not to disturb the doctors, please. Part of your job is to be as invisible as possible. Thank you."

Her voice, a dull monotone, made me wonder how many times she'd given that speech. I took a Xeroxed copy of a fuzzy floor plan and scanned the maze of hallways. A large irregular and blackened out "F" sat dead center in the heart of RAL. It wasn't dissected and labeled room by room like the other corridors.

It was the area that housed Cally.

"What about F?" I asked.

"F is off limits. You're expected to keep your mind on your duties and not loiter in the doorways. Any infractions will result in immediate dismissal." She shot me one last withering glare before returning to her papers.

I didn't even ask the woman's name. I decided to save my questions for Amanda.

For the next three hours I circled the halls, stopping in one room after the next, dumping garbage buckets and sweeping floors. Half of the rooms were offices; the others were labs, some of which resembled science classrooms. I'd hoped to meet some of the doctors or technicians en route, but the halls remained empty. By the time I'd finished, my spirits were low, and I felt physically drained. Much more than usual.

When my shift finally ended, I met Amanda for dinner. "Normally I have a lot more energy. Do you think my extra weight is slowing me down?"

"No, RAL is a lot more work than the outer halls. Carrie's shift for the day would end once she left RAL, so consider yourself off the clock now." She giggled as she watched me fighting to stay awake over my bowl of chili. "Go on, Margo. Get some sleep. You'll feel better in the morning."

I finished eating dinner and retreated to my room, dragging my throbbing feet to the bathroom for a relaxing soak in the tub. With each passing moment I grew achier, and so weak that

I started to worry I was coming down sick. The bubbles in the tub soothed me as I slid into warm water and leaned my head back against an inflatable bath pillow.

“Margo?!” Amanda’s face matched her voice. “Good Lord! How long have you been in there?”

I sat up quickly and realized I was still in the bathtub. The bubbles had fizzled out, the water cool. Struggling to remember, I mumbled, “I dunno. What time is it?” I reached for the folded towel beside the tub. My arms quivered like soggy spaghetti noodles.

“Nine fifteen.”

“Damn!” I wrapped the towel around my gooseflesh covered body and stepped from the tub as water swirled down the drain. “I knew I was tired, but I’ve never fallen asleep in the tub before. I better get in bed before I pass out on the floor,” I said, half joking. Amanda rested a palm against my back and supported my elbow as I shuffled from the bathroom.

A bed never felt as good as that bed at that moment. I didn’t even bother to turn off the light.

It was so dark I didn’t realize I was awake at first. *Amanda must have turned off the light.* I fumbled with my alarm clock and checked the time. Two forty-seven. I groaned in frustration and glared into the darkness. As tired as I was earlier, and as badly as I needed the extra sleep, I knew I wasn't dozing back off. Now what?

RAL.

Like a child tugging at my sleeve, I couldn't shake it off. Corridor F would be as inaccessible that afternoon as it had been yesterday, but I was desperate to get inside. And I was pretty damn sure my key wouldn't open Cally's door.

But Amanda's key would.

No, I could never do that to her! Of course, no one would question if she checked into RAL during the middle of the night. If I tried to sign in with my key, however, someone would demand an explanation. Plus, I didn't have authorization to enter Cally's room, and Amanda did. *I just want to see her; I won't disturb her. And I'll have the key back before Amanda wakes up.*

Now...where does she keep her key?

The light beeps of the keypad as I entered my birthday seemed deafening in the otherwise undisturbed silence. I tiptoed through the doorway and waited until the door closed completely before flipping the light switch. I squinted against the harsh fluorescent lighting as I approached the window slowly. "Where are you, Cally?" I whispered.

The enclosure appeared deserted. The rumpled pink blanket lay empty under the tree. I sighed, pulling a chair from the computer table, and sat facing her terrarium.

Finally the small creature swaggered from behind a trunk.

She stopped in the center of the room and sat on her haunches. Amanda was right about one thing—she was not a cat. Covered in blonde fur with a long tail that curled around her hind legs, she appeared very feline from behind. But her legs were longer than a cats, and her front legs weren't legs at all, but skinny arms. Her fur-gloved hands were delicate, like that of a small child. Distinctive purring slipped through the speakers. I still didn't buy that she was a fairy, but whatever she was, she seemed harmless.

With a quick jump she disappeared behind a tree trunk. I crept to the window and knelt. Maybe if she didn't see me, she'd come back out into the open.

As I slowly lifted my eyes over the edge of the window, I came face to face with a little girl. A little girl with a fur-covered head, almond shaped black eyes, and a tiny mouth. I stared slack jawed as her adorable features curled into what looked like the beginnings of a smile.

She didn't smile, however. She hissed. A loud, screeching hiss that revealed the points of two tiny razor-sharp fangs.

"Holy shit!" I screamed, falling back on my ass.

"Margo! What the hell are you doing in here?"

If I wasn't already on the floor, I would've toppled over when Amanda burst into the room. I knew I was in deep trouble, but at the moment I was relieved to see her. "I, uh..."

"Great. Now she's wide awake." Amanda scowled at me. "I can't leave until she goes back to sleep, you know."

"I'm sorry. I didn't realize," I said weakly. No reason I could formulate would justify why I'd stolen her key to break in during the night, so instead I tried to be helpful. "What if you feed her? Maybe that would tire her out."

"It's not feeding time yet," she said, running her hands through her mussed hair. "Best I can do is give her a snack. I doubt it will work, but it's worth a shot."

She opened the door to the left of the glass and turned on the light. Inside was an anti-chamber, not much bigger than a short hallway. There was a panel of switches on the wall and a recessed locker to the left. "Wait here."

Amanda pulled a small sack and what appeared to be an oxygen mask and backpack out of the locker.

"What's all that for?"

She shook the sack lightly. "Snacks for Cally. She can have one or two a day at most. And this," she lifted the backpack, "is extremely important if you plan to enter her living space."

"Why?"

"Cally breathes Carbon Dioxide. This portable oxygen tank allows us to go inside and take care of her."

"Doesn't she bite?" I couldn't shake the image of those fangs coming at me.

"Heavens, no! She's quite docile... you just startled her." She slid the mask over her nose and mouth and continued, her voice muffled, "Once I turn on the oxygen mask the outer door will lock, so don't try to come in. I'll only be a few minutes."

I watched from the window as Amanda carried the sack into the room and sat on the floor. Cally circled and pounced like a playful kitten, letting Amanda stroke her fur as she nibbled the snacks offered to her. They played together for a few minutes, then Cally settled back onto the pink blanket and curled into a ball.

The door opened with a rush of chilly air. Amanda replaced the snacks and oxygen equipment and exited the room briskly. "Come on, let's go. I need to salvage a few minutes of sleep before work."

"Amanda, I'm really sor—"

"Forget about it. No harm, no foul. No one else has to know."

"Anything you say," I murmured, glancing over my shoulder at Cally. But she wasn't asleep. Alert and upright, her shining black eyes locked on me. Then she yawned, revealing more than just a pair of sharp fangs. Her canines were twice as long as the rest of her teeth, but they were all sharp points, like a mouth full of miniature spearheads. And her tongue was pointed as well, not to mention a peculiar shade of purple. I shuddered and followed Amanda out of the room.

To my surprise—and relief—Amanda was in good spirits Friday night. I'd avoided her all day because I expected her to lay into me for stealing her key. But when we met for dinner, she appeared upbeat, asking how my day had been.

"I'm tired, but not as much as yesterday," I replied, working on my second plate of cheese fries. "I think I'll take a plate of fries upstairs and watch some television tonight."

"Sounds like fun. I'd join you, but I have a long night ahead of me." She pushed her plate away and sipped her soda. "Cally has been very restless today. I'm going to spend some one-on-one time with her. Try to wear her out."

"Are you sure that's safe?" Sudden worry for my friend killed my appetite. "I don't think she's as tame as you say."

Amanda laughed. "Why is that?"

"I don't know. Maybe it's her weird hiss or that mouth full of barracuda teeth." I shrugged, realizing how cowardly I sounded. "I guess she just doesn't like me."

"I think you're wrong. Most fairies are mischievous and rambunctious, but not actually mean-spirited. Cally has been raised by humans, so she doesn't know how to use her powers. You'd be surprised how gentle she really is." She finished her soda and stood. "Are you too tired to come with me?"

I hesitated. "I don't know, Amanda. Seriously, I get a weird vibe from her."

"Which will disappear once you see her in action," she insisted. "Look, I'll be there with you, so there's nothing to worry about. I promise!"

"Well…"

"Please?"

I had to admit, I still wanted to know more about the

creature. *Quit being so paranoid. Amanda was playing with her last night.* If Cally were dangerous, she would never have gone in there without protection.

"Okay, I'll go. Wouldn't be the first time I've been wrong about something. Just let me change my clothes first. Carrie's jeans are cutting off my circulation. Size ten, my ass!"

Amanda was teaching Cally sign language. The little girl was a fast learner, and eager to show off her new skills. She ran to the window to show me each new word she learned, and before long I had forgotten how uneasy she had made me. Her antics kept me laughing so hard I was in tears.

They played for nearly an hour before Cally curled up on her blanket. Amanda crept from the room and shut down the oxygen tank. We watched Cally napping, her purrs rattling the observatory speakers.

"Thanks for talking me into coming with you," I said. "I think I just let my imagination get the best of me. Cally is amazing."

"Yes, she is."

"How do they plan to breed her if she's the only one they've found?"

Amanda took a three-ringed binder from the table. "I was assigned research right after I arrived here. You'd be amazed at the information I've found so far. This file contains everything we know about her." She wiggled it in front of my eyes. "You can read it if you want."

"Sure!" I accepted the notebook as a loud crackling interrupted our conversation.

Amanda pulled a hand radio from her hip. Dr. Banks' fuzzy voice invaded the room. "Amanda, would you be kind enough to assist me in the office? I'm having difficulty locating some of the project files."

"Yes sir," she replied. "I'll be there immediately." Turning to me, she said, "Margo, would you do me a huge favor?"

"Probably."

"Could you wait here until I get back and keep an eye on Cally for me? She's out for the night, I think, but I don't have time to shut everything down at the minute. I won't be gone long."

"No problem," I said, opening the book. "I'll read the file while you're gone. Take your time."

The door shut behind her. Sudden scratching on the glass startled me. I looked up to see Cally pressed against the window. She gestured wildly with her hands. I struggled to remember the words Amanda taught her. Game? Play? Bath?

Snack!

It was almost as if someone had whispered in my ear. I frowned, slowly closing the notebook, and laying it on the desk. Cally hopped in place like a hyper child. I knelt in front of her, the glass between us.

"I don't remember… did Amanda feed you?" She shook

her head. "No, I don't think she did either." I sat on my heels, unsure of what to do. The anti-chamber door was still unlocked. Cally had exhibited no signs of aggression towards me. Besides, she really did look hungry. "Eh, what the hell!"

The small backpack rested comfortably over my shoulders. I placed the translucent plastic mask over my nose and mouth, took the sack of treats from the locker, and turned on the air tank. A large push button by the door sucked the oxygen from the room as the seal around Cally's door released. It swung open on mechanical hinges.

I stepped inside.

We stared at each other momentarily, and she looked as edgy as I felt. *Be calm. She probably senses fear.* I extended a shaky hand.

"It's okay, Cally. I brought you some treats. See?"

She shuffled closer. I pulled a biscuit from the bag for her. Her eyes brightened and she pounced, landing at my feet with her small hands outstretched. Gently, she accepted the snacks I offered and carried them to her blanket. I slipped out of the room unnoticed as she enjoyed her treats. After putting everything back in its place, I left the anti-chamber. Feeling relieved, I took my seat by the table and reached for the book.

It was gone.

I searched the room wildly, certain I'd left the book on the desk. But it wasn't there. Wasn't on the floor or in the trash, either. Amanda was gonna be pissed if she found out what I'd done. Did I leave it in the snack locker? I grasped the doorknob as something inside Cally's habitat caught my eye.

The notebook.

I was certain I left the book on the table, but there it was, laying a few feet from Cally's bed. I rushed into the anti-chamber, repositioned the backpack over my shoulders and the mask over my face, and turned on my air. The air swooshed from the room as the door swung open.

It was there on the floor, not even ten feet away from me.

But as I bent to pick it up off the floor, I heard an ominous click. Reaching for the knob, I realized the door had locked behind me. I shook the handle frantically, but it didn't budge. The book fell from my hands and papers cascaded around my feet as I tried to escape.

Amanda returned, and I pounded on the glass for her attention. "I'm trapped in here, Amanda! The door locked behind me!"

I could hear her voice clearly through the speakers. "Give me a few minutes. Sometimes the lock is quirky. There's at least a days' worth of air in that pack, so don't worry."

She was so calm, so unaffected, while I was fighting hysteria. *Chill out. She knows what she's doing.* I forced myself to relax, sitting cross legged on the floor and gathering the scattered notebook pages as she fiddled with the lock.

As I clipped handfuls of loose papers into the binder, my eyes happened to glance over a single page still clenched in my hand. It was a sheet of loose leaf covered in notes printed in Amanda's tidy handwriting. Bold letters immediately caught my attention.

"Caligo Mediocris Imperium Project, or darkest fairy control project. Objective: study specimen Viscus Edo Caligo Mediocris, or flesh devouring darkest fairy, to determine transformative properties and possible applications for human genetic manipulation."

I wasn't entirely sure what it meant. Flesh devouring? What kind of flesh was Amanda referring to? I scanned the page further, freezing on a highlighted paragraph at the bottom of the page.

"When exposed to oxygen, the specimen transforms into an obligate carnivore, which can feed for up to ten days before returning to its passive state. (Or 1 day per 20lbs of red meat, depending on size of carcass.) It is important to maintain a strict environment of undiluted Carbon Dioxide until feeding time. Caligo Mediocris must feed at least once a month to maintain its health."

That much I understood clearly.

An odd buzz, followed by a rush of cool air, invaded the chamber. I heard a single beep as a sign lit up above the doorway.

OXYGEN: ON

As if on cue, Cally floated off her blanket, onyx eyes fixed on me. Her blonde furry body darkened, flattened, and transformed into a leathery canvas stretched taut over a sharp skeleton. Bat wings emerged from her spine, and the rows of spearhead teeth elongated until they curled under her chin. Her purr, which earlier had been so endearing, deepened to a growl.

The anti-chamber was now filled with people, with Amanda and Dr. Banks sitting in the center. "The oxygen is on!" I screamed at them. Dr. Banks nodded and said something to Amanda, and she smiled, giving me a thumbs up. Flinging myself against the door, I screamed, "Let me out! Hurry!"

"Mar-go." My name was a hiss falling from unnatural lips. I turned to face the black monstrosity hovering at my back. Her purple pointed tongue snaked through the air and caressed my face, leaving slimy saliva trails on my skin. Circling my neck, she used it to lift me off the floor.

I tried to kick my legs and pry myself free, but my limbs felt soggy. My skin numbed under the slick of her saliva, like I'd been swabbed with Novocain. Her tongue wrapped around my windpipe and made it hard to breathe. "Cally, please don't," I wheezed.

Unable to break away, I watched her sniff me over like a hungry dog. She lifted her barbed claws and gestured. This time I recognized the word immediately.

Snack.

About the Author

Jezzy Wolfe is a poet and author who has appeared in numerous anthologies and publications. Her debut poetry collection, MONSTRUM POETICA, was released in 2021 from Raw Dog Screaming Press. Her work has also appeared in Smart Rhino's *Zippered Flesh* trilogy as well as their *Insidious Assassins* and *Asinine Assassins* anthologies, Crystal Lake's *Shallow Waters* anthology, Western Legends' *Unnatural Tales of the Jackalope*, *Space & Time Magazine*, and the legendary *Weird Tales Magazine*, just to name a few. When she is not hiking trails or being chased by her ferrets, you can find her on her blog at jezzywolfe.wordpress.com, and on Facebook at www.facebook.com/jezzywolfeauthor.

Locks of Loathe *appeared in* ZIPPERED FLESH: TALES OF BODY ENHANCEMENTS GONE BAD! *from* Smart Rhino Publications, February 2012

To the Victor Goes the Soil *originally appeared in* Morpheus Tales' Special Flash Edition *of* Morpheus Tales eZine, ©October 2009, *and again in* Support the Little Guy eZine Issue #2, February 2011

Hell Does Not Bring Fire *appeared in* Weird Tales Magazine Issue #365, November 2022

Small Claws, Small Guns *appeared in* ASININE ASSASSINS *from* Smart Rhino Publications, August 2021

Lucious *appeared in* ZIPPERED FLESH 2: MORE TALES OF BODY ENHANCEMENTS GONE BAD *from* Smart Rhino Publications, February 2013

Return by Fire *appeared in* Sirens Call eZine, Winter Edition, Issue #56, December 2021

Love Me, Love My Alpaca *appeared in* The World of Myth eZine, Issue #56, December 2017

Sanguinary *appeared in* Sirens Call eZine, Winter Edition, Issue #56, December 2021

All Will Turn to Gray *appeared in* ZIPPERED FLESH 3: EVEN MORE TALES OF BODY ENHANCEMENTS GONE BAD! *from* Smart Rhino Publications, October 2017

War Dance *appeared in* UNNATURAL TALES OF THE JACKALOPE *from* Western Legends, June 2012

Met Halfway *appeared in* HARVEST HILL: 31 TALES OF HALLOWEEN HORROR *from* Graveside Tales, October 2009

Mother, Mad *appeared in* Space and Time Magazine Issue #137, June 2020

Reap *appeared in* UNWELCOMED: STORIES OF HAUNTINGS AND POSSESSIONS *from* ZombieWorks Publications, November 2022

Agnus Dei *appeared in* INSIDIOUS ASSASSINS *from* Smart Rhino Publications, January 2016

Branching Out *appeared in* Necrocastizine, Issue #002, January 2019

Fellow *appeared in* THE SHE WOLF WAS HERE *from* Jennifer L. Miller's Contributing Authors, March 2021

A Grim Fairy Tale *originally appeared in* THE 2009 LADIES AND GENTLEMEN OF HORROR from Sonar4 Publications, October 2009

Made in the USA
Middletown, DE
05 March 2024

50274191R00179

13 ¿Quién fue presentado a César por Cleopatra?

Sosígenes de Alejandría, recomendado a Julio César por la reina de Egipto para reformar el calendario, lo reformó en 45 a. C.

14 ¿Qué ordenó el emperador Augusto?

En el año 8 d. C. hizo corregir los errores del calendario juliano y ordenó que durante algunos años no hubiera años bisiestos.

15 ¿Qué otros calendarios hay?

Entre otros calendarios utilizados están el musulmán, el budista, el chino, el hebreo, el hindú, el maya, el azteca, el japonés y el persa.

OBSERVACIÓN DE LA NATURALEZA

16 ¿Qué observó Darwin?

El gran naturalista inglés Charles Darwin, padre de la teoría de la evolución, llegó al archipiélago de Galápagos en 1835 a bordo del bergantín *Beagle*. Vio una gran variedad de tortugas gigantes y pinzones, y observó que diferían de una isla a otra.

17 ¿Quién descubrió la atracción de la gravedad?

El físico Isaac Newton (1643-1727) descubrió esta fuerza de la naturaleza al observar una manzana caer de un árbol.

¿LO SABÍAS?

Todas las copias del libro de Darwin *El origen de las especies* se vendieron en un día.

18 ¿Quién inventó la vacuna?

El médico y naturalista inglés Edward Jenner vio en 1782 que, tras tener contacto con vacas infectadas de viruela, las ordeñadoras quedaban inmunizadas, y se le ocurrió usar agentes patógenos extraídos de los animales para inyectarlos en personas, creando la primera inyección «vacuna».

19 ¿Qué descubrió Alexander Fleming?

Este médico y biólogo escocés descubrió en 1928 la primera sustancia antibiótica, la penicilina, tras ver que la presencia de moho inhibía el crecimiento de los cultivos de bacterias.

20 ¿Quién dijo que la Tierra no es el centro del universo en el s. XVI?

Cuando aún se creía que el Sol y los planetas giraban alrededor de la Tierra, Copérnico observó que el brillo de Venus y Mercurio era variable, lo que le llevó a pensar que no estaban siempre a la misma distancia de nuestro planeta.

21 ¿Quién superó la barrera del sonido en 1947?

El piloto Charles Yeager, a bordo del avión cohete experimental *Bell XS-1*, alcanzó una velocidad superior a 1.191,60 km/h (o *Mach 1*, la velocidad del sonido en el aire).

22

¿Qué usó Franklin?

Cuando inventó el pararrayos, Benjamin Franklin utilizó una cometa a la que le añadió una punta de acero. La hizo volar durante una tormenta para probar que la punta atraía la electricidad de los rayos.

23

¿Qué le pasó a G.W. Richmann?

En 1753, el científico alemán quiso repetir el experimento del pararrayos, pero cayó fulminado por una descarga eléctrica mucho más potente que la recibida por Benjamin Franklin.

¿LO SABÍAS?

Nikola Tesla fue el primero en intuir que las radiaciones eran muy peligrosas.

¿LO SABÍAS?

Marie Curie ganó dos premios Nobel.

24 ¿Qué descubrió Wilhelm Röntgen?

En 1895, el científico alemán descubrió los rayos X.

25 ¿Qué hizo Marie Curie a finales del siglo XIX?

La científica polaca descubrió la radiación del átomo observando que minerales con uranio hacen que el aire alrededor conduzca la electricidad.

26 ¿Quién usó los rayos X?

El primer uso de los rayos con fines médicos se debe al británico John Hall-Edwards.

¿LO SABÍAS?

El primer estudio sobre los rayos llamados luego «X» fue de Nikola Tesla.

LUZ Y CIENCIA

27 ¿Quién inventó la óptica moderna?

Ibn al-Haytham, conocido en Occidente con el nombre de Alhacén (*ca.* 965-1040), fue un científico islámico que estudió la refracción y reflexión de los rayos de luz.

28 ¿Cuánto tiempo llevó tomar la primera fotografía?

Nicéphore Niépce obtuvo la primera fotografía de la historia en 1827, para la que necesitó un tiempo de exposición de 8 horas; logró fijarla sobre una placa de peltre.

29 ¿Qué descubrió Bonaventura Cavalieri?

El matemático italiano retomó en su obra El *espejo ustorio*, escrita en 1632, los estudios de Arquímedes (siglo III a. C.) sobre geometría de la parábola para proyectar un espejo curvo capaz de concentrar los rayos de luz en un punto.

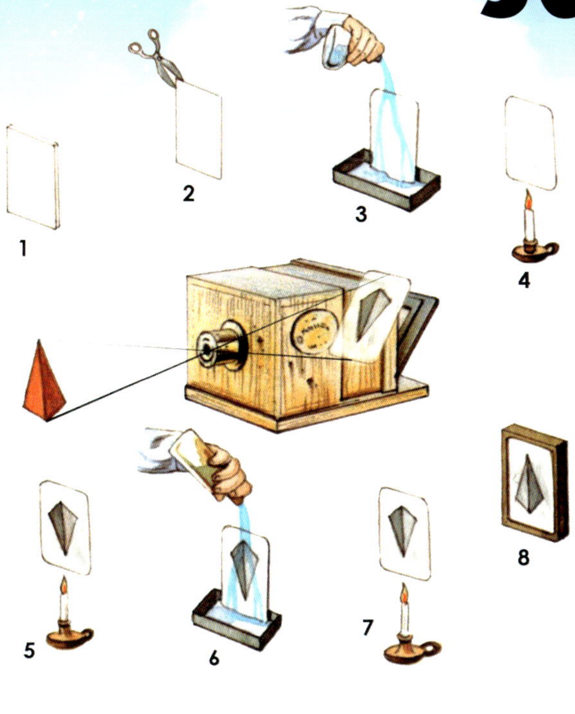

30 ¿Qué es un daguerrotipo?

Es el primer proceso fotográfico completo, desde la preparación hasta el revelado, realizado en 1837 por el pintor e inventor francés Louis Daguerre, en colaboración con Nicéphore Niépce.

31 ¿Qué fabricó George Eastman?

El empresario norteamericano, apasionado de la fotografía, construyó en 1888 la primera máquina fotográfica al alcance de todos y fundó Kodak.

INVENTOS Y DESCUBRIMIENTOS

32 ¿Cómo inventó el telescopio Galileo Galilei en el s. XVII?

Utilizó el catalejo, invento del holandés Hans Lippershey, colocando en sus extremos una lente convexa y una cóncava.

33 ¿Quién descubrió colores en la luz?

El científico inglés Isaac Newton, al estudiar la dispersión óptica, vio que un rayo de luz que pasaba a través de un prisma de vidrio se descomponía en varios colores; al atravesar un segundo prisma el rayo de luz blanca se recomponía de nuevo.

34 ¿Qué es la bomba neumática?

Es una máquina que se utiliza para sacar agua de un pozo y que consiste en un fuelle con el que se introduce aire, que impulsa el agua. La primera máquina neumática fue construida por el alemán Otto von Guericke en 1654, pero cuando la noticia llegó a Inglaterra también Robert Boyle, que estudiaba las propiedades del aire y el vacío, construyó otro modelo.

35 ¿Para qué utilizó el telescopio Galileo?

En 1610 Galileo utilizó su invento para mirar la Luna, el planeta Júpiter y las estrellas. A partir de sus observaciones creó la teoría heliocéntrica (los planetas giran alrededor del Sol), que anteriormente había sido postulada por Copérnico.

36 ¿Quién inventó el círculo Dou?

Este instrumento, que servía para medir con precisión los ángulos en campo abierto, fue inventado en torno a 1610 por el geómetra holandés Jan Pieterszoon Dou. También se conoce como «círculo holandés».

¿LO SABÍAS?

Robert Hooke inventaba instrumentos para experimentos científicos.

37 ¿Qué científico descubrió la célula?

Examinando la caña de azúcar con un microscopio construido por él mismo, en 1665 el inglés Robert Hooke apreció cavidades, separadas por paredes, a las que llamó «celdas» *(cell)*, de donde deriva el término «célula».

38 ¿Cómo se midió el metro?

Para establecer esta medida se acordó que sería la diezmillonésima parte del cuadrante de un meridiano terrestre. Para calcularlo, se midió un arco (un trozo) del meridiano de París, entre Dunquerque y Barcelona; se calculó la longitud del cuarto y se dividió.

39 ¿Quién descubrió organismos unicelulares?

El holandés Antoni van Leeuwenhoek (1632-1723), óptico y naturalista, al perfeccionar el microscopio de Hooke logró aumentar casi 300 veces una imagen. De este modo consiguió observar por primera vez protozoos y bacterias.

¿LO SABÍAS?

Hooke sostuvo que los fósiles eran restos de especies extinguidas.

40 ¿Quién describió el teodolito?

El primero en ofrecer una descripción de este instrumento, que se utiliza para obtener ángulos verticales y horizontales y utilizarlo en las triangulaciones, fue el humanista alemán Gregor Reisch, que lo mostró en su *Enciclopedia* en 1512.

41 ¿Quién fue el primero en registrar el sonido?

Aunque muchos piensan que fue Thomas Alva Edison, en realidad en 1854 el francés Édouard-Léon Scott de Martinville construyó un instrumento capaz de registrar en superficies adecuadas el sonido de la voz y transcribirlo en signos, pero sin reproducirlo.

42 ¿Qué era la pascalina?

Fue el nombre dado a la máquina construida en 1642 por el científico francés Blaise Pascal. Se considera la máquina precursora de las calculadoras.

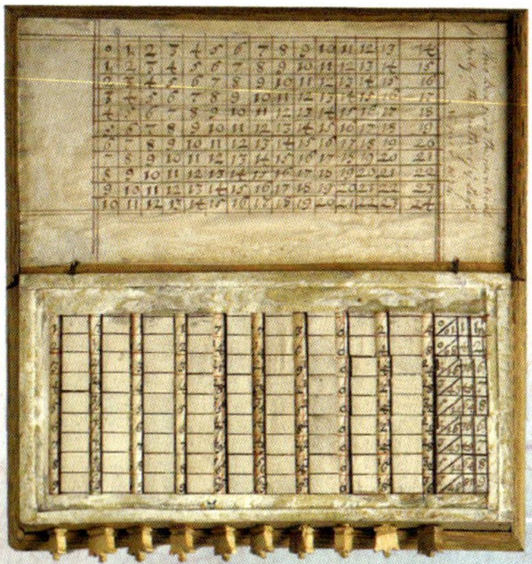

43 ¿Qué inventó Napier?

Tras introducir los logaritmos, el matemático escocés John Napier inventó un instrumento de cálculo compuesto por varillas de marfil, sobre cada una de las cuales iban inscritos los primeros múltiplos de un número; utilizado en 1617, el instrumento se llamó «ábaco neperiano».

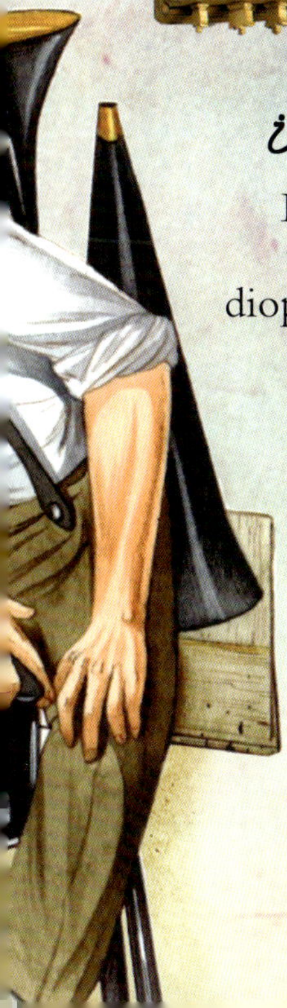

¿LO SABÍAS?

El antecesor del teodolito fue la dioptra (siglo III a. C.).

44 ¿Quién inventó el disco gramofónico?

En 1876, Thomas Alva Edison había construido el fonógrafo, que para registrar el sonido utilizaba un cilindro vertical.
En 1887, el alemán Emile Berliner sustituyó el cilindro por un disco que giraba horizontalmente: el disco gramofónico.

45 ¿Qué pasó con la máquina de coser de Josef Madersperger?

El genial sastre alemán inventó en 1839 la máquina de coser que lleva su nombre. Había invertido 30 años y todos sus ahorros en ella, pero la falta de dinero impidió la producción y solo quedó un prototipo.

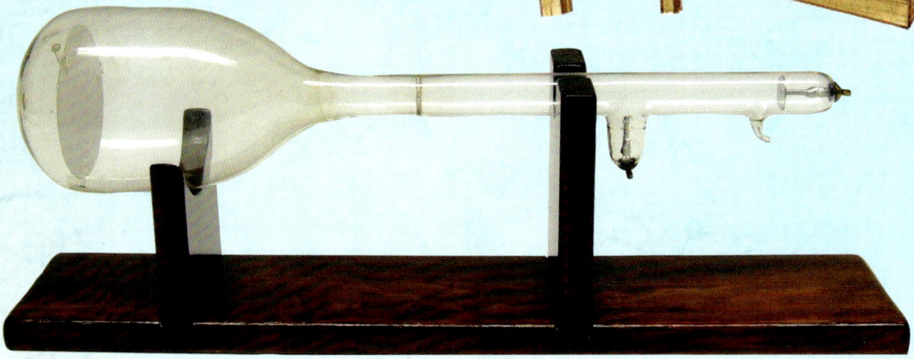

46 ¿De dónde viene «rayos X»?

En 1895, el físico alemán Wilhelm Röntgen descubrió radiciones que permitían ver el interior de cuerpos opacos al atravesarlos. Como eran radiaciones desconocidas, se las llamó con esta letra.

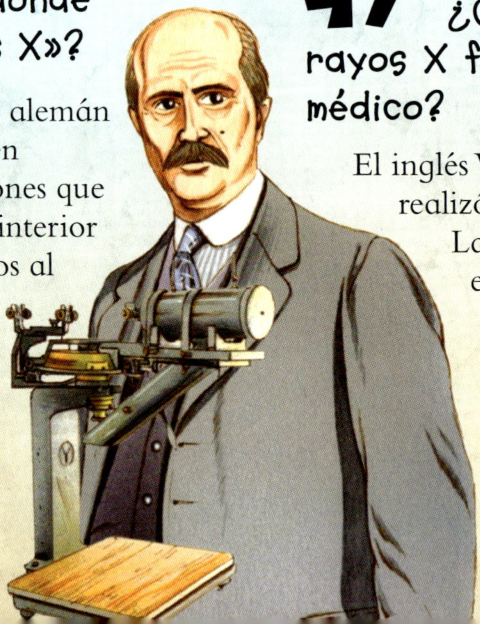

47 ¿Quién usó los rayos X fuera del campo médico?

El inglés William Henry Bragg realizó, junto a su hijo William Lawrence, el primer espectroscopio de rayos X y dio inicio a la nueva ciencia del estudio de la estructura cristalina. Por estos trabajos obtuvieron el premio Nobel de Física en 1915.

48 ¿Quién inventó los alimentos envasados?

En torno a 1796, al francés Nicolas Appert se le ocurrió una idea para bloquear el deterioro de los alimentos con calor y cierre hermético.

49 ¿Qué inventó el ruso Paul Nipkow?

En 1883 fabricó un disco para la «escansión» o barrido en línea de imágenes, base de la transmisión a distancia y de la televisión.

¿LO SABÍAS?

Hoy las señales son transmitidas en forma de *bits* digitales.

50 ¿Cuándo se fabricó el primer televisor electrónico?

Fue en 1927, y lo hizo el inventor estadounidense Philo Farnsworth, apenas dos años después del modelo electromecánico del inglés John Logie Baird. Para ello había inventado antes un disector de imagen (tubo de televisión), el cual se utilizó hasta finales del siglo xx.

51 ¿Qué fue la «guerra de corrientes»?

Fue una disputa entre Thomas Edison, partidario del uso de la corriente continua, y Nikola Tesla y George Westinghouse, que defendían la corriente alterna, más fácil de transportar a distancia.

¿LO SABÍAS?

El primer gran suceso transmitido por la televisión fueron las Olimpiadas de Berlín de 1936.

52 ¿A quién se debe la palabra «voltio»?

Al italiano Alessandro Volta, que fabricó la primera pila eléctrica en 1799, cuyo funcionamiento ilustró en el Institute de France el 7 de noviembre de 1801, ante Napoleón Bonaparte.

53 ¿Con quién discutió Volta?

Tuvo una disputa con Luigi Galvani, que defendía la electricidad animal diciendo que era necesario el músculo animal para que hubiera corriente.

¿LO SABÍAS?

El sustantivo «pila» deriva de su característica estructura, una pila de discos superpuestos.

54 ¿Quién inventó la dinamo?

El físico italiano Antonio Pacinotti construyó, en 1859, un generador de corriente continua reversible, capaz de funcionar como motor eléctrico, que se considera la primera dinamo.

55 ¿Qué inventaron los hermanos Chappe?

Claude e Ignace Chappe inventaron el telégrafo óptico, un sistema de comunicación basado en la combinación de las posiciones adoptadas por grandes brazos móviles visibles a distancia.

56 ¿Cuándo se descubrió la doble hélice del ADN?

La particular forma de la estructura del ADN o ácido desoxirribonucleico fue detectada en 1953 por James Watson y Francis Crick, quienes, por su descubrimiento, ganaron el premio Nobel.

¿LO SABÍAS?

El telégrafo óptico de los hermanos Chappe fue presentado a Napoleón Bonaparte.

57 ¿Qué afirmó Copérnico en el s. XVI?

En su tratado astronómico *De revolutionibus orbium coelestium*, publicado en Núremberg en 1543, el famoso astrónomo polaco afirmó que el Sol estaba en el centro de las órbitas de los planetas que componían el sistema solar. Su tesis fue denostada.

58 ¿Quién estudió el cielo antes que Copérnico?

Uno de los estudiosos del cielo, Aristarco de Samos, planteó en el siglo III a. C. los movimientos de revolución y rotación de la Tierra.

59 ¿Qué inventó Eratóstenes?

En el siglo III a. C. construyó un modelo de la esfera celeste (esfera armilar) empleando anillos fijos para representar el meridiano y el horizonte, y móviles para la rotación de los astros.

60 ¿Quién construyó el primer catalejo?

Aunque la paternidad de este invento aún es incierta, la primera solicitud de patente fue depositada en 1608 por el holandés Hans Lippershey. A partir de él, Galileo pudo construir después el telescopio.

61 ¿Qué construyó Isambard Kingdom Brunel?

Este ingeniero de origen británico que vivió en el siglo XIX es uno de los científicos más innovadores y versátiles de todos los tiempos. Realizó trabajos en varios campos, ideando puentes colgantes, galerías, líneas férreas, grandes barcos (como el *SS Great Eastern* de 210 m de eslora), hospitales prefabricados y otros muchos útiles ingenios.

62 ¿Cómo evolucionó el microscopio?

Gracias a su desarrollo, los científicos pudieron observar la anatomía de la célula. El italiano Marcello Malpighi, padre de la histología, confirmó en 1675 la existencia de las células en tejidos vegetales.

63 ¿Quién inventó el abrelatas?

Con la aparición de la lata para envasar la comida en 1810, hacía falta una herramienta que permitiese abrirla fácilmente: en 1858 Ezra Warner inventó el abrelatas, utilizado durante la Guerra Civil estadounidense.

64 ¿Quién fabricó la primera ametralladora moderna?

Hiram Maxim, estadounidense naturalizado británico, puso a punto en 1884 la primera totaltamente automática, capaz de diparar más de 500 proyectiles por minuto.

65 ¿Qué construyó John Harrison?

Este genial relojero inglés inventó el cronómetro marino, el instrumento que permite determinar con precisión la longitud en alta mar; trabajó ininterrumpidamente desde 1728 a 1772 para perfeccionar los modelos que había realizado.

66 ¿Quién utilizó el cronómetro de Harrison?

Hubo cinco diseños del cronómetro, construidos por Harrison a lo largo de décadas. El H-4 (el cuarto) fue utilizado por el explorador James Cook en una de sus expediciones.

67 ¿Qué hizo Blaise Pascal?

Blaise Pascal inventó en 1642 la pascalina, la primera calculadora. También verificó en 1647 los resultados obtenidos por Evangelista Torricelli en los cálculos de la fuerza ejercida por la presión atmosférica: pidió a su cuñado que subiera a una altitud de 1.000 m y comprobó que, a mayor alitud, menos presión.

¿LO SABÍAS?

El español Manuel Jalón Corominas inventó la fregona en 1964. En Estados Unidos ya existían otros tipos de aparatos fregasuelos con cubo, y de ellos sacó Manuel Jalón su idea.

68 ¿Qué científico introdujo el término «barómetro»?

Fue acuñado por el irlandés Robert Boyle. Él fue también quien, en 1662, enunció la ley física que afirma que la presión de un gas perfecto es inversamente proporcional a su volumen.

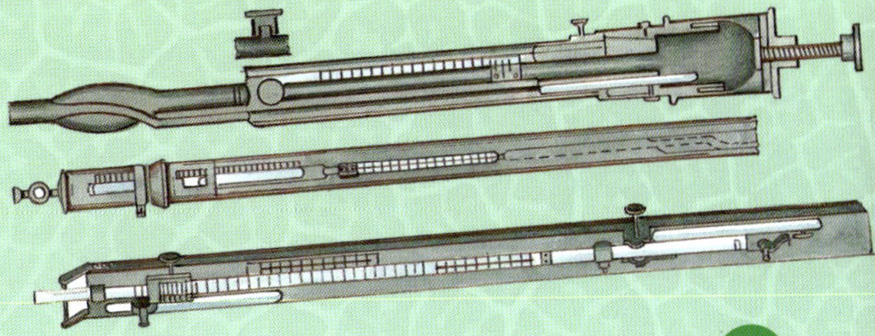

TRANSPORTES

69 ¿A quién se debe el invento de la máquina de vapor?

Precursora de los transportes a vapor, su invención se debe al herrero inglés Thomas Newcomen, que en 1712 construyó el primer motor de pistones impulsado por la presión del vapor y utilizado para extraer agua de las minas. Sin embargo, fueron las innovaciones aportadas por el escocés James Watt a partir de 1765 las que permitieron un uso generalizado de la máquina en el transporte y la industria.

¿LO SABÍAS

El primer automóvil híbrido, eléctrico y con motor fue desarrollado por Ferdinand Porsche en 1900.

70 ¿Quién construyó la *Locomotion*?

El ingeniero inglés George Stephenson y su hijo Robert construyeron en 1825 la locomotora que hizo el primer viaje de tren entre las ciudades de Stockton y Darlington, llevando 38 vagones cargados de carbón y trigo.

71 ¿Quién proyectó el *Clermont*?

El *Clermont* fue el primer barco de vapor, y fue construido en 1807 por Robert Fulton, ingeniero estadounidense. El barco navegaba por el Hudson y enlazaba Nueva York con Albany; podía transportar 30 pasajeros.

72 ¿Cómo funcionaba la primera máquina de vapor?

La eolípila, construida por Herón de Alejandría en el siglo II d. C., era una esfera que se mantenía en rotación por efecto del vapor, que ascendía con fuerza por dos delgados tubos opuestos en forma de «L». El vapor se producía calentando agua en el recipiente de la parte inferior.

73 ¿Quiénes fueron los primeros en volar?

Los franceses Jean-François Pilâtre de Rozier y François Laurent d'Arlandes, en 1783, fueron pioneros de la aviación, realizando el primer ascenso de un globo tripulado inventado por los hermanos Montgolfier.

74 ¿Qué altura alcanzó el globo Montgolfier?

Cuando De Rozier y D'Arlandes hicieron su viaje, sobrevolaron París a una altitud de casi 1.000 metros.

75 ¿Quién se lanzó primero en paracaídas?

Fue el inventor francés André-Jacques Garnerin, que el 22 de octubre de 1797 se lanzó desde un globo a una altura de 350 metros.

76

¿Quién fue el primer astronauta?

Fue el ruso Yuri Gagarin. El 12 de abril de 1961, a bordo de la cápsula espacial *Vostok-1,* efectuó un giro completo alrededor de nuestro planeta antes de volver a la Tierra después de 88 minutos de vuelo.

77

¿Quién fue el padre del planeador?

El alemán Otto Lilienthal estudió a fondo el vuelo de las aves y construyó varias «cometas voladoras», con las que realizó muchos vuelos hasta el 9 de agosto de 1896, cuando murió al caer desde 17 m.

78

¿Qué profundidad alcanzó el batiscafo *Trieste*?

El 23 de enero de 1960, con Jacques Piccard y Don Walsh a bordo, el *Trieste* tocó el fondo de la fosa de las Marianas, la depresión oceánica más profunda del mundo, situada en el océano Pacífico al este de las islas. La profundidad alcanzada fue de 10.902 m bajo el nivel del mar.

¿LO SABÍAS?

Un batiscafo ha de ser capaz de soportar la fuerte presión del agua.

GRANDES **NOMBRES**

79 ¿Quién fue Cresques Abraham?

Fue un cartógrafo y el probable autor, junto con su hijo Jehuda, del *Atlas catalán*, el mapamundi más importante del periodo medieval, que fue realizado hacia 1375 en Mallorca, donde convivían judíos, musulmanes y cristianos.

80 ¿Quién hizo el primer mapamundi moderno?

La primera reproducción a escala de la Tierra (que aún no incluía el continente americano) es el globo terrestre del alemán Martin Behaim, elaborado entre 1490 y 1492 en Núremberg.

¿LO SABÍAS?

Se atribuye al griego Anaximandro (siglo VI a. C.) el primer mapa de la Tierra rodeada por el océano.

81 ¿Por qué es famoso Gerard Kremer?

El gran geógrafo y matemático, más conocido por su nombre latinizado Gerardus Mercator, inventó, en 1569, un sistema de proyección cartográfica que hoy aún se conoce por su nombre y es el más usado en cartas náuticas. Construyó también un globo celeste.

82 ¿Qué papa fue astrónomo?

El monje benedictino Gerberto de Aurillac, que se convirtió en papa en 999 con el nombre de Silvestre II, fue un profundo conocedor de la ciencia árabe. Construyó modelos de las esferas celestes y del globo terrestre para enseñar astronomía.

83 ¿Cuál fue la aportación de Leonardo da Vinci a la medicina?

Una de sus numerosas contribuciones a la ciencia fueron sus dibujos anatómicos, que alcazaban un altísimo nivel de detalle. Los que representaban la estructura craneal, o los sistemas muscular y esquelético y las válvulas cardiacas, son valiosos documentos del que puso las bases de la anatomía científica incluso bajo condiciones muy difíciles de estudio.

¿LO SABÍAS?

Leonardo diseccionaba los cadáveres de los criminales sin que se enterase la Inquisición.

84 ¿Qué inventó Barsanti?

El ingeniero y sacerdote Eugenio Barsanti construyó en 1856, junto con Felice Matteucci, el primer motor de combustión. El invento fue patentado por Matteucci 20 años después, para reivindicar la paternidad frente al alemán Nikolaus August Otto.

85 ¿Cuándo nació el cine?

Hacia finales del siglo XIX Thomas Edison inventó el kinetoscopio, y en 1895 el *cinématographe* fue presentado por los hermanos Lumière. Este aparato permitía la visualización por varios espectadores al mismo tiempo.

¿LO SABÍAS?

Tras varios intentos no satisfactorios de sincronizar el sonido con las imágenes, en 1927 se proyectó el primer largometraje sonoro, *El cantor de jazz*.

86 ¿Qué rodaron los hermanos Lumière?

Estos cineastas precursores realizaron en 1895 decenas de películas breves sobre temas de actualidad y documentales, así como escenas de carácter familiar y género cómico.

87 ¿Qué máquina calculadora ideó Alan Turing?

El famoso matemático y lógico inglés concibió a principios de la década de 1940 el modelo abstracto de una máquina ideal capaz de realizar los complejos cálculos que permitieron construir *Colossus*, un potentísimo mecanismo calculador que, durante la Segunda Guerra Mundial, permitió a los británicos descifrar los códigos de *Enigma*, una potente máquina usada por Alemania para cifrar y descifrar mensajes.

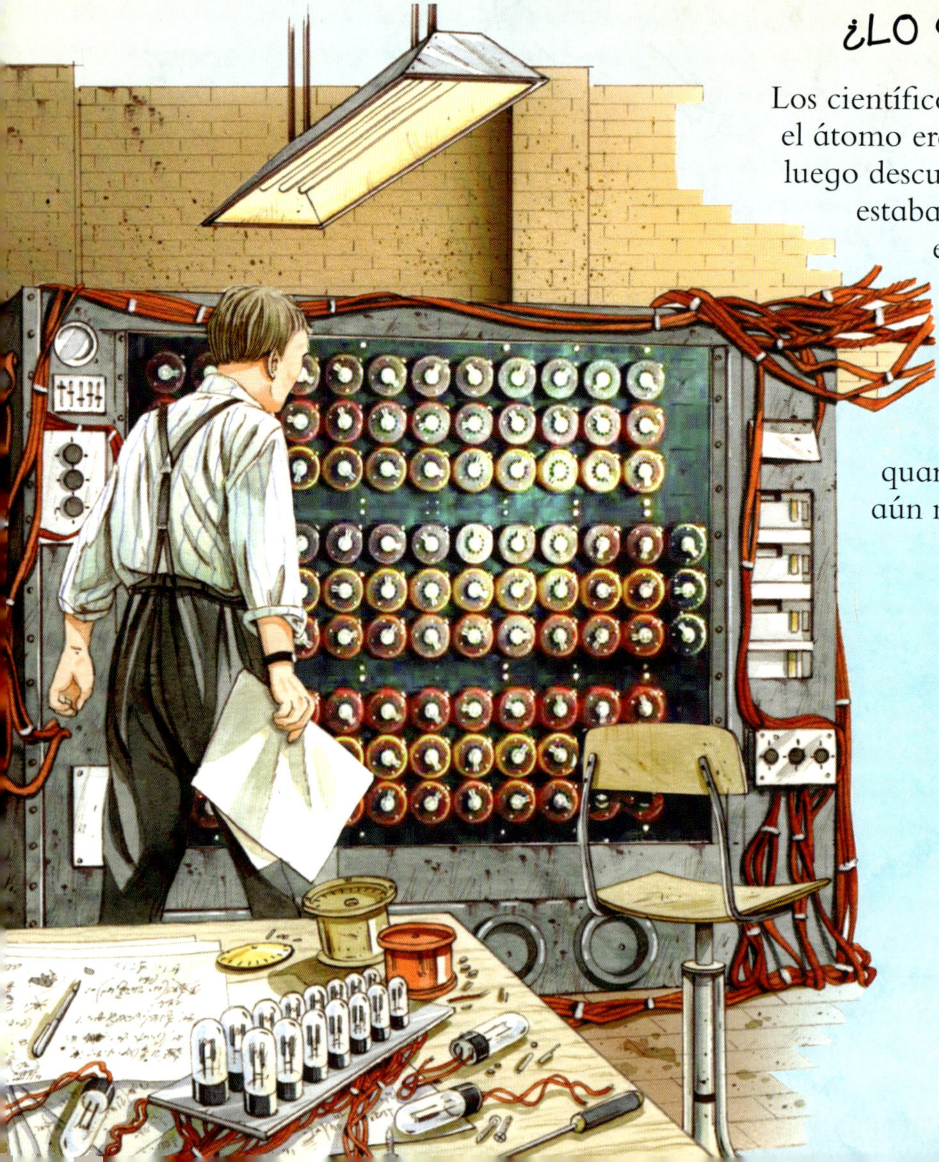

¿LO SABÍAS?

Los científicos creían que el átomo era indivisible; luego descubrieron que estaba formado por electrones y un núcleo de protones y neutrones, compuestos a su vez por quarks, partículas aún más pequeñas.

88 ¿Qué científico inventó la cámara de niebla?

Este instrumento, empleado para detectar partículas subatómicas, fue inventado por el físico británico Charles Thomson Rees Wilson en 1899.

89 ¿Quién intuyó el potencial de los ordenadores?

Ada Lovelace y Charles Babbage imaginaron a mediados del siglo XIX el comportamiento de los ordenadores antes de que la tecnología fuese capaz de fabricarlos.

90 ¿Quién es el autor de la ecuación más famosa?

Albert Einstein, en 1905, incluyó la célebre fórmula $E=mc^2$ en un artículo en el que exponía las bases de la teoría de la relatividad.

91 ¿Cómo se traduce la ecuación $E=mc^2$?

La energía de un cuerpo en reposo (E) es igual a su masa (m) multiplicada por la velocidad de la luz (c) al cuadrado.

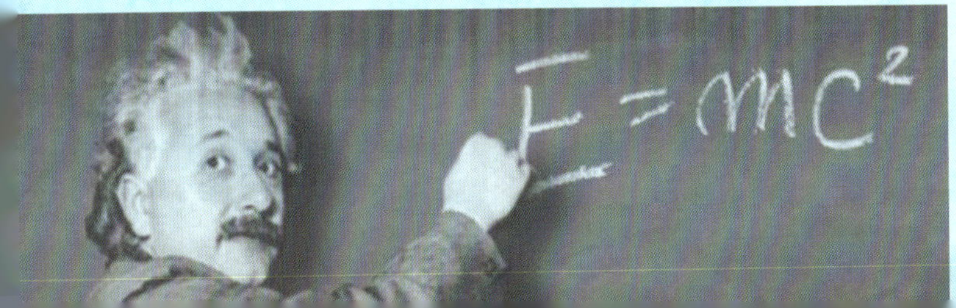

¿LO SABÍAS?

Albert Einstein obtuvo el premio Nobel en 1921.

92 ¿Qué construyó Nikola Tesla?

En 1898, en el Madison Square Garden, el inventor de origen serbio asombró al público con una demostración de un pequeño robot sumergible teledirigido por radio. Sus investigaciones abarcaron casi todos los campos: termodinámica, radiaciones, energía solar, rayos X y cósmicos, fotografía, fluorescencia, automática, robótica, electromagnetismo...

¿LO SABÍAS?

En 1900, aparte de señales, se logró transmitir voz y música.

93 ¿Qué consiguió el ruso Popov?

En 1896, el físico Aleksandr Popov logró transmitir la primera señal en alfabeto morse a una distancia de 250 metros.

94 ¿Quién fue Jagadish Chandra Bose?

Fue un físico indio que, en 1894, demostró la propagación a distancia de las ondas electromagnéticas: hizo sonar un despertador, que provocó la explosión de una carga mediante una señal de radio.

95 ¿Cuándo realizó Marconi su experimento?

Guglielmo Marconi logró transmitir una señal a distancia hasta el otro lado de una colina el 8 de diciembre de 1895.

¿LO SABÍAS? Desde Génova, en 1930, Marconi encendió las luces de Sidney con una señal de radio.

96 ¿Quién defendía la corriente alterna?

Nikola Tesla peleó por la utilización de la corriente alterna, que resultaba más fácil de transportar que la continua, de la que era firme partidario su rival Thomas Alva Edison.

MECENAZGO CIENTÍFICO

97 ¿De dónde procede la palabra «mecenas»?

El noble romano Cayo Mecenas fue un impulsor de las artes del siglo I a. C. Apoyó a artistas como Virgilio y Horacio, y se volcó tanto en su patrocinio que desde entonces se llama «mecenas» a todo aquel que ayude económicamente a artistas y científicos.

98 ¿Cuál fue la gran época del mecenazgo?

El Renacimiento fue la gran época del mecenazgo de las artes y las ciencias. Gracias a los mecenas fue posible la figura del humanista, un entendido en todas las ramas del saber.

99 ¿Quién creó la Casa del Saber?

Harun al-Rashid, quinto califa de la dinastía abásida que reinó entre 786 y 809, fundó en Bagdad este importante centro de estudio del que formaron parte, entre otros, el padre del álgebra Al-Juarismi, el químico y médico al-Razi, el astrónomo Thabit ibn Qurrá, los hermanos Banu Musa y el filósofo Al-Kindi.

101 ¿Dónde se impulsó mucho la ciencia?

En el Occidente islámico, especialmente en Al-Ándalus, durante los siglos IX-XI, la ciencia fue ampliamente financiada por los emires y los califas, interesados sobre todo por las ciencias aplicadas: las matemáticas, la astrología y la medicina.

100 ¿Quién ayudó a Leonardo da Vinci?

El gran genio de los siglos XV y XVI fue acogido por muchas cortes renacentistas italianas: Florencia, Mantua, Venecia, Roma y Milán. Estuvo al servicio de Ludovico el Moro y de César Borgia. Tras ser llamado por Francisco I, pasó sus últimos años en Francia, donde murió.

¿LO SABÍAS?

En marzo de 2017 falleció el gran mecenas de la ciencia española Pere Mir, quien creó la Fundación Cellex.

Índice onomástico

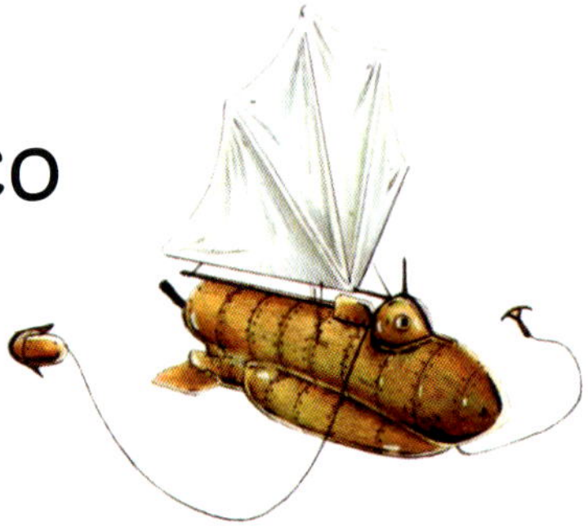